VISIONS OF DRYTVAARTE

JOEL A.T. ROOS

Illustrated by
D.D. Wazz
and
Joona "Tulikoura" Kujanen

Published by New Generation Publishing in 2020
Copyright © JOEL A.T. ROOS 2020

First Edition

ISBN: **978-1-80031-910-3**

www.newgeneration-publishing.com

New Generation Publishing

Dedicated to my father
D.D.W

CONTENTS

Have you ever had a memorable dream that you have spoken about to your friends? You can only remember short visions of the dream, and you are unable to build a comprehensive picture of it. This is exactly what this book is about, a distant dream you could not quite understand. Some of these visions end suddenly or even repeat themselves. More than anything, it describes and defines emptiness as a form of storytelling and asks its reader to understand the absence of depth...

MINIMAL LITERARY ART

NATURE ABOVE MAN

Landscapes Of Drytgastadl

500 Old English Miles

DRYTVAARTE

Drytvaarte was based on a flat plane of existence and it was surrounded by a vast sea. Above Drytvaarte was the shield of the sky with its numerous and ever-shining stars, the sun and the four moons. Seasons of the year appeared all around in Drytvaarte simultaneously and usually summers were warm and winters cold. Drytvaarte was a world where the length of a year varied. The variation was caused by the magical breathing of the existence. However, summer and winter were always the longest seasons, whereas spring and autumn appeared for a shorter time. A year in Drytvaarte was about four hundred days. Summer and winter lasted about one hundred and fifty days and the remaining hundred days were rather equally split between spring and autumn.

In Drytvaarte, there was no concept of a 'month'. Instead, people referred to a specific day of the current season. For example, one could say that this is 'the sixty-second day of the winter'. After the one hundred and fiftieth day of the same winter, people began to talk about the first day of spring, and so on. These days also defined certain annual celebrations and festivals around the world. For instance, people of Dyveln celebrated their legendary tale of Night Bear on the fifth day of summer.

Winters in Drytvaarte were usually cold and plentiful with snow. It was the time when the sun was weaker and darkness fell earlier during the day. Icy winds and drowning snowfalls did not make the situation any easier for the ones who lived in the world. However, the last thirty days of winter were usually milder, and often people had various celebrations to its glory.

"It was such a cold winter that it felt as if someone had thrust an icy dagger through my life."

Spring was regarded as a time of rejoicing and hope. It was the season when the snow started to melt and the sun became stronger. All the cities, towns and villages were filled with traders, adventurers and travellers. For many, this was the season when one could finally go and meet his or her distant friends. Therefore, spring was often called 'the season of many meetings'.

"Ah yes, spring brings friends together!"

Summer was usually the time when the world was in its most active state. The sun was shining and the nights were shorter and less dark. Travellers were frequently visiting towns and used the long days and warmth in their advantage.

"It was such a beautiful summer! We walked in the forest during the night and it was so peaceful and the spirits of the forest were dancing and celebrating as we arrived at a small lake. Her eyes were as beautiful as the forest around us. They had that soothing glimmer in them; I could have watched them for all time."

Autumn was the time when the world turned darker and wetter. Farmers gathered their goods and prepared for winter alongside other people. Landscapes were bursting with different colours as leaves started to drop one by one, leaving only pine trees green. Hard rains and blowing winds were not surprising during these times, and the sun was once again getting weaker.

"Autumn is the son of winter; it still has not learnt to be cruel enough."

'The shield of the sky' was a name that was common all around the world. It was used to describe everything that the sky held. The firmament had one sun, which appeared from the south and disappeared to the north. Its appearance varied, depending on the season. During winter, the sun was weaker and showed itself for a shorter time. During summer, the situation was the opposite. The peoples of Drytvaarte had given the sun multiple names, and therefore plenty of tales revolved around it. It was often regarded as an ancient power that watched over the world.

"Winter is the poison of the sun."

The shield of the sky had four moons and, unlike the sun, the moons simply appeared in the sky when the sun went down. They were placed in the sky so that the entire world was illuminated by them equally. The only exception was the moon in the northeast, which tended to be dimmer than the rest. Plenty of stories were told about these pieces of the sky, but the moon of the northeast had a special reputation, and sometimes it was referred to as 'the tear of a star'.

"So sad is that one moon, so dim and dying. It is like a forgotten crystal, like a freezing winter morning. It is like the tear of a star."

Drytvaarte's timeline was somewhat mysterious and no mortal knew when the world had begun, or when it was going to end. It could be said that Drytvaarte was an eternal world. The magical breathing of the existence was a massive part of the world's history and how the world changed throughout the ages. These cycles each lasted a varied amount of years. For instance, some cycles lasted for about a thousand years, whereas some only a few hundred.

In the beginning of every cycle, the world was strong in magic. This was the point when the existence was breathing its magic out cheerfully. As time went by, the magic started to weaken and disappear. Eventually, the existence ran out of breath and the magic became non-existent. This brought with it the end of a cycle. It always took a few centuries for the existence to inhale and start the cycle process again with its magical blow. Essentially, the peoples of Drytvaarte did not even notice these cycles, since the time gaps were beyond most folks' lifespan.

Most of the peoples of Drytvaarte did write their history down, but since most of the cycles were so long, the majority of the writings of the past were gone within some thousand years. The peoples did acknowledge that the world was probably older than one cycle, but simply did not know that much about the past.

The start of each cycle also meant that the world had more magical occurrences, and people were more likely to have magical powers if they were born in the early centuries of a cycle. Magic was a complex matter in the world of Drytvaarte, which usually manifested itself in the form of a miracle or a curse. Nevertheless, spell casters were always a rare sight in the world and many peoples lived their lives without even knowing about such matters.

STRUCTURE OF THE COSMOS

Above all was Hasgastadl, which was the home of the halmhendens, an influential folk, whose story also defined several other peoples' lives in the world. In Hasgastadl, the halmhendens had halls of wood and stone, echoing with knowledge of the past and of worlds that existed a long time ago. Hasgastadl was an island surrounded by a sea that ended in a dreamy mist and darkness.

Between Hasgastadl and the shield of the sky was Glauesk, which was the void separating the home of the halmhendens from the world of Drytvaarte. It was a space of darkness, with dim lights singing in the distance. Through Glauesk, the halmhendens were said to descend to the world of Drytvaarte.

· Below Glauesk was Blesk, which was called 'Loft World' by the few people who knew about its existence. It was an invisible place somewhere, being most likely an existence of its own. Like the name suggested, it was a large complex of wooden lofts and rooms, with multiple doors and secret hallways. The place was created and used by many ancient forces and halmhendens as a resting place before they reached Drytvaarte.

Taivaarte, or more commonly known as 'the shield of the sky' was the home of everything that lived and moved in the skies. It was the home of the sun, the moons, the stars and the clouds that travelled the world. Taivaarte was the sky for the mortals and it brought light and dark to Drytvaarte. It was the torch of nature living its life above all people, dying and coming to life every day.

Drytvaarte, also known as 'the shield of the soil', was created by the ancient powers and spirits of the cosmos for the mortal beings to dwell in. It was a vast plain of existence with numerous lands. The continent named

Drytgastadl was one of the largest, and was often referred to as Drytvaarte, as the peoples who dwelled there knew of only one world.

In the very deep roots of Drytvaarte was Kulus, 'the well of earth', which served as a passageway for the spirits to build the world. In the process, some of the spirits became too independent and destructive, and the creative powers had to find a place to remove the disparaging spirits. It was decided that the spirits would be thrown into Kulus and kept there until the end of time. The spirits of destruction became hateful towards the rest of the powers after their imprisonment. The abandoned spirits promised that they would swallow all the nefarious creations in the world, and possess them as their servants, if the well was opened.

Many ancient books suggested that there were numerous hidden passages to the large cave complexes of Kulus, which were in the depths of Drytvaarte. The place had plenty of great bonfires, which burnt eternally in their dark halls. Just like in many other magical places in Drytvaarte, there were certain stone halls and hallways with ceilings that appeared to look like starry skies.

Below Drytvaarte was Hauesk, also known as 'Cellar World', which was created by halmhaers. Just like Loft World, it was a place that did not exist physically anywhere. It was claimed to be somewhere between Drytvaarte and Alasgastadl, serving as a dreamy passage for the folk of halmhaer in their attempt to reach Drytvaarte. It was a world filled with ethereal and infinite forests and lakes, where many stone formations were worshipped and odd rituals took place. Hauesk had many spirits and malevolent beings, who were not welcome in the world of Drytvaarte.

Alasgastadl was the home of the halmhaers, often called the 'glass bottle world' or the 'great glass throat of the world'. It was a place surrounded by the realm of night, where night was said to reside during daytime. Many ancient legends suggested that Hasgastadl and Alasgastadl changed places as the day moved forward. During the day,

Hasgastadl shone with the shield of the sky, but when the night came, Alasgastadl took over and the realm of night descended upon Drytvaarte.

REGARDING THE PEOPLES OF DRYTVAARTE

Drytvaarte's long past had seen many peoples and realms. One of the most successful of these peoples were manfolk, whose ability to overcome adversities was exceptional, considering their short lives. Manfolk forged legends on their own, which set the way for their traditions and ever-burning spirit of honour.

Some peoples in the world were blessed with magic and halmhendens were particularly gifted sorcerers. Stala, the creator of halmhendens, gave the people tall and noble frames, which commonly emanated mysteriousness. Halmhendens with their white hair and purple eyes were wizards and wanderers, often following the great bidding of Stala.

Elves looked very much like manfolk, apart from their longer and curved ears. Their people's fate became uncontrollably entwined with Stala, who ended up dividing the folk. Regardless, the mighty lore of the elves was seen like a play, and every elf played a part in it. Act after act, the elves moved the story forward, simultaneously doing their best to prevent other people's influence.

Only a few folks in the world could drink ale like dwarfs, as they were particularly keen to feast and drink their beer. Short in stature, the long-bearded dwarfs were brave and curious in their nature, often discovering clandestine places. These adventures were usually encouraged by the folktales of their kin, enlightening the dim and veiled dimensions of the world in olden starlight.

Cold north defined its people and gelders were no exception. They were as tall as manfolk and their broad bodies hurled through the fields of snow, as the protection of Caolfveld watched upon their earthly journey. Gelders with their earth-grey skin and braided beards were outstanding hunters and warriors. Their call lay within their people and the eternal northern landscapes.

Drytvaarte was not spared from evil either, as the world had its malevolent inhabitants as well. Yrtar, the dark spirit behind gabyrs, gaberleks and hurthallans roamed the lands in shadows. Hurthallans were his strongest creations and their ugly but resilient figures reminded some people of gelders. Gaberleks were not as robust, but equally ferocious in their bloody ways. Lastly arrived the gabyrs, who were the most versatile nefarious beings the world had ever seen. They reminded one of gaberleks with their soil-coloured skins, sharp teeth and thin hair.

Some evil was not great in numbers, yet they could inflict indescribable destruction. Even the name 'Vilhiildes' brought shivers to the few people who were unfortunate to know about their existence. These demonic beings were crafted by Atrurionas and their tall and lean forms were surrounded by black spells and freezing ice. Their light-blue hair and empty eyes absorbed light, as their forsaken weapons decayed the life around them.

HALMHENDENS

Didly Didly Mazz

"I still remember the halls where we were born. The candles and the great crystal star hanging from the ceiling. We were listening to the words of the seer, who told us to cast our influence upon the lands. We were told to live in the waves of the world, to smell the rain in the air, to feel the gravel in the soil. I stood up from my wooden chair as I joined the others, who were prepared for the journey to the world below. The corridors were full of our kin, carrying more candles, which filled the air with white smoke. I carved my name to the stone slabs, which were covering our home's marble walls. The shadows filled the small dents of our scriptures in the faint light of the corridor. I could see the names around me that were long gone, the ones who were now looking at us, far beyond in places without time.

"It was the moment when I arrived. The world was full of magic and wonders. The sky singing its song, the stars shining like a silver blade covered in frost, I looked up and did not see my old home any longer. I was to make this place my new home, a story that would affect this world with its splendours and miracles. It was a night of memories, which were so old that the world would never remember them. The land was trembling around me and the ground broke in front of us. Behind the thick wall of disorder, we could see the walls rising in the lands. I could see home again – and so the gates opened."

Stala and sixteen other forces dwelled in the village of Körpihimgat, where it was always an early summer morning. The sky was full of canvasses of stars and its colour was dim blue, showing signs of a dawn. The time to create a new world was at hand and Stala was going to be in an important role shaping it. Stala, who was well known for his ability to channel and shape magic, was given the responsibility to stabilise the new world with a magical flow. Stala lived in a small wooden hut where he gazed at the endless starscape, which waved against the eternal and dim summer night skies. For centuries the forces contemplated, and finally a great wave was unleashed, where the first inhale of magic took place. In the moment began the magical breathing of the existence, which surrounded Drytvaarte.

Stala possessed immense powers, and his attitude towards using magic was often doubted by the sixteen others. Very few trusted him and it was common for the sixteen to bemoan how he happened to have the keys to the magical flow and channelling. Many had a reason to fear, as Stala openly expressed his desire to have a world where only the immortal powers would live and magic would be pure. Stala could not understand why the rest of the forces wanted a world for mortal folks. He thought it was nonsense and a waste of higher knowledge. Stala was also tired of living in Körpihimgat and Loistesse with the others, despite it reminding him of olden times and glorious ages of the past, which he profoundly missed. Körpihimgat was a place, which had wooden houses and small gardens usually plentiful with strawberries. Sometimes these strawberry shrubberies built playful walls around the homes of the forces, where they had dwelled in silence.

To prevent Stala doing anything unpreventable, the sixteen other forces prohibited him to enter Drytvaarte, as they feared his unpredictable nature. Stala was furious about the decision and could not understand the lack of gratitude after he had been the centric character in the creation of the world. For numerous years, Stala gathered his energy and began to brew an alternative plan. After many clandestine nights, Stala finally created Hasgastadl, where the first step of his scheme took place. In the stone halls of Hasgastadl, Stala channelled his energies together and so came to be halmhendens. Each of his creations carried Stala's magic and his primary spectre resided in Hasgastadl, sending the halmhendens to Drytvaarte. However, occasionally Stala manifested himself into a halmhenden and secretly travelled the world as well. In this form he had relatively fewer powers, as he was outside the source of his might.

This was a way for Stala to experience Drytvaarte, and his plans began to grow rapidly. Firstly, he built Blesk, which was also named Loft World, and for many halmhendens it was a resting point between Hasgastadl and Drytvaarte. To ensure his status in the world, Stala wanted to protect the place, which also gave access to his domain. Stala met many spirits, who had arrived in Drytvaarte after its creation and asked them to establish another layer around Blesk. In return, Stala channelled pure magic for the young spirits, who were thirsty for success. The spirits of Husmyrsket created a dreamy world of endless wooden rooms with stoves and benches. In these dim rooms, the spirits resided and no conflict would follow them, as it was declared a world of amity. Through Husmyrsket, Stala could guarantee that Blesk and the access to Hasgastadl remained safe for halmhendens and their allies.

"If you are too afraid to say your opinion aloud, then you are not even worth of that opinion."

If someone tried to understand Stala or his actions, one had to comprehend with nature, where no chaos or order reigned. He could hurt and do evil, yet somewhere inside him was light that crackled like a candle in the wind. He did not draw his desire to control from any reason that could be understood with a clear purpose. He simply was, and in his wake many others suffered, creating an alternative atmosphere of another truth. He would not turn any subject upside-down, instead he would erase their meaning from the aether. He was a nullifier, not a destroyer, but other forces and mortals saw him as the embodiment of anti-cosmos.

Stala had an ambitious plan, which later was named 'the inevitable motion'. Stala sent his halmhendens to Drytgastadl, where their first task was to find the richest locations of the magical flow. The search took innumerable years, which gave time for Stala to focus on his other plans. It was important for the creator of halmhendens to secure his power in the world and his plot was to make other affecting forces as weak as possible. He could not directly drain their powers, but he could turn them against each other. His schemes were noted by several other moving energies in the world and his reputation preceded him everywhere.

"Loneliness and incomprehension of words detached me from this purposelessness, when I drifted away from everything that I once deemed familiar. I observed myself as an outsider and I saw no hope. Only the end welcomed me in every predetermined turn and gave me the determination to seek for alternative paths. I was cursed with this mind, with this desire to live forever through words, which I would never finish. They stole my right to be free and put my mind inside a prison, where I would always be the adversary. Perhaps for me it was the acceptance of fate, just like the acceptance of death. Yet, I could not die, but I could be the enemy of them all. I was finally complete."

The only person who Stala trusted was Elsfala, who was his brother, and the two had experienced infinite lifetimes in lands now long forgotten. The only place which connected them to these times was Körpihimgat and Stala kept visiting the village. In here resided Raune, an elderly woman who at first seemed just an ordinary farmer, loving her strawberry shrubberies. The truth was that she was the oldest of all energies in the world and she had decided not to enter Drytvaarte, as she knew what was to come. Stala and Elsfala spoke with Raune, who told Stala that every other force in Drytvaarte would never understand him, but his role would be necessary. The world would need Hasgastadl, Kulus and the beacons of day, and Stala's presence would make them happen.

Raune also warned Stala and Elsfala that vilhiildes would attempt to take over Drytvaarte, as they had always tried with the previous lands. She asked Stala to join other forces in Kajoste, where the vilhiildes would initially try to destroy Oblivion of Heroes and enter Drytgastadl. Stala followed her suggestions and fought alongside several other energies. It was the only time in his life when he was not openly distinguished from the other forces. After the conflicts, Stala met Bethelbas Skaiwon and Bovenkauv, the only energies in Drytvaarte who did not clearly despise his presence. Especially, Bethelbas was the only one who brought something new to Stala's life, which so far had been occupied by empty chaos. It was perhaps love, which for Stala was the deepest bottom of the unknown oceans, and he decided to sojourn in Kajoste for some time. Bethelbas liked Stala as well, which won the trust of many others, including Father Storm. Bethelbas, Stala and Father Storm travelled to Selkelgen, where their friendship tightened. At least that is what Bethelbas and Father Storm believed.

Stala saw potential in the storm elves, who were Father Storm's folks. He knew that in Drytgastadl the halmhendens would need warriors and the elves would be a worthy army for the task. Stala wanted to capture the essence of the cosmic order in the world and he planned to build three beacons of day. However, Stala and the halmhendens lacked certain abilities to see the strings of energy in the world. Stala met Taipaleita Foltaanvielta, whose family possessed these skills and were willing to help Stala. The family, Stala and Father Storm travelled to Drytgastadl, where several other forces also helped to build the beacons of day. For Stala, the purpose of the beacons was to enable more magical flow to Hasgastadl and give a better access for his people. Being oblivious of Stala's plans, many forces thought that his ideas were for the greater good and order of the aether.

However, there were vilhiildes, who never wanted this order to happen and were hoping to take the world down. They wanted to get to the olden days and one way to do that was to find a way to Loistesse. Stala's beacons were preventing it from happening, which caused major conflicts between the two factions. It was also an age when Stala was betrayed by Elsfala, who joined the vilhiildes. Elsfala had grown tired of Stala's eternal struggle with the rest of the world and now his plans to lock the magical flow and lands together were going to prevent the lives of many other ancient forces. An already instable Stala became more erratic, as he saw Elsfala joining Atrurionas, the leader of vilhiildes. According to Elsfala, the vilhiildes represented the necessary evil to bring down his silent supremacy, which was going to ruin the world ultimately.

The first realm of halmhendens, Moltraugad, was finished in the same age and the realm had the well of Kulus below it. The realm was also near the mountain of Odomnan, where Atrurionas resided with the mightiest of vilhiildes. The land was called at the time Välkehtgen and different elven realms existed there as well. Stala decided to keep Kulus hidden and claimed that its true location was in the east from Välkehtgen, making many other forces seek in the wrong place. Kulus was originally a passageway for the original spirits, who were part of Drytvaarte's shaping. Stala intentionally built Moltraugad on the top of the well, as he knew that some of the spirits had turned destructive and were most likely trying to get out. Nevertheless, his idea was to harness the energy from the spirits and use them against Atrurionas and Elsfala.

Much later in time, vilhiildes and halmhendens fought over Moltraugad. Stala had been waiting for the moment to use Kulus against his old enemies, who were now at his doorstep. Stala intentionally opened the well, which blasted a great wave outside it, destroying everything around it. Stala and his adversaries lost their physical form in the battle and the whole of Moltraugad turned silent. Stala woke again in Hasgastadl, where his spectre dwelled, and wondered what had happened. It seemed that Raune had lied to him and had tried to erase him from the world by giving him the wrong location of Kulus.

After the loss of Moltraugad some of the halmhendens killed themselves, which made Stala avenge their treachery by creating Alasgastadl and condemning them there. Stala called the fallen ones halmhaers and they ultimately became his mirror image of fury and bitterness. Stala abandoned the realm and established Worlgaltrin and Hurlgaltrin in Galtreken, which were now his last standing fortresses in Drytgastadl. When Stala finally thought that the world would not challenge him, the peoples from the east appeared. The manfolks and elves by the shores of the inland sea of Yeldes caused trouble to halmhendens by conquering their establishments and taking some of their magical items. One could say that this started the downfall of halmhendens in Drytgastadl, where only some of the mightiest of halmhenden families kept supporting Stala, and his ongoing battle against rest of the world.

RIDGE OF SORCEROUS ATMOSPHERES

Moltraugad was a large realm which consisted of stone halls, corridors, bridges and chasms. Parts of it were built inside large hills, which painted the landscape with ethereal atmosphere. Only a few trees were present, but the land was plentiful with small lakes and rivers, that shined under the sun and the moons. The realm's northern parts continued as several massive wooden fortresses, which belonged to the wide variety of houses of the realm. These castles were built by the river, which expanded north from Moltraugad and large bridges connected these buildings together.

Moltraugad was built in a very short time, as the magic involved was strong and could aid halmhendens significantly. The realm literally rose from the foundations of the world and made the soil bow in front its majesty. In the middle of the creation were five halmhenden families: Cinderei, Ruswall, Rauwos, Hefetga and Altull. They had been blessed by Stala and their members and allies would shine amongst the halmhenden ranks throughout the coming years.

The land where Moltraugad rose was called Välkehtgen and it had a good variety of peoples living in its lands. For Stala, Välkehtgen had a special purpose, since it had the strongest flow of magic in Drytgastadl. Raune had told Stala that here lay the well of Kulus, which originally served as a gateway for the spirits, who were part of Drytgastadl's creation. Stala felt a familiar connection to the land and it appeared as if it had been part of him a long time ago. Stala had always had the ability to sense different atmospheres which occupied the minds of mortals and immortals. Upon the arrival to Välkehtgen, Stala sensed something exceptionally baffling.

Välkehtgen indeed had a specific atmosphere and mood to it. It seemed that all the peoples living there lived a very certain way of life, which was described as eternally youthful, excitingly tipsy and sincerely hopeful. This was concerning for Stala, as it all reminded him of something long-lost, that happened to be irritatingly blurry and nostalgic. Stala remembered how he used to store atmospheres and moods and how his collection was nearly complete. The memory led him to times which were full of fierce battles. His last recollection reminded him how Atrurionas took something from him, something that had now returned around him like a waft from freshly baked bread.

Stala was aware that he was most likely the only one in the world to have the atmosphere of Loistesse in his mind. It was the clearest memory of the place anyone could have, without still living there. It also happened to be his most precious atmosphere and he was very protective over it. Atrurionas was aware of this and had a great desire to acquire it from Stala, which led to an inevitable clash.

Atrurionas and Stala had been enemies since existence was young, but Atrurionas' motivation to destroy Stala was not based completely on their adversary. He also wanted to have the access to Loistesse, where Yrtar, the creator of hurthallans and gaberleks occasionally resided. Atrurionas and Yrtar were fighting each other as well and his plan was to enter Loistesse and finally challenge the old enemy. This meant that the motivations for all the actions in the conflict were mostly based on the long past, which did not exist anymore. The memories of those ages still lingered in the minds of Stala, Yrtar and Atrurionas, who seemed to be the only ones caring.

Whilst Stala had his confrontations with Atrurionas, the halmhendens of Moltraugad did a lot of background work. Many influential houses of sorcery were founded by the river that led north from Moltraugad, where they specialised in atmospheres. Stala ordered the families of Rauwos, Altull and Hefetga to leave the realm and establish further strongholds in the east. Ruswalls and Cindereis were left to rule Moltraugad, which at first seemed to work well. However, Stala did not know that the two families were not willing to share power and their opinions of Stala were not particularly confident either. One could say that the story of Moltraugad was destined to end with misery and Stala's occupation with the conflicts drew too much attention away from the ones who were going to betray him.

The most crucial turn in the internal relations of Moltraugad happened when a piece of Hjardabristallum's western sky fell near the realm. This piece was one of the atmospheric keys that could possibly enable access to the lands of the past. At the time, Ruswalls were led by Aulvan and his supporters happened to find this stellar illustration of the western sky. It could possibly offer the access to Loistesse, and Aulvan decided to keep the illustration hidden from his competition. The piece of the sky contained atmosphere, which Stala wanted as well, but Aulvan had the idea to use it for the benefit of his own family. He personally thought that the halmhendens did not belong to Drytgastadl and Stala had condemned their kin there.

The leader of the Cindereis, Eawotel, discovered Aulvan's secret schemes through her spies and decided to threaten him. Eawotel was going to tell Stala about Aulvan's actions, causing distress and pressure for his family. One day, Stala suddenly arrived to Moltraugad, as he came to warn about a large army of vilhiildes marching towards the realm. Upon his arrival, Eawotel met Stala and told him that she had something important to tell. However, it all had to wait since it was more important to focus on the defence of the city than make Stala more worried. The battle commenced, which gave Aulvan and his family enough time to plan a bold scheme. Their idea was to assassinate all the Cindereis before they could inform Stala about the piece of the western sky. Whilst the fight was raging, the Ruswalls confronted the Cindereis near the large river of Moltraugad. Ruswalls thought that the family of Cinderei was not expecting anything, but this misconception led to a tragedy.

Eawotel Cinderei, who was very talented at gathering information, had prepared for the ambush, which surprised the attacking Ruswalls. Their family was completely overrun and slain to the last halmhenden, leaving Cindereis enough resources to make it look like the doing of vilhiildes. Eawotel quickly sent her best warriors to the quarters of the Ruswalls to acquire the piece of sky, which was taken to the house of Cinderei in the shadows. The whole battle had provided enough coverage for such a daring operation, which kept Stala ignorant of the situation. After the battle was over, halmhendens gathered and Stala spoke to the realm's leading characters. He was angry about the loss of many important halmhendens, especially the Ruswalls.

Stala later came to Eawotel and asked about the subject she wanted to discuss about before the battle, but the halmhenden told that she could not remember the matter any longer. Some of the halmhendens who knew about the scheme watched in horror as Eawotel lied to Stala, who gathered his troops and headed out of Moltraugad. Later Eawotel was confronted by Ruswall's loyalists, who said to have their vengeance. Yet, they would not want to tell Stala about it, as they saw the conflict too personal of a subject between the families. Besides, Stala would most likely not even believe Ruswall's supporters, since they were usually arguing with him and their relations had suffered throughout the ages.

The darkest secret which Eawotel possessed was that she was Elsfala's and Atrurionas' ally. Their clandestine alliance had not been revealed to anyone and their aim was to reach Loistesse together. Eawotel could not take the piece of sky for vilhiildes in Odomnan, as it faded when taken away from the halmhendens, and the vilhiildes could not simply approach Moltraugad either. It was a stalemate that required the death of Stala and the fall of Moltraugad. For Cindereis, it was a long wait, since the fight against the vilhiildes was going well and the other halmhenden families were strongly united. It left no other option than to wait in the shadows and begin a slow corruption.

While dark thoughts were occupying the background of the realm's future, many halmhenden families saw it in a brighter light. Stala, who had spread his knowledge about different atmospheres, had inspired many houses to specialise in the matter. For instance, a large room was built for different atmospheres, which connected Moltraugad to the soil of the world. These square-shaped holes in the wall breathed air, which could alter anyone's mood or mind. They were ancient passages and the halmhendens could absorb any atmosphere there. It became the archive of old knowledge and was an imprint of many forgotten places, such as Körpihimgat, Loistesse, Selkelgen and Kajoste. For example, Stala believed that Kulus was perhaps one of these gateways of atmosphere from Loistesse, since Raune had mentioned it in the past.

Atmospheres became an essential part of halmhenden magic, which kept growing rapidly. Several crafting guilds were founded and the most famous of them was Afwlanda and Eksholsat. The company found a way to add an atmosphere to any object, such as clothes, jewellery or tools. The item that was imbued with a certain atmosphere received its qualities as well. Whatever had happened in the place and time of the atmosphere gave features for the item, and it could alter the wearer's mind, memory or abilities. To reduce the effect, many of Moltraugad's talented wizards learnt how to cut the atmospheres and lessen their effect, which occasionally led to a complete detachment of mind. Hiririndul Vost was a master at cutting atmospheres and he commenced a mission to reconstruct the memories of Körpihimgat and Loistesse, which were claimed to be still in the air of Drytgastadl.

The obtainment and shaping of the atmospheres ultimately began to determine the minds of the halmhendens, who dwelled in Moltraugad. The problem was that majority of the most sought-after atmospheres were the ones which were not part of Drytgastadl. The memories of Körpihimgat and Loistesse filled the minds of the halmhendens and many lost their sense of the surrounding world. They shaped the minds in a way that altered their realisation of sizes, distances, pace and time. For some halmhendens, Moltraugad became the whole world, when they moved inside its halls. Every room in the city felt like a piece of a land and the illusion trapped their comprehension tragically.

It brought up the suggestion amongst Moltraugad's scholars that these atmospheres and memories were as tiny as grains of gravel. That could possibly also mean that Loistesse, Körpihimgat, Selkelgen, Kajoste and many other places were just fabricated dreams by the energies of the world. They felt like large places, but were just everyone's shared imagination and past, and now only their atmospheres had remained. Perhaps these places never existed but they had been shared by the majority of the people of Drytvaarte. Whilst the halmhendens were engaging themselves with the atmospheres, Cindereis were taking steps towards Moltraugad's loss. It was all coming together.

Atwair was a shady character, whose job was to sneak people to Odomnan. Some folks in Välkehtgen had turned on the side of vilhiildes, but had kept their alliance secret. Atwair was the solution, as he could disguise anybody who travelled in the land and he guided several groups back and forth to Odomnan and the surrounding Välkehtgen. The curtain of the forbidden night caressed the skins of the travellers, as Atwair showed the path to Atrurionas. Cindereis had used Atwair's services several times, but ultimately troubles were coming their way. Atwair approached Cindereis near Moltraugad and told that there was someone observing the shadowy traffic near Odomnan.

The investigator was a rogue halmhenden named Alveas Vean, who had heard from dwarven sources about the legends of how pieces of the western sky fell near Moltraugad. It had ignited his interest in the tale and how it had changed the relations in the land and his home. To his surprise, no one seemed to know anything about it, which increased his fascination even more. Alveas knew that something was happening and the folks were either lying or were forced to do so. Alveas visited several houses in Moltraugad, which were located around the great river leading north. Inside one of the establishments, Alveas happened to come across a familiar face, which belonged to Molsa Cinderei. The investigator had seen her several times in the company of Atwair, who had taken people to meet Atrurionas.

Alveas noted that the mood in Moltraugad had begun to change. The halmhendens had become blithe and neglecting towards life. They had stopped caring about values and everything had turned meaningless. These elements also brought up occasionally pure hatred towards life itself, as the halmhendens had started to live in a world of insignificance. Alveas discovered that it was part of Atrurionas' plan, who smuggled certain atmospheres to Moltraugad with the help of the Cindereis. The family took imbued items, which contained Atrurionas' creations of emptiness and disdain towards all life. These atmospheres disheartened even the strongest minds, which had inspired an annulling change in Moltraugad.

One could suggest that this was also one of the elements which enabled the birth of halmhaers. Its crippling disposition took over the realm's people and Moltraugad's end commenced. All other atmospheres had disappeared in a short time and when Stala returned to the realm, he was confused and angry. The creator of the halmhendens researched the general atmosphere, which felt hostile and fragile, leaving only one exception. Stala had finally got a trace of the hidden piece of the western sky, the presence of which was clear after all other moods had faded. It was the only atmosphere remaining in Moltraugad, which origin was outside Drytgastadl. Stala found the piece of sky inside one of the houses, which was commonly used by the Cindereis. Stala could not understand what had happened to his creations and why his folks were behaving oddly. Stala acted and invited an old friend, named Afvid. He was a mysterious man with a flute, which was also known as the melody of the dancing truth.

Stala was ready to execute every single traitor in the realm, but he wanted to get a final confirmation. Stala told Afvid to play his flute in a way that revealed all the ones who had ever had secrets or ill intentions towards him. Afvid walked and playfully kept leaping in Moltraugad, whilst performing with his instrument. Stala was observing in the distance and saw when certain halmhendens began to dance and chant against their will. In their spontaneous songs, they were forced to reveal their darkest secrets and Stala kept listening with the shine of blood in his eyes.

Stala captured all Cindereis and their accomplices and executed them mercilessly. No one in the family was spared, as Stala was utterly blood-crazed with his revenge. Simultaneously, Stala claimed that the whole of Moltraugad had been an illusion set by Raune and rest of the world, who wanted his death. It could be said that it was not too far away from the truth. Raune had intentionally told Stala about the well of Kulus and hoped that he would build Moltraugad. In Raune's eyes, Stala's chaotic side and evils were supposed to be trapped in Moltraugad, while the rest of the halmhendens in the east would get a chance for a better life. Raune had always said to her accomplices, that regardless of the outcome, Stala brought balance to many matters in the world. Only if his death failed, the cycle would continue, until a new adversary would replace him.

Once again Stala's death failed and Atrurionas attacked Moltraugad with all his strongest vilhiildes. Stala planned a defence, which was not strong enough to keep their old enemies out. This time the halmhendens who had been scheming with the vilhiildes were dead, so the only way to end the struggle was to defeat the other side entirely. Stala watched as his realm fell and meaninglessness conquered his mind. He knew that Kulus, regardless of its authenticity, would change the situation if opened suddenly. Stala travelled inside one of the halls of Moltraugad, where the presumed mythic well was located. Upon the opening, a great blast howled through the whole realm, killing everyone in its wave, absorbing the piece of sky as well. The age of Moltraugad had ended with tears and blood and only in its silenced halls dwelled the confused vilhiildes, who got trapped inside the lingering atmospheres.

RESIDING IN YESTERDAY

Many decisions were made before Drytgastadl took its final shape. The events before its time were complicated and relations between several forces were deeply rooted to the original mythology of the existence. Elsfala, who was Stala's brother, had always watched his older sibling striving and he was not happy. Perhaps it was envy, but Elsfala had several plans to change Stala's course of actions. Raune and Elsfala were part of an ancient alliance and their relationship with Atrurionas was not a warm one. However, when the age of Drytgastadl began, it offered the two an opportunity to change the situation, which had been mostly dominated by Stala.

Raune and Elsfala spoke with their old enemy Atrurionas, whose vilhiildes were threatening Drytvaarte. A truce was impossible, but at least both sides agreed that it was essential to remove Stala from the picture. Raune refused to join Atrurionas, but Elsfala was keener to side with the lord of vilhiildes. There was a profound reason behind his willingness to join his old enemy and betray his sibling Stala, becoming obvious later in time. When Elsfala saw the great halmhenden families, who came from Hasgastadl, Elsfala mirrored some of Stala's powers and added his own agents to the families. Amongst these halmhendens was Eawotel Cinderei, whose family members believed Elsfala's illusion and that Eawotel had always belonged to the family.

Eawotel grew in one of the mighty houses of Moltraugad and spent many days wandering in the nature. She had a superior relationship with the land and its atmospheres, which many other halmhendens could not see or feel. Eawotel could gain information from the environment in its purest form, without being physically in a location. She became an effective spy, who told tales to her friends in a form of poetry and chant. She was aware of her origin and was waiting for the day, when her energies would grow stronger. From the very first decades of her life, she was frustrated with the simplicity of life and other living beings, given her undefinable yearning towards lost times, through which she had never lived.

Eawotel often spoke about the lost lands and locations, which she regarded more interesting than the present. Her mind was living in forests, lakes and shrines of old times, which wisdom had faded. For her, life was useless if one could not become part of the legends and songs. Eawotel was also a strong defender of the idea that nothing should be written down of these ancient days. One could say that this also helped her to fight Stala, as she saw him as a force taking halmhendens away from the mythic silver era. Eawotel was often seen worshipping old shrines built by Välkehtgen's oldest folks. According to her diaries, these people were descendants of the lost lands, whose duty was to remind the whole world of Körpihimgat and Loistesse.

While Eawotel was practicing her traditions, she was also an agent of Elsfala, who was also ally of Atrurionas. Eawotel had grown her influence within the family and her opinions about Stala were not a secret to most members of her family. She was a deceiving manipulator and could turn her whole family against Stala. However, it was not hard, as the majority of Cindereis were already frustrated with Stala and his absence and elusiveness. Eawotel met Atwair, a mysterious stranger, who had offered his services to Elsfala and Atrurionas. Atwair could pierce through night and atmospheres, while making its travellers undetectable. Atwair's abilities gave Eawotel the chance to visit Elsfala and receive further plans regarding Moltraugad and Stala.

Eawotel spent a lot of time in Odomnan with Elsfala and Atrurionas and learnt everything about their elaborate plan to take down Stala and Moltraugad. It included elements and spells, which opposed meaning, order and continuity, making them dangerous for all living beings. However, all the opposing elements applied only in Drytgastadl, which Atrurionas and Elsfala tried to escape. It was common for both to tell Eawotel tales of Loistesse's glorious past, whose yearning call kept them awake at night. Eawotel also found out that Raune had been the only force remaining in Körpihimgat, after the rest of the energies created Drytgastadl.

Raune became a legendary character in Eawotel's mind, which interested her. Elsfala did not like to talk about her at all and Atrurionas had been her enemy, so that did not help the situation. Eawotel thought that Elsfala and Atrurionas were both envious of Raune, who had not left the lost lands and now their longing to return was increasing drastically in their minds. It was perhaps a mistake for both and for the most part irreversible, but it did not stop Atrurionas and vilhiildes trying. Nevertheless, Raune would have never wanted Atrurionas back, so his absence or even vanishing would been a huge favour for the rest of the world.

Eawotel took her knowledge of Körpihimgat, Loistesse and Raune to the house where she was raised in Moltraugad. Here, Eawotel studied the subject night and day, looking at the sun go up and down. Eawotel also liked to study outdoors and she often moved her table and chair around the land, whilst looking at the sky. She became very passionate about Körpihimgat and often dreamt about it. After seeing many self-absorbing dreams, Eawotel decided to commence her travels around Välkehtgen and find clues of the tales, which were told by Elsfala. On her journeys towards the west, Eawotel met people who reminded her of the tales in the old books of the lost lands. She started to see a pattern in the peoples and their lore began to unfold in front of her, making clear hints towards the long-gone world.

After innumerable weeks of travel, Eawotel arrived in the western shores of Drytgastadl, where she stared at the sea and felt something acquainted. A vision emerged in the horizon and her world turned to encounters of several visions of mystery. She felt the arrival of Körpihimgat and the power of Raune, who embraced her entrance with warmth. The old lady rose from a chair, which was next to a little fireplace, and greeted Eawotel. The garden outside the house was simple and well maintained and Raune's wooden cottage was full of items, which emanated tales of old. Eawotel's eyes glimmered as she sat next to Raune, who smiled and offered her wine.

Raune and Eawotel spoke and became friends after a few days. Raune took Eawotel around the lands, which she had previously tried to imagine. All the places were disappearing and they had a forgotten and sad feeling to them. It would have made anyone teary, as the two looked at the spruce forests with rivers, lakes and ruins of places that once used to shine with life and stories. Raune told Eawotel that the lost lands had no future, but perhaps Loistesse still had some hope left. Raune explained that there was a reason why these places were called the lost lands, and there was a reason why they were all gone. All the heroes and realms once there had diminished and their heirs continued the tale in Drytgastadl, which Raune had accepted after many years of mourning.

Eawotel and Raune's friendship strengthened and Raune asked whether Eawotel would like to live in Körpihimgat, despite its vanishing presence. According to Raune, there was not much hope left anywhere and most of the things in life were now meaningless. The more Eawotel looked and listened to Raune speaking, the more convinced she became that Atrurionas was one of Raune's sons. The father was Paulrosy, and he had been the very spirit of Körpihimgat who, unfortunately, had started to fade a long time ago. Raune had refused to leave his side, when the rest of the energies created Drytgastadl and other places.

Raune said that Eawotel was the daughter she had always wanted. She had the future in her and the time of

Stala, Elsfala and Atrurionas was over, giving Raune another reason not to come to Drytgastadl. Eawotel thought that perhaps she could bring the rest of the Cindereis to Körpihimgat, as she had grown keen with the rest of her family. Even if Elsfala and Atrurionas would arrive to Loistesse, they would only fight Yrtar and most likely destroy each other, which was only beneficial for Raune. Eawotel saw light in the plan and returned to Moltraugad with hopes of taking forward the scheme.

Many factors changed when a piece of the western sky dropped near Moltraugad. Ruswall's supporters found the illustration and brought it secretly to one of the houses, which was mostly in control of their family. Eawotel, whose skills had taken her to the leading ranks of the Cindereis, acted as soon as she sensed the rare item in the domain. The piece of the sky radiated of Loistesse and Aulvan sealed the illustration to the Ruswall quarters, which had highly decorated study rooms and houses inside the grand keep's many levels. Eawotel had to get the piece of sky, since the Ruswalls were planning to use it to get to Loistesse, leaving everyone else in Drytgastadl. However, Eawotel was perhaps the only halmhenden in the realm who could have used its guidance to lead her own halmhendens to the land.

Eawotel's presence had been tainted by her visit to Raune, which was sensed by a few individuals in the world. Eawotel was oblivious that her visit to Raune's home had left a mark on her, which altered the atmosphere around her. More than anything, Eawotel was utterly ignorant to the fact that she was also Raune's creation, and just moving atmosphere herself. The glory of Loistesse was within her and even Elsfala did not know this, who kept thinking that Eawotel was his creation alone. The reason why Raune never revealed this to Elsfala was a mystery, but Eawotel could understand that she was an agent of Raune, working hard to destroy Atrurionas as well. Their alliance was a lie and Elsfala was fighting two fronts, against his brother

Stala and against the lord of the vilhiildes. It was only a matter of time until the great plot would be revealed.

Eawotel's time slowed and she watched the realm shattering into pieces of irrelevance. She was in a state of understanding the meaning of hidden paths, which Raune and Elsfala had shown her before. Eawotel was finally in the crossroads and it was time to decide. Her personal desires crossed with the bigger picture, which did not seem to give her a break from the unceasing torment and pressure of the coming days. She did not have faith in herself, as she had understood the senselessness in such a thought. At some point, Eawotel shared more thoughts with Raune that she had ever shared with anyone else, making her want to leave Drytgastadl as well.

Eawotel returned to Odomnan and met Elsfala, who asked about her long absence. Eawotel was honest, but could not reveal all the details that had changed her ability to observe and to be controlled. Elsfala did not see any change in Eawotel, but Atrurionas could sense it. The great leader of the vilhiildes summoned Eawotel to his fortress, which floated in darkness, longing and rage. Atrurionas looked through Eawotel's eyes, who stood in the halls of the vilhiildes and showed no emotion. Even the air had turned dark, when Atrurionas sensed that Eawotel could bare his atmospheres of the anti-life. The lord of the vilhiildes touched Eawotel's forehead and spoke words of poison, which took her deeper into the world of meaninglessness. Eawotel lost it all and the deliverance was complete, but its purpose had been revealed to the wrong authority. Atrurionas told Eawotel to commence the intense corruption of Moltraugad, as her mind had been set to rot it piece by piece.

Atrurionas detected that Eawotel had been in Körpihimgat, but she had enough willpower to resist revealing the plan. Eawotel began to smuggle specific atmospheres to Moltraugad, forged by Atrurionas. Its energy caused halmhendens to lack all enthusiasm, concern or interest, slowly causing a downfall. Eawotel could no longer stop, as she was partly controlled by Atrurionas. Eawotel also had her plans to acquire the piece of the western sky from the family of Ruswall, who had become hostile against the Cindereis. Eawotel confronted Aulvan Ruswall, who was the leader of the family, and threatened to tell Stala about their scheme. This was of course just a lie, which was an attempt to solve the situation peacefully.

Eawotel commenced a plan to defend her family, as she could sense how the Ruswalls were planning their assassination. When Stala came to Moltraugad, speaking about a hurling wave of attacking vilhiildes, Eawotel put together a plan to ambush the Ruswalls, who most likely were going to use the battle as a disguise to kill all Cindereis. Well prepared, the Cindereis defeated the Ruswalls, who thought their secret attack while the battle was raging would give them an advantage. The situation turned dark for the Ruswalls, who were slain to the last halmhenden. Eawotel stole the piece of sky and took it the family quarters, which was known for its large wooden halls, tall windows and musty smell.

Eawotel wanted to escape Drytgastadl more than anything and Raune decided to appear in Eawotel's dream. In here, she told Eawotel to travel one more time to Körpihimgat and leave everything else behind. The piece of the sky, which had fallen from Hjardabristallum's creation, was going to destroy everything in Moltraugad as its atmospheres were changing too rapidly. During the same night, Eawotel took only her most essential items and escaped in the shadows towards the west. The journey was as long as it had been previously, but this time Raune was already waiting for her in the shores. The old lady explained that Eawotel's role in the story was coming to an end and her presence had increased the sky illustration's power. Now it was silently waiting in the dark until Stala would open the well and the piece of the sky would attempt to charge through it. This process could bring the end to Stala and Atrurionas, if they were to fight in Moltraugad.

SOJOURNER OF THE FABRIC HORIZON

The sky was grey and rainy when Hiririndul fell in the air. Drops of water glistened on his skin and his eyes looked at the disappearing familiarity of his home. He could remember Stala's hand on his head and a smile, which blessed him with beauty and emotion. He had become an illustrator of moods and a cutter of atmospheres. His sole purpose was to collect memories of Loistesse and Körpihimgat, which were floating in Drytgastadl. As the halmhenden fell from the sky, he went through several layers of feelings, reminiscences and fates, which led him to a place of questions and obscurities, to a new home below the grey sky.

Hiririndul resided in a forest near the realm of Moltraugad and his hut was modest and lacked decorations. He had a fireplace and in front of it he studied books, which he had received from Stala. The pages in the books were still empty, but it was his task to fill them with stories so the ages of the lost lands would never be forgotten. Every time Hiririndul walked in the forest and breathed its brisk air, he could take a book and write about an atmosphere that surrounded his mind. The stories filled the books and he had to cut them to chapters, which could weaken their energies. Quite often, Hiririndul met characters of the past in his journeys and they begged to be written down in the tales, so they could finally live forever. Hiririndul was filled with mercy, as he wrote down entire families, who burst out laughing and crying, as their spectres danced on the forest floors after innumerable years.

Hiririndul met the family of Bolkke, who had gone through a colourful past in the lost lands. Hiririndul met its two members by a small forest lake, where a father and his daughter were fishing and looking at the sunset above the trees. Hiririndul sat next to them and they all were quiet for a while, still staring at the water. Emcan, the daughter, could sense that Hiririndul was not local and offered him water. The thirsty halmhenden accepted the gesture and greeted Taabe, who was Emcan's father. The three got into a conversation, which was a beginning of an unexpected friendship. The halmhenden learnt that Emcan and Taabe were the last two remaining members of the family, as everyone else had fallen in the wars of the past. Bolkkes had lived in Loistesse and Körpihimgat, where their family had been full of brave warriors. Unfortunately, all that glory was now gone and only their minds could remember the legends.

Hiririndul discovered that the family had been involved in the conflicts that also included Stala, Raune and many other relevant energies of the world. Bolkkes were fighting Stala, Elsfala and their sister Äevel, who Hiririndul had never heard about. Taabe explained that he had slain Äevel in the Battle of Furnhastes, which used to be Stala's mountain hold in Loistesse. Elsfala accepted the defeat, but Stala could never forgive the loss of his sister, who had been more important to him than his brother. Stala swore to slay the whole family of Bolkke, but for their fortune, Raune intervened after the war. Bolkkes were only a small part of the whole conflict, but they had happened to be the ones who ceased the world with the death of Äevel. Raune could no longer watch the madness and Paulrosy's energy collapsed. Körpihimgat and Loistesse began to fade and Raune forced amity upon the land. Stala raged and told Raune, that nothing in the world would stop him finding the family. This was also one of the several reasons why Raune allowed Körpihimgat to wither until only one village was left. This gave time for many folks of the lost lands to travel east to Välkehtgen, taking a large toll on mortal beings. Some people faded with the world, whereas some remained there, just like Emcan and Taabe.

Hiririndul understood that Stala was glad to leave Loistesse, as it reminded him of Äevel's death every day.

He wanted to forget the misfortune and since he could not find Bolkkes due to Raune's protection, he decided to wait until Drytgastadl would see its dawn. Hiririndul had learnt more about Stala than anyone could have ever told him, and he joined Emcan and Taabe on their adventures. The three travelled around the lands and Hiririndul's books lit the world around with its strings of light. Hiririndul met many folks, who kept asking that their stories would be written down to his books, as they gave hope of remembrance. The faint golden spectres and distant voices hugged Hiririndul, whose hand was writing constantly. He was celebrated with every moment, and the halmhenden could feel the warmth in his heart.

It is impossible to say if Hiririndul had a piece of Stala's goodness and love, which he had personally forgotten. It all seemed to come together when Taabe and Emcan showed the forgotten mountain hold of Stala. On the stairs sat a character, who raised her head when the three approached her. Taabe could not say a word, as he stuttered the name of Äevel. The woman rose and her beautiful but tired face had motionless eyes. She stepped towards the three and could remember Taabe, who remained speechless. Hiririndul was confused, but he could sense stronger atmospheres than before. Äevel and Taabe agreed that the madness had taken over them and the hate was to be left behind forever. Hiririndul could not understand any of it, as the conflicts behind Loistesse were more complicated than the very lives they were living.

Hiririndul spoke of how he was willing to show the path to Stala, and Äevel agreed, only if he would help her to end the insanity of the world. Hiririndul had to write about Äevel in his books, otherwise the world would eventually forget about her, making it a battle against time. Hiririndul dedicated the last page in his book for Äevel, who needed time before she could get to Drytgastadl. Meanwhile, Hiririndul commenced his journey back home, as he had filled all his books with places and characters of the lost lands. Hiririndul had to use his ability to leap between the dreamy fabric, which reigned between the old and new. He could leave his body while he was sleeping and bid his farewell to all the spectres, who had kept him company. It was time to make his way back home, through undefined paths between dreams and waking hours.

Hiririndul wrote in his memoirs that he believed that Loistesse, Körpihimgat and Välkehtgen all existed simultaneously in the same place, it was just the matter of seeing through the dreamy fabric that separated them. The books that Hiririndul wrote were holes in the fabric and through them the people on the other side could access Drytgastadl. Hiririndul had seen some folks doing the leap themselves, but for a few it had been a pure impossibility. For instance, the family of Bolkke could not escape Loistesse entirely and Hiririndul's help was essential for their survival, including Äevel. The more Hiririndul travelled between the fabric, the more he could sense Stala's mark and energy. He believed that Stala had been part of creating the dreamy walls between the old and new, but did not know his deepest purpose behind its distant and elusive magic.

The fading of Körpihimgat and Loistesse was upon its remaining folks, when Hiririndul finally returned home. The halmhenden created a small library inside his hut, which included all his books that had been with him on his travels. Hirindul did not have any time to waste and he set out of his hut to find Stala and tell everything about his experiences. As soon as the halmhenden stepped out of his home, Stala and several of his bodyguards greeted him. Hiririndul was stunned, as Stala approached him and his presence filled the air with freezing seriousness. Stala smirked at Hiririndul, who could not say a single word in front of the sudden arrival. Hiririndul followed Stala, but was prevented entering his own home, where Stala was reading the books. Hiririndul tried to tell Stala about his sister, but the bodyguards hit him on the ground, making him confused about the treatment.

Stala saw the largest book on the working table, which was in the middle of his little hut. When Stala opened it, he saw familiar names, which made his leather glove covered fists tighten. Without further hesitation, Stala threw some of the books into Hiririndul's fireplace, which he had set only a moment ago. The books burnt, leaving a sorrowful mist in the air and Hiririndul felt a melancholic blow in his mind and heart. The halmhenden struck one of the guards and charged in, only to see the book, which included Bolkkes, in his fireplace. Hiririndul screamed and begged Stala to reason his actions, who kept watching the flames with a cruel smile on his face. Hiririndul stared at Stala, who did not know that the very last page of the same book was about his sister Äevel. The halmhenden said nothing, as the warm air waved on his face and Stala looked at his collapsed posture. Hiririndul received a lifelong task from Stala to find his enemies and write their stories down, so he could prevent them coming to Drytgastadl.

"That was the end of reconciliation."

Hiririndul became a tool of Stala to hunt his old enemies from the past and let their tales burn in the pages. Hiririndul hated the task and his spirit resisted the malevolent plan. The halmhenden travelled as much as he could and tried to find Äevel, Emcan and Taabe, but the search left the halmhenden in despair. Even the places they had visited had turned grey, forgotten, empty of memories and warmth. They no longer had a meaning or a past and they had been utterly nullified by Stala, leaving only a few atmospheres left. Hiririndul made haste and swiftly saved these moods and the folks, who were helpless and miserable. The halmhenden brought a secret booklet and saved many details about the fading lands, before the wave of oblivion stormed and great silence set upon it forever.

Hiririndul took the atmospheres with him and led the people past the fabric to Välkehtgen, where smiles returned to their faces. Hiririndul kept doing his secret journeys whilst he was hunting Stala's enemies, who he had to find, or else Stala would have suspected a betrayal. He was in a difficult situation, safe directions existing only where Stala's eyes were absent. Hiririndul also met a large swan, who took his saved peoples and atmospheres to Välkehtgen, where the bird's majesty speckled the land with future. It did not take long until Hiririndul became a hero of the almost-forgotten folks, who established stone statues in his honour. They could be found everywhere in Välkehtgen, but the halmhenden himself remained oblivious to such tributes.

Hiririndul's operations were interrupted when Stala commanded the halmhenden to build the hall of atmospheres, where all the major moods and memories would reside. Hiririndul had to bring all his books to the halls, where several others under his command built the hall, which had a large terrace on its roof, surrounded by four massive hills. In here, Hiririndul channelled, shaped, cut and altered the atmospheres under the eyes of Stala, who used their energies to build his version of Loistesse. Hiririndul knew the direction Stala was going with his plans. The creator of the halmhendens wanted to see a forged past of Loistesse, which did not include any of the losses or enemies he had faced. Maybe Stala was hoping to see some happiness in this fabricated past. Nevertheless, Hiririndul kept travelling and bringing back forces, some of which were possibly also Stala's enemies, making it a dangerous dance on a blade.

Stala liked to travel as well and was usually seen moving around the lands with his trusted bodyguards. Eventually Stala came across statues, which were done in the honour of Hiririndul. Stala inquired the peoples about the stories revolving the commendations, which unmistakably were dedicatory to Hiririndul. Stala did not show any emotions when he heard about Hiririndul's secret actions, but inside he was cutting the mark of a traitor to his dead body. Hiririndul, who did not know about the statues, worked in the halls as usual when he was confronted by Stala. The force behind the halmhendens had brought his sword and Stala's eyes were as lifeless as the deed he was going to perform. Hiririndul, who did not beg for his life, proudly stood in front of Stala, who pierced him with his weapon. Hiririndul fell on his knees and told Stala about the book, which had Äevel's spirit inside.

"She wanted to see you, she had longing in her eyes and a reason in her head to stop you from all of this madness. Her grace was trying to reach you, and yet you burnt her return, like you are going to burn yourself away. This world will cast you down and it is you who shall be forgotten eventually. No statues shall stand in your honour, only piles of corpses."

OF HOW THE NEW LIGHT BURNT THE YEARS

A few tales suggested that Hiririndul did not die when Stala thrusted his sword through the halmhenden. Hiririndul had spent so many years in the lost lands that he had become part of the spectres, who resided on the other side of the fabric. It is believed that the halmhenden wrote himself to the books and went to sleep, which enabled him to return to Moltraugad. However, only his body returned, and not his spirit and mind, which kept living in the fading world. Hiririndul believed that he could prevent the fading and help everyone to return Loistesse. He had simply begun to hate Stala and did not want anyone to live under his rule, thus doing everything to avert the happening. Hiririndul's death in Moltraugad did not erase him from the world, but made him stronger in the dreamy world, which was occupied by the lost folks. It is possible that it gave him enough energy to channel certain atmospheres, which provided stability and home for the forgotten peoples of the past. Regardless, he was celebrated as a hero on both sides of the fabric.

After the great blast, which erupted from Raune's Kulus, Moltraugad quietened and only some vilhiildes remained there. The beings were captured and held in a prison-like environment, which made them think that the fallen Moltraugad was the whole world. Everything inside the hill halls was interpreted as certain parts of the world, where the vilhiildes had resided or travelled before. Even the small windows, which brought light to the chambers of Moltraugad, were thought to be the sun and the moons, when their pillars of light sieved the air in the musty halls. For outsiders it would have been a melancholic sight, when the vilhiildes were utterly mesmerised by the broken enchantment of the lost realm.

The vilhiildes who had any sanity left, renamed all the places in Moltraugad to correspond with their history, which tricked them to think even more that the illusion was true. The most popular place was the western wing of Moltraugad, which was on the top of the grand hills. It was accessed via stairs and the vilhiildes kept running there, thinking that the place was Loistesse. Eventually the stairs crumbled and many vilhiildes fell to their deaths. Some legends told that some of the beings believed so stubbornly in Loistesse, that they could run up the invisible stairs to the western wing of Moltraugad, often ending up killing themselves. In the end, all the insanity silenced the realm and only some of the vilhiildes remained there, sleeping in a hazy dream. Perhaps somewhere in their abyssal spirits they could sense the numbing madness, which made them furious and reckless with black magic, drowning Moltraugad in eternal darkness.

DISTANT LANDSCAPES PAINTED HOME

Moltraugad was mostly built on the rocky hills, which were as tall as small mountains. It had several halls underneath the hills and parts of the rocky hilltops had castles, bridges and other sorts of establishments. Many of these buildings were dedicated for either living or studying magic. The whole realm sat on the top of the hills, which crossed the landscape south to north and the only exception was the western wing of Moltraugad, which expanded towards the point with another ridge. In many ways, Moltraugad had mysterious and distant atmosphere and many said its views were wistful and naturally beautiful. It was not uncommon to see the halmhendens playing string instruments on the rocky hillsides and honouring their homely landscapes.

The rooms, chambers and halls of Moltraugad were carved into dim stone, which often were glistening with exquisite textures and layers of earth. The halls were commonly very tall and had stairs going alongside the walls, which enabled the halmhendens to reach the hilltops and other buildings. On the same levels were small windows that illuminated the dim bottoms of the realm's marble floors. In places like these, the halmhendens implemented several different atmospheres and moods. Their purpose was to serve as a source of inspiration or study, which could help the halmhendens to understand the world better. For instance, one of the largest halls was the celebratory chamber, with long tables and enormous wine casks, enjoying the atmosphere of happiness and hope.

At the end of hill range was a river, which kept going further north and northwest. Alongside its stream were many of Moltraugad's most revered and abstruse houses. They were usually made of wood and their glass windows were unnecessarily large and decorated. Many of these establishments produced talented halmhendens, who lived in the wooden castles and wings. They usually included several gardens and small lakes, where the halmhendens studied and practised rigidly. Many of the buildings also had bridges that connected them together like towers of oak, building impressive structures over the river. All in all, the whole realm was carefully built and outsiders could have never believed that its beauty would fall one day.

SPELLBOUND IN LIFE AND DEATH

The halmhendens of Moltraugad were different to the rest of their kin, as they were remarkably enthusiastic about the atmospheres and moods. Their involvement with such energies drained them from certain traits and usually left them with a straightforward, but powerful identity. The halmhendens of Moltraugad were always looking forward to focus on a specific subject or action, so they could try their energies and abilities. For many, it was a competition of magic and mystery that in many ways was the root of Moltraugad's downfall. The folk would rather have their discussions through sorcery than normal conversations, which reflected their worldviews successfully and comprehensively.

The people of Moltraugad did not care about opinions or individual traits, as all of them were irrelevant in front the bigger picture. The folk did not care about the methods, if the aims very successfully achieved. Controversially though, it was the same reason why so many of the halmhenden families in the realm became each other's enemies. They all thought to be the owners of the whole domain, which sparked many confrontations. One could say that the realm lacked order of status and no one was willing to take orders from others, even from Stala. This meant that generally the halmhendens of the realm were elusive, arrogant and overly passionate, which for outsiders was often too much to handle.

AS THE FORT WAS HIS RIGHT EYE AND THE WELL HIS LEFT EYE

After Moltraugad was founded, Stala ordered the families of Rauwos, Hefetga and Altull to move east, where their mission was to establish further halmhenden strongholds. The idea was to capture the whole world's magical flow and channel all of it to Hasgastadl, so Stala could gain full control of his fate. The creator of the halmhendens noted that the further he travelled east, the less the old influence of the lost lands was present. Since the old atmospheres were still surrounding the halmhendens in Moltraugad, Stala asked the three families and their supporters to travel eastwards. They were to journey until they were outside the influence of all of these ancient atmospheres.

When the halmhendens travelled towards the east, they began to wake from the enchantment, which was still reigning in Välkehtgen. Step by step, the world became clearer and fresher for the halmhendens, who had dwelled in the obscure dreams of the lost lands. Stala had told the halmhendens to build Worlgaltrin and Hurlgaltrin in an area where the dreamy atmospheres ended. Stala hoped that the halmhendens in the east had completely clear minds and could be free from the fascination of the past. When the halmhendens arrived in Galtreken, they were finally detached from it grasp and the building process for Worlgaltrin and Hurlgaltrin began.

The halmhendens began to build their establishments around the land, which included the city and several smaller fortresses. The largest fort was built to the mountains of Jarlidan, south from the chasms, which were close to the city of Worlgaltrin. The two large chasms also needed bridges, which helped the halmhendens to travel around the lands and enabled all sorts of trading between their settlements. Everything in the halmhenden realm was done with pure magic and the stone buildings rose rapidly, including gardens and commons. In a matter of a few years, the folk had established a busy realm, which mainly focused on binding magic to different items. Stala was proud of these halmhendens, but was afraid to lose all their creations in the future. The creator of the people ordered Hurlgaltrin to be built east from the city, where it served as a channel of magic. The place was built inside a cave which the halmhendens had grown to like.

Hurlgaltrin's cave was a mysterious place and many halmhendens carved their names into the walls, so the location remained protected. The well of Hurlgaltrin was unswervingly coupled with Hasgastadl, which is why the well was made exceptionally deep. The cave that continued north was filled with silvery halmhenden runes, which had small blurry bolts of light travelling in the air in the cave ceiling. The lights occasionally moved the runes around, creating beautiful patterns on the glimmering cave walls. Its mood was soothing and longing, as if it reminded all its dwellers of something wistful.

The legends tell of an age when some halmhendens presumably travelled from Hurlgaltrin to Hasgastadl and back. The runes in the walls opened small gates, which took them to the halls of their kin. However, the runes were not the only interesting details within the cave, as it also had small spruce forests inside it. The cave extended towards the north and the forest inside it had a sky, which made the place look as if it was outside the cave. In these spruce woods resided trolls, a small folk, who lived inside their tiny wooden huts. They were ancient folks and had dwelled inside the cave for innumerable years. The trolls and the halmhendens made a pact when the well was built to the southern end of the cave's opening: the trolls could preserve and hide the halmhenden magical items in their mysterious little world and in return the halmhendens protected their home.

As people, the trolls were not interested in riches, but were deeply protective over nature and animals. Halmhendens could trust the folk, as they knew that the trolls were not interested in taking advantage of their magical items. As a sign of alliance, the runes of the halmhendens flew to the spruce woods and made the trees shine during night time. For many of the halmhendens, Hurlgaltrin had turned into a place of peace, contemplation and preservation. Stala considered the place to be perfect for hiding and conserving the magical items. The propinquity of the well could help halmhendens to send all the magic to Hasgastadl if a disaster was to occur.

The three leading halmhenden families of Worlgaltrin were Rauwos, Altull and Hefetga, and their plans were to experiment with magic, so the halmhendens could prepare for the coming days. The family of Rauwos was led by Tuolan and Vhyolan, brothers who shaped stone, soil and metals with ease. They had founded a guild of magic with the rest of the leading families, where spells were classed into different categories. They called them visible and invisible sorcery, which were also divided into flowing and draining magic. The halmhendens were training rigorously to control both sides of the sorcery, which abled them to control lifespan and many other ethereal assets. It was common that when the halmhendens learnt spells, they bound parts of themselves to items, dividing their personal qualities to useful objects.

Tuolan and Vhyolan learnt to manipulate both sides of the sorcery and connected them to a flawless flow of spells. The brothers were favoured by Stala and he carved special runes for them in Hurlgaltrin. The runes were keys to Hasgastadl and if the brothers had to face their end in the cave, the runes could save their spirits in aether, without letting them disappear. The brothers were grateful of the major gifts by Stala, who had been observing the expansion of the halmhenden realm in Galtreken. Vhyolan decided to dedicate the rune to his left eye, which could make him look through it, despite being somewhere else. The binding made Vhyolan's actual left eye weak, but his guarding eye was always observing Hurlgaltrin and its entrance.

Vhyolan was set to be the watcher of Hurlgaltrin, and Tuolan became responsible for Worlgaltrin's defence. This irritated Oasven Altull, the warden of Worlgaltrin, who was a fine example of how Stala's desire to control was passed on to the people. Oasven was intelligent but arrogant and cruel and he did everything to ensure that the Altulls would control Worlgaltrin. The halmhenden had already gained several enemies, as he claimed that whole region of Galtreken was part of the halmhenden realm. Oasven demanded that the land would be left only for their people and all others should leave. Halsurs, who were a noble folk living in the eastern mountains of Galtreken, had already found an enemy in Oasven and their conflict was only a matter of time.

The halsurs were created by Belfares, and they were tall and slim folks with bronze coloured skin, fair hair and bright eyes. Their people were upright and honourable and were often seen wearing helmets with feathers and wings. Belfares had created homes for the people, which were on the mountainsides and forests. Halsurs lived inside enormous stone mansions and vast terraces which offered great views to the west, where the open landscape whispered contemplatively. Belfares and his people liked statues and decorations, which mostly were made of marble and white stone. Oasven hated all their beauty and perfection and he was certain that there was time to force them out of Galtreken.

Oasven was perhaps the strongest manifestation of Stala's will to control and influence people. His family and their supporters began to remove other halmhendens from the important roles in the realm, to guarantee that the Altulls would reign forever. Stala began to question Oasven and arrived to Worlgaltrin for an inspection. The creator of the halmhendens met Oasven, who let Stala understand that other halmhenden families were not trustworthy and had tendencies to challenge Stala's leadership. Oasven's power had grown so immense, that many other halmhendens were afraid to contest the family that now controlled most of Worlgaltrin's aspects. Oasven, who was a charismatic speaker, convinced Stala that everything was in order in the realm, which luckily for him was also supported by his peers.

Stala, who had plenty of trouble in Moltraugad over the centuries, let the family of Altull flourish in Worlgaltrin. The family of Hefetga were too preoccupied crafting magic, and Rauwos had too many responsibilities guarding the realm. One could say that the leader of the family was obsessed with Stala and he did everything to become like him. Oasven had read all the stories regarding the lost lands and Stala's fight with other ancient powers, which made him look like an invincible, ethereal warrior king. Oasven was aware that Stala liked a lot of Vhyolan and Tuolan and he had to do something about the brothers, who could have appeared more competent than him.

After some time, Oasven removed Tuolan and Vhyolan from their roles as the realm guardians, which came as a surprise for the public. Even Stala arrived to Worlgaltrin and demanded explanation from Oasven, who had been scheming during the darkest hours of the night. Oasven had heard from his spies that the brothers of Rauwos had met Belfares and halsurs in the east several times over the years. The brothers were discussing amity, but for Oasven it was an opportunity to accuse Rauwos of betrayal. Vhyolan and Tuolan happened to be in the east when Stala arrived in Worlgaltrin. Oasven crafted stories of how the brothers had left the realm to gather an army with halsurs to attack Hurlgaltrin.

Oasven, Stala and their army rode to the east, where they arrived in the home of the halsurs. Vhyolan and Tuolan were inside one of the mansions when the battle commenced. Stala let Oasven command the forces, as he trusted his judgement. Little did he know that the halsurs had never planned anything against the halmhendens, nor had they built an alliance with the Rauwos. In a summer rain, the homes of the halsurs were destroyed and their whole kin slain, only leaving Vhyolan and Tuolan alive, who were captured and battered unconscious. Stala, who had believed Oasven's stories, gave the brothers a chance to explain themselves, who had been completely ambushed by Oasven's warriors.

Tuolan and Vhyolan watched the fallen homes of the halsurs and Belfares, who had been slain and hung from one of the marble statues. In the early evening light, the brothers defended their lives and told Stala how Oasven was behind a scheme to control Worlgaltrin. Stala had no reason to execute the brothers, and for Oasven's disappointment, let them keep their lives. Stala could not prove anyone right or wrong and demanded an armistice between the families. He had already seen a few issues in Moltraugad and he did not want them to happen in Worlgaltrin, which was supposed to represent the future of halmhendens. Reluctantly, the beaten brothers returned to Worlgaltrin with Oasven, Stala and rest of the forces, and their return raised many questions.

Despite the family of Rauwos calling for justice, Stala did not change the ruling family to another one. Altulls had received a lot of support and the majority of halmhendens were on their side. The family of Rauwos was falling out and they had been put into a corner like a pesky wolf. Vhyolan had decided to do something about the situation, but he intended to keep his plans to himself. Even Tuolan did not know that Vhyolan was about to change the course of Worlgaltrin forever. Oasven had become so arrogant that he walked everywhere alone, as he was sure that no one dared to hurt him. His favourite place was the large common, which was north of Worlgaltrin's city. The garden had statues and long straight stone paths, which had beautiful engravings in them. In here walked Vhyolan, whose heart did not pound for fear, but for pure hatred.

Oasven, who met Vhyolan in the common, smiled and mocked the halmhenden, whose stone-cold eyes remained absorbed in anger. Oasven was so certain of his status that he let Vhyolan get too close to him, who suddenly took a dagger out of his cloak and stabbed Oasven in his stomach. Oasven screamed and tried to call for help, but Vhyolan stabbed him again in the throat and began pounding his knife into the dying halmhenden repeatedly. Oasven was already gurgling, but Vhyolan kept hitting the halmhenden and his clothes got drenched in blood. The wolf had bitten, and no longer was his heart heavy. Every stab had won a page in the books of legends and his name would be feared, hated and respected till the end of times.

The death of Oasven caused a massive storm in the realm, and search for the murderer began. Oasven, despite being generally a popular leader, had many enemies, which gave enough cover for Vhyolan. The halmhenden had not told anyone about his deed and the family of Rauwos remained oblivious of the act. Soon, the realm's leading families were summoned to a meeting, which was supposed to solve the situation and find the murderer. Altulls, Rauwos and Hefetgas met in the hall of Worlgaltrin, where the families and their supporters had gathered around with worried minds. Amongst the nervous halmhendens sat Vhyolan, who was the calmest of them all and his facial expression switched between amused and dull.

The dubiety increased in the realm and the search was fierce. During this time, Vhyolan told his brother Tuolan that if something happened to him, he and rest of the family should flee to the north. Tuolan became troubled and understood that Vhyolan had been behind Oasven's death. Unfortunately, the chatters and actions of the brothers had been observed by a spy of the Altulls, who had been following them for some time. When Vhyolan and Tuolan discussed the clothes he wore during the murder, the spy discovered that Vhyolan had not burnt them. Instead, Vhyolan had kept them hidden, as the blood of Oasven tainted the coat and its energy resisted fire. The family of Altull happened to be famous for fire related magic and its force ran in their blood.

The spy managed to sneak into Vhyolan's chamber and find the clothes, which he had tried to wash with water. The thief took the clothes and returned to the house of Altull, where he showed the blood tainted coat and its insignias, which belonged to Rauwos. Ultimately the situation was revealed in front of the whole assembly of the leading families, where Altulls showed Vhyolan's coat. The meeting nearly turned into a fight between the families as Fejerne Altull accused Vhyolan of Oasven's murder. Vhyolan laughed and denied all knowledge, pointing out that the spy fabricated the coat. At that moment, Fejerne took the coat and threw it in the fire, which was in the middle of the chamber. The piece of cloth resisted the flames and Fejerne shouted how the blood of Altull was on the coat. Vhyolan charged at Fejerne with rage in his eyes, but the fight was stopped by Stala, who had stormed into the chamber. His intervention calmed the situation and the hearing continued.

Vhyolan was found guilty of Oasven's murder and he was sentenced to prison. Stala did not execute Vhyolan, since his powers were bound to Hurlgaltrin and it was too late to remove his rune and eye from the place. The only way to keep the balance in the realm was to imprison Vhyolan in a place where he could do no harm, but still possess parts of his powers. Vhyolan showed no emotion, when Stala drained some of his energies away and sent him to the prison of Kejeskrip, north of the city of Worlgaltrin. Tuolan and the rest of the Rauwos left the realm to the north, where they began to dwell in forests, hiding from the other families, who saw them as traitors.

Whilst Vhyolan was going to be in the prison, Worlgaltrin went forward. The realm was ruled by the Hefetgas, who had focused mostly on the crafting of magic and their powers had risen from the shadows, whilst everyone else had focused on fighting each other. Dakel Hefetga, who led the family, possessed the skill to manipulate already existing spells, which had been bound to the world naturally during its creation. Any item that had gone through specific times or an event gathered features from the previous bearer's life and transferred the traits to its new carrier. Dakel took all these stories and used their energies to create something useful for the halmhendens, who were desperate to adapt the world that surrounded them. The halmhendens realised that any item that had been carried by a revered warrior could possibly carry a hidden skill in the item, which could teach anyone to be a better warrior unnaturally fast.

The magical items helped halmhendens to survive, but they also attracted plenty of attention from other people. For instance, there were folk named asg and they were the original energies behind manfolk. The asg began to raid many of the halmhenden settlements and their desire to obtain magic was unbelievable haughty. Manfolk, who came to exist later in time, never knew of the asg and they were mostly forgotten in time, regardless of their undeniable mark which scarred halmhendens. Dakel Hefetga did not want to stop the creation of magical items, despite many of them ending in the hands of the asg. Instead, the halmhendens intentionally created bad items, which they let the asg capture and get corrupted by. At first, the idea was great, but later turned out to be a failure, which set the halmhendens on a path of obliteration.

When halmhaers appeared in Drytgastadl, their very coming stirred up the situation even further. Stala watched with grim thoughts as the halmhaers moved through the world, causing inevitable destruction. The family of Rauwos, who had left Worlgaltrin, resided north of the realm in Pimenn and Hillfort Lands. Their leader, Tuolan Rauwos, saw the fading of the halmhendens and the coming of halmhaers, who were the harbingers of the end. The beauty and marvel of their realm was disappearing and the age of separation had begun, which ended the fragile unity of halmhendens for all time.

Ultimately, a company of powerful halmhaers saw the opportunity to take over Worlgaltrin. The halmhendens who dwelled there were no longer strong enough to defend the realm and their folk had separated, causing a great fracture in magic. The halmhaers, who stood against worldly sorcery, captured Worlgaltrin and slew all the remaining halmhendens in the city, including Hefetgas. The commanders of the halmhaers were Silmost Phaer and Mund Phaer, who were particularly vicious and bitter in spirit. The commanders of the halmhaers tried to conquer Hurlgaltrin as well, but its defence was too strong and the sacred cave, and the well, did not bend in front of their spells. The plan was to gain access to Hasgastadl from Hurlgaltrin, but after the scheme failed, the halmhaers decided to destroy the beacons of day as an alternative option. The idea was to destroy and drain their powers, so the world's order would collapse and Alasgastadl would clash with Hasgastadl.

Despite the halmhenden separation, there were many adventuring kinsmen who defied the plans of the halmhaers. One of the leading halmhendens enforcing unity was Sauenge Partal. She was an adventurous lady, whose wealth and skills gave her an opportunity to gain reliable allies, such as the storm elves. Stala and Father Storm had their relations in Selkelgen, and now in Drytgastadl it was time to work together for a stable future. Lady Partal worked with Captain Foltad, who was a storm elf leader from Ikirias. The two and their forces chased halmhaers in search of the beacons of day. The task, which took considerable time, was successfully completed, but the conflict was far from over. Upon the discovery and securing of the northern beacon of day, Partal, Foltad and several others learnt that Worlgaltrin had been taken over by halmhaers.

The War of Hulstakn began when Partal, Foltad and their company returned from the north. Along the way,

Partal had met Tuolan Rauwos, who was planning to free Vhyolan from the prison of Jarlidan and let him join the battle. The halmhaers were quick in their response and an intense fight occurred everywhere in Galtreken. It took several days for Tuolan to bring his brother from Jarlidan, whose guards were no longer inspired to do their obligations. Nevertheless, Vhyolan was weak after the imprisonment, but his brother hoped that Vhyolan could regain his powers before the conflict would be over. The war had indeed gathered powerful characters on its fields, including Hurastil, a legendary hero from Kajoste, who knew Father Storm as well. The elves who fought alongside the halmhendens rejoiced in the presence of Hurastil, whose polearm pierced halmhaers mercilessly in their ranks.

Ultimately, the war ended after Hurastil slew Mund Phaer, the remaining halmhaer commander. The conflict had been devastating on both sides and had caused a great downheartedness amongst halmhendens and Stala. The creator of the halmhendens was utterly exhausted after the fall of the realms and his people, making him remarkably quiet. Stala retreated to Hasgastadl, where he was going to remain silent for many years, without saying a word to anyone. The remaining halmhendens stayed in Drytgastadl, where they were left to survive in a changing world. Some of the halmhendens even claimed that Stala had lost his sense of the world, which made him abandon his own folk and plans. The age of separation had ended, and the time of utter fading had begun for their people. Its winds were blowing heartbreakingly and only the whispering roads reminded them of what once was.

Sometime after the events, all halmhendens of Worlgaltrin had either died or disappeared. Their people were still in the world, but were rarely seen by other folks, making them beings from legends. This crushing downfall struck the halmhendens with an intensity that could be compared to an eternal funeral of one's parents. The people never recovered, and the last leading family left was

Rauwos. Tuolan, Vhyolan and the remaining members hid in the shadows of Worlgaltrin, where they saw how Galtreken was looted by manfolk and other peoples from the east. Tuolan, who had kept staring at remoteness for several years, had finished his tale in his mind and no reward was awaiting anyone. There was no other option than to demand justice from the peoples of the east, even if it took the remainder of his life.

Tuolan left to Aetari, Dyveln and Ylvart, where he commanded the return of the magical items of the halmhendens. Only a few depictions of the encounter survived, but it is said that the halmhenden stood proudly in front of the manfolk, who spat on his face and ridiculed him. Even the spear that pierced his stomach did not change his empty face, which was tired and scruffy from all the years of fighting. Vhyolan knew what was going to happen, and he had bid his farewell to his brother, knowing that he would not come back. Everything had become meaningless, which meant that perhaps the curse of Moltraugad was not in the place, but in the minds of halmhendens. Even Stala did nothing to help the situation and he kept sitting on his throne in Hasgastadl contemplating mournfully. It all had come to an end, which disheartened the whole people and everything that once meant something for them.

The last story regarding the family of Rauwos concerned Vhyolan. The halmhenden had wandered aimlessly for some time and his thoughts were not accepting the defeat. The world had changed, but it did not stop Vhyolan planning revenge against all the realms that once pillaged Worlgaltrin. Vhyolan asked the storm elves of Ikirias to join his efforts to defeat Aetari, Dyveln and Ylvart, but the elves declined the offer. Vhyolan had begun to see the alteration, which defied the past order of the world. Old friends no longer shared the same aims and old enemies no longer cared about your existence. It all burnt Vhyolan's heart, who travelled to the north to meet gelders. Once there, he promised Worlgaltrin as a reward if he could feel victorious in front of his enemies once more. The gelders accepted the offer and the War of the Returning One began, giving Vhyolan one last chance to reclaim glory.

The war was relentless and quickly turned out to be a mistake, which the gelders began to withdraw from. Vhyolan, whose great plans crumbled, waited in Worlgaltrin for the armies of Aetari, Dyveln, Ylvart and Podfrud, to finish the long story. The unmotivated gelders could not hold the attackers and Vhyolan fled the city, having the intention to reach Hurlgaltrin. The escape at first was a success, but his absence was noted and a group of his foes began to chase him in the snowy landscape. When the halmhenden reached Hurlgaltrin, he was surrounded by his pursuing foes. In here, Vhyolan knew that his death would be meaningful and in the hands of the runes. The halmhenden fought courageously, but there were too many enemies and ultimately Vhyolan was slain by Faerkroll, the grand lord commander of the sky elf guard. This was the final day of Worlgaltrin and Hurlgaltrin, sealing its fate forever from halmhendens. The kinsmen who had survived occasionally visited Galtreken, but the realm never saw a new dawn, and became like a beautiful painting that deteriorated in tears.

THE EYE OF THE NULLIFIER

When halmhendens appeared in Hasgastadl, the sky was quiet and its serene chant whispered like a gentle choir. Stala smiled and his hopes glowed around his face as he struck energy to his creations. Amongst the halmhendens were many exceptional individuals and one of the greatest had a name: Vhyolan. The halmhenden was part of the family of Rauwos, who represented a different wave of their people. Vhyolan and his brother Tuolan were Stala's friends and they often spoke about the coming days and shaping magic. However, even Vhyolan's brother Tuolan did not know that Vhyolan had a particular role in Stala's plan. Vhyolan carried an atmosphere, which Stala had crafted just for Worlgaltrin. The atmosphere surrounding Vhyolan was empty and all the energies around it were absorbed inside it wherever he roamed. Vhyolan was essentially a walking archive, set to live his life in Drytgastadl and gather as much information as possible for Stala's continuous plans. One could even suggest that halmhendens were not even his prime creation, but Vhyolan's work helped Stala to create something more successful.

Vhyolan Rauwos received a gift from Stala when the days of Worlgaltrin and Hurlgaltrin were young: a rune, which shone in the cave of Hurlgaltrin and bound the friendship between Vhyolan and the creator. In truth, Vhyolan was the very eye of Stala and all the energy he gathered, Stala could see and learn in Hasgastadl. Vhyolan also shared a lot of thoughts and knowledge with Stala, explaining a lot of the choices he made in his life. For instance, the family of Altull carried energies in them, which Stala wanted to leave in the past. They had somehow survived and were attached to the family when Stala shared parts of his powers and knowledge with his fresh creations.

Vhyolan knew that Stala could not personally kill Oasven or other Altulls, as there was a chance that he would have destroyed a piece of himself in the process. Vhyolan never spoke about the topic with Stala, but his visions were telling him to taint his blade one day with the blood of Oasven. Vhyolan also kept seeing Raune in these dreams, which suggested that Stala had given Vhyolan the part of him which still perhaps appreciated and missed Raune. The two had complicated relations in the lost lands, with a peculiar balance between respect and hatred. For Vhyolan, all these stories were mysteries, chapters of a life which he did not experience but somehow remembered. For example, Vhyolan always had a reoccurring dream where he danced with Raune in Körpihimgat in the small strawberry garden of the lady. One could even propose that perhaps Vhyolan was a manifestation of him, which Stala wanted to show to Raune one day. Maybe the halmhenden was supposed to be evidence that he was willing to build a better world.

Vhyolan was full of life and he travelled a lot in Galtreken and in the surrounding lands. The halmhenden had several developments, which consisted of forging alliances and preventing questionable foes rising in the north. Stala preferred to give Vhyolan the freedom to travel, as he also gained new information through his encounters. One of Vhyolan's friends was a halsur named Ulgarta, who was a tall warrior with a winged helmet. The spear-bearing warrior invited Vhyolan to join his adventures, which mostly took him to Northlands, later known as Hillfort Lands. Vhyolan enjoyed Ulgarta's and his sister Haelgarta's company, who were brave fighters and excellent at using lengthy weapons like spears and axes. The siblings taught Vhyolan many things about the lands outside Galtreken and one could say that Vhyolan even learnt to laugh with the two.

Northlands had many early folks, who were ruled by shadowy ladies and lords, who either fought each other or raided towns outside the land. Ilvaine was a grim lady of the north and her greedy and scruffy servants stole the mythic marble chest from the halsurs. The chest contained the beauty, craftsmanship and knowledge of the people and its absence drained the lives of the halsurs. Haelgarta and Ulgarta mustered a warband and asked Vhyolan to join them on a quest to the north to reclaim the chest. Vhyolan, who had not experienced war, was very keen to see blood and glory with his own eyes. The marble chest was created by Belfares and Lemmesujelten and its theft gave Vhyolan and many others an opportunity to set their foot on a path of adventure and battle. The quest took many weeks and during the time Vhyolan did not only partake in battles, but met new powers of the world, which had not dwelled in the lost lands.

The energies called themselves asg and they were the forces who ultimately brought manfolk into the world. They looked exactly like their later creations, but were somewhat more ethereal in presence. The asg and Vhyolan discussed life several times and the halmhenden often told tales of lost lands. The young energies habitually gathered around Vhyolan, who sat by a campfire and told many legends about Loistesse and Körpihimgat. Vhyolan did not understand his own words, as he was sharing stories he did not experience personally, but were in his memory through Stala. Nevertheless, the tales were a huge success and the asg were envious of such a glorious past, giving them inspiration. The asg began to nurture heroes and send them all around the world to create epics and challenge beasts and evils. Eventually, from these peoples ascended manfolk, who would spread around the world. Sadly, Vhyolan did not know at the time, that some of these heroes were the beginning of Aetari, Dyveln and many other peoples, who partly caused the downfall of Worlgaltrin.

When the asg were living their mythological ages, Vhyolan absorbed some of their legends and energies. Stala saw the tales through Vhyolan's eye and they made him distressed. Stala could see Hasgastadl in flames as manfolk hurled their flaming swords in the sacred halls of his people. The creator of halmhendens wasted no time as he summoned Vhyolan back to Hurlgaltrin and forbade Vhyolan to partake in Haelgarta and Ulgarta's journeys. Something had got inside Vhyolan and its roots were the dawn of the manfolk, waving its blade at the halmhendens in Stala's nightmares. Perhaps Stala was resentful of the asg, who were young and independent from the burdens of the past. He saw something special and concerning in them simultaneously. It was as if Stala wished that it was the asg he had created and not the halmhendens.

The Altulls, who ruled Worlgaltrin, had been tightening their grip over the realm and many other families had retreated to their own houses. Everyone had to work together, but the atmosphere was tense and emotions windy. Tuolan Rauwos had remained in Worlgaltrin when Vhyolan was in the east, and his obligations as a warden of Worlgaltrin had been boring. Upon his return, Tuolan was glad to see Vhyolan, who spoke of Northlands and the peoples who resided there. Tuolan recognised that Oasven had begun to speak of armies and war quests to conquer all the surroundings lands to prevent all their possible enemies entering Galtreken. Tuolan and Vhyolan and many others thought it was an insane idea, as the other peoples were not warmongers.

Oasven was jealous of Vhyolan and Tuolan, and he tried to find any reason to remove the brothers from their ranks, so he and his family could alone rule Worlgaltrin. The family of Rauwos and their supporters lived in their mansions, north from the city, which gave their family an advantage over many others. Oasven was not able to spy on the family of Rauwos as easily as the others, who resided within the walls of the city. Vhyolan, who was frustrated about the absence Stala, travelled east to speak with the halsurs. Here, Vhyolan met his old friends and warned them of Oasven, who had already caused trouble in their lands. The possibility of a war was lurking in the shadows and the bold warriors of halsur were hesitant, but willing to fight for their lives if necessary.

Belfares, who had regained the marble chest, kept inviting Vhyolan and Tuolan to his realm, as he considered the two as friends. The three had established a trust, which showed a spark of hope in the middle of Oasven's actions. However, Vhyolan's and Tuolan's travels east had been noted by Oasven, who had assigned a scout to gather information on the two brothers. Oasven was suspecting a betrayal and he was using any reason to kill the brothers. At first, the two were removed from their ranks as wardens of the realm, which finally got the attention of Stala. The creator of the halmhendens was furious when titles given by him were removed from the brothers of Rauwos. Oasven, who was a skilful speaker, spoke with Stala and claimed that the brothers were going to ally with the halsurs and attack Hurlgaltrin.

Stala gave a permission to assemble forces and travel east to see what Vhyolan and Tuolan were planning. Stala was suspicious of the situation, but had promised Oasven a chance to prove his competence. Vhyolan and Tuolan were eating food and sharing mead with Belfares when the army of Worlgaltrin attacked. Stala had no time to stop Oasven, who charged with his cavalry to the towns and mountainside mansions, slaying halsurs swiftly. Oasven had notable preponderance and his force could easily surround the small realm, giving the people no time to speak or properly defend themselves. Only the brothers were spared, who were brought in front of Oasven and Stala. Vhyolan, whose mouth and forehead were bleeding, looked at all his dead friends and the smiling Oasven, whose face shone of power and confidence.

The brothers of Rauwos returned to Worlgaltrin with the army of Oasven and Stala. Tuolan or Vhyolan did not talk with Oasven, but Stala kept looking at Vhyolan, whose bloodstained clothes and face was full of anger and vengeance. Stala sneered and rode next to Vhyolan and subtly handed him a dagger, which was covered in familiar runes. Vhyolan looked at the gift and smiled under his bloody face, which showed a sign of relief and satisfaction. Without a single word, the company returned to the realm after several days of travel and Vhyolan began to think about his fatal move.

"I must unleash my anger, otherwise I might hurt myself. It is a call of my inner echoes, which no one can prevent, a true sign of awakening. I have hated him since the day I met him and finally I will end his life, which will release me from this anger forever. It is the greatest reward I have received from the almighty Stala and I shall make it memorable like the end of a long war. I am reborn through this deed; every drop of his blood will bring me joy beyond expression. I will stab him until he is dry like gravel, a pitiful husk understanding his mortality, begging for a drop of life, which I will drink with his tears. If my anger could inflict its fury upon the family of Altull, I would vomit molten hate upon their people and see them cry for mercy, as their bodies would diminish into oblivion."

Where there was life, there was death as well. Vhyolan killed Oasven in one of the gardens of Worlgaltrin, where he used to walk alone. Oasven had become too bold and he believed that no one dared to touch him, as his influence swept over the realm like a lash hitting a pitiful servant. Vhyolan approached him and stabbed him repeatedly, making his stomach a muddle of pain, which showed his mortality. Darkness fell over Vhyolan's world and his life was fulfilled with meaning. It was the path he was always supposed to walk and now it was glowing stronger than ever before. In the struggle against Oasven, Vhyolan lost his other eye completely, yet its vision of Hurlgaltrin remained strong.

When the whole world is against you and when the world does not believe you, it is a waste of time to say any words either. The only thing one can do is smile and behold how the world does not have any hold of you. Vhyolan had these thoughts, when he faced the council that sentenced him to prison. The eye of Stala remained open and the two saw the same future of flames and destruction, where Worlgaltrin was going to fall. Yet, Vhyolan and Stala remained stubborn and kept the spirit alive. Vhyolan's energies were removed, but it all had a meaning, as he was concealed from the death that was awaiting the realm. His isolation kept the past and future alive and his thoughts would dwell in the musty prisons, waiting for the day to reappear.

"They thought that I lost my freedom, but in truth, I was finally free from their inevitable ending. I only had to wait until it would happen, so I could challenge the enemies that would destroy us. I would face defeat, so I would receive knowledge of power of the new world. This I would take to Stala and with its energy, we would forge a weapon beyond life and death, one day making the world bend on its knees."

Indeed, the imprisonment of Vhyolan had a meaning, which no one could have ever understood. He was the atmosphere that Stala was protecting, and the events that were going to happen could have jeopardised his life if he was outside the prison. When the time was right, Tuolan freed his brother from the dungeons of Jarlidan, where his thoughts had manifested into a raging serpent. The blood of a dragon was flowing in Vhyolan when Tuolan broke through Jarlidan and the unmotivated guards left the fort. Vhyolan was weak and his energies were gathering slowly, but it did not prevent him seeing a new dawn, designed by the mighty Stala. It was the era of conflict, and halmhaers had appeared in the world, calling true warriors of halmhendens for the final battle to determine the fate of their people.

When Vhyolan was recovering, he asked how his life could have been different. He seemed to be the only one who could literally see the whole picture and destruction, which was going to abolish all the achievements of halmhendens. It was the time of the War of Hulstakn and it pushed Vhyolan's desire to recover. Meanwhile, Stala was building his relations with the storm elves, who helped the halmhendens to fight over Worlgaltrin. Ultimately, Vhyolan missed the battles, but heard about how Hurastil, a great champion of Kajoste slew the halmhaer commander Phaer in the final battle.

Vhyolan continued his own endeavours, whilst watching over Hurlgaltrin and its people. He had finally understood the structures of the past and now everything was clearer to him than before. According to Vhyolan, all of the lost lands were somewhere in Drytvaarte, but enough time had passed that their locations had been forgotten. The halmhenden believed in a cycle, which also gave an interpretation for each previous age. Vhyolan wrote about how Loistesse, Kajoste and many other places were indeed in the same world, but their mythic status had made them appear as if they had never existed. He also added that the cosmic fabrics and curtains were possibly the reason behind the separation of place and age.

Simultaneously, Vhyolan was concerned about Stala and his neglectful attitude in Drytgastadl. The creator of the halmhendens was no longer present and he was said to appear worn and sad. Vhyolan had understood that Stala did have plans for the future, but his mind was no longer able to interpret them. Vhyolan wanted to prove to him that halmhendens could one day rise and be worthy of his new plan. The halmhenden began to approach many forces who opposed manfolks and began to build up alliances. Vhyolan tried to gather as many halmhendens as possible, but the remaining kinsmen declined after the age of separation ended.

Nevertheless, all of this did not prevent Vhyolan from carrying out his coming revenge on manfolk. For uncountable years Vhyolan travelled and tried to find fighters, who wanted to destroy Aetari, Dyveln and many other realms. It seemed that very few were keen to join the halmhenden cause and he was often seen as an old bitter man, desperately wanting to achieve something impossible. Occasionally, some gabyr clans joined Vhyolan's ranks and he even managed to wake wars in the lands of the manfolk and elves, but the efforts were not enough. Vhyolan even asked the storm elves, who also refused to join the war. In the end, the halmhenden ran out of allies, which made him approach gelders: warriors of the north.

Vhyolan was aware of the gelders and their struggles of the past. The halmhenden offered Worlgaltrin for the people, which was too tempting for the gelders to reject and they decided to join Vhyolan's plan. The War of the Returning One began and it was the one final chance for Vhyolan to prove his worth to Stala. The early steps of the war were successful for Vhyolan, but later the conflict turned against itself. The gelders had to return to the north, where their realm was attacked by gabyrs and Vhyolan's sanity was coming to an end. In the Battle of Worlgaltrin, the armies of Aetari, Dyveln, Ylvart and Podfrud defeated the remaining gelders, and Vhyolan escaped to east, where his plan was to reach Hurlgaltrin.

In the cave of Hurlgaltrin, Vhyolan fought his last battle against miscellaneous warriors of different backgrounds. The halmhenden was certain of his death, but at least his passing would happen in Hurlgaltrin. In the cave, his eye and runes danced as the halmhenden battled the foes that had been pursuing him for days. Everyone was tired, but the desire to win was overwhelming. Vhyolan slew a few of his opponents and finally fell to the ground, where his life was taken by the sky elf Grand Lord Commander Faerkroll. The halmhenden's passing grabbed him like a stream of warm water and his eyes finally closed, sending his spirit towards the ancestral halls in Hasgastadl.

"For many years I have travelled on this earth. Many adventures and stories I have witnessed. What have I seen? I really do not know. Maybe I have seen love and hate and all that lies in between. Maybe it all was just a spell that

made me forget how cold this world is. Maybe it was all a dream that I saw a long time ago. Who knows, but I am here to leave a mark on this place, drifting in this desolation, which the people around me call life. It would be easy if we all knew were we all are going. But then again, who would define those roads of hope? Who would give you the keys to the knowledge that would release you from this meaninglessness and frustration?"

THE GLASS THROAT OF THE WORLD

When the realms of Halmhendens began to fall after numerous conflicts and internal troubles, some of the halmhendens could not bear the defeat and ended up killing themselves. Stala decided to punish the ones who had decided to take their own lives and built a massive glass bottle in a place that was said to be underneath the world. The place was so large that it had forests and lakes inside it and it bore the name of Alasgastadl, the glass throat of the world. The loss of many halmhenden lives had caused large imbalances in the world's magical constructs and had turned some halmhendens into halmhaers. Ultimately, these folks were eternally bound to oppose magic and Stala thought that it was best for the halmhaers to be captured in Alasgastadl.

The glass bottle world was also surrounded by the realm of night that reigned under Drytvaarte and it was said that when the night came, it took over the world's skies. It is unclear whether Stala and the force of night were friends or enemies, but at first there were no clear adversities. Meanwhile, the captured halmhaers realised that they could possess enormously strong magical abilities that were the very opposite of spells. The abilities could remove, absorb and destroy pure magic, which ignited the flame of revenge in the hearts of their newly-forged people.

When the years went by, the halmhaers grew in population and their magical skills became stronger and fiercer. The people built large stone mansions and towers to practice their magical art. The most important part was the founding of Celtenvalan, the great vault of spells. Celtenvalan became tremendously successful in the leadership of Galestrade and Plenehalasam, the two mightiest halmhaers.

Alasgastadl's presence developed so strong that it started to absorb magic from the world itself, affecting the magical breathing of the existence. The halmhaers were first certain that they could destroy the whole world's magic with Alasgastadl, but this failed as the world started to produce more magic in its own pace.

The magical breathing of the existence also disturbed the realm of night, which regarded the glass bottle world as a threat. This started a struggle, where the night constantly tried to get inside Alasgastadl and end the small world of halmhaers. The folk acknowledged the hostility of the night, so they began to plan how to protect their coming days. When the tower of Julostal was built by Plenehalasam, the woman remembered a friend who she met during the journey to Alasgastadl. The friend's name was Aringolasvasulbarad, a large flying creature resembling a dragon that was hollow like a spectre. It could fly through different layers of the world and had the wingspan of a mountain.

For decades Plenehalasam tried to contact the flying creature and eventually Aringolasvasulbarad arrived into the realm of Alasgastadl. The creature promised to help halmhaers in their return to the world, if it could get the realm of night as its home. This was a hard bargain for the halmhaers, but seemed an inevitable trade, as the realm of night was their foe as well. The deal was sealed and very soon Drytgastadl felt the approaching storm, which was percolating from the glass throat of the world.

Many halmhaer schemes occurred in Drytgastadl and they caused great despair on several personal levels. However, the people never managed to become a threat to the world and remained shadowy wanderers and grim rulers of forbidden places. Their situation remained the same until a group of adventurers found a way to enter the realm of night, and with their ship they approached the glass bottle world. Nelleffe Atmoryn and a man named Abyss sailed in the realm of night towards Alasgastadl with their crew and they were approaching the world so fast, that the ship broke through the glass wall. Water began to fall into the glass bottle, eventually drowning the surprised halmhaers, leaving only the ones who were outside Alasgastadl alive. The glass throat of the world had been finally shut.

"I am dead, or will be dead soon. I cannot tell the difference anymore, since I am already living a deceased life. I do not want the feeling to be with me, but I cannot do anything about the constant consciousness that makes me solely dull. I am not going to live long, but I will at least work hard to leave something to this world. So, I beg to the forces of this world, give me enough time to at least finish my work, before I disappear to the oblivion. My mind is a disease either fooling me or then it is telling me that the end has come. Regardless, all the words are useless, because my illusions are taking me somewhere I can finally rest. Farewell."

PEOPLES OF DRYVAARTE

PART 2

ELVES

Diddy Diddy Wazz.

According to the legendarium of the elven peoples, they lived a long time ago in a place named Selkelgen. In these lands dwelled four great powers who were called Mother Sky, Father Storm, Pearl Wind and White Hat. The four powers had mostly focused on building mighty mansions and fortresses, but eventually they became lonely in their empty halls. The boredom sparked a desire to create mortal folk, who could share the world with them and furthermore, achieve great deeds.

Mother Sky created her elves and put the families of Holsgerv and Oldanhalv to lead them. These sky elves were blessed with intelligence and tranquillity and the two families were successful from the very beginning. The firmament was rejoicing their presence and every step sparked light where no one else had previously trod.

Father Storm saw the creations of Mother Sky and became envious, since her creations were so graceful and noble in his deep blue eyes. Father Storm did not want to be overshadowed by Mother Sky's folk, so he made the storm elves cunning and ambitious. Father Storm called the families of Sadetske and Proikelt the mightiest bloodlines, and rulers of their people. One could say that this started the friction between the two major powers, as their creations competed for success.

Pearl Wind, who had lived with Mother Sky and Father Storm, made the shore elves, as she hoped that the elves would explore the seas and protect the lands from possible foes. The folk of shore elves manifested from her thoughts and were known for their bravery and yearning for adventure.

The protector of the mountain elves flew frequently in the air like a white serpent with memorable headwear. This was the reason the power was called White Hat, as his appearance resembled a snow-covered mountain side. White Hat hoped that his creations would be the fiercest ones, so he gifted his elves with arrogance, a daring attitude and will to challenge.

During the years of Selkelgen, the situation between the four elven peoples became incredibly intricate and challenging. It seemed that the elven folk had started a journey and a story that would last forever and the ages to come would only play as a stage for their grandeur. Eventually, a war began between the elven families and numerous alliances and treaties were made, which defined the relationships of the elves for rest of their days. The War of Selkelgen ended when Mother Sky escaped on the top of the shield of the sky. Father Storm built a massive bridge of water to the skies, so he and his loyal guards could sail and face the mother. On the firmament, the enormous ships of the storm elves crushed trough the waves and beheld Mother Sky's fury. Father Storm shouted for Mother Sky, who appeared from above. In the shadows, Mother Sky had created her most powerful creations, great silvery birds, which were now descending upon the storm elf ships. The greatest and final battle of Selkelgen's days had begun.

The shield of the sky, which had turned into a sea, witnessed a clash that lasted for weeks. Mother Sky lost many of her silver birds and had no other choice than to break the whole sky apart. The firmament fractured and the seas and the ships fell from the skies. It is believed that due to this legend, Selkelgen disappeared and washed all the elves to the inland sea of Yeldes in Drytgastadl.

"The waves were hitting the shores with such a vehemence that even some of the stone cliffs broke. The sky was roaring and the thunder was striking its spears of light down to the depths of the earth. I could see them struggling in the waves as they were gasping for air. So many of them were washed onto the shore, exhausted and confused they stood up on the shores. They were arguing over matters I could not understand, but it appeared that their ancient parents were in a conflict. For days I was with them, hearing tales about Mother Sky and Father Storm, who gave birth to their kin. One day, the oldest of them, named Heledvilas, ordered the people to scatter, and to find

separate homes since it had become impossible to live together. In the following days, the folks left in different directions, to places where they could find peace and good life.

"I was invited to a celebration, which was led by the new high queen. The long tables were full of delicious dishes and chalices of delightful wine. The bards were singing and playing their flutes, as the brisk autumn evening was sending its last light upon the field of our celebration. These people confused me, as I felt how gracious they were, but simultaneously they were hiding something. I could not read these folks, as if they were too cunning and powerful. Nevertheless, I could at least tell that behind their noble appearance lay a wolf that should not be threatened"

Ultimately, the tales of Selkelgen became folklore in the minds of the elves after their arrival in Drytgastadl. No one knew whether anything had ever happened, nor if Selkelgen had ever even existed. Nevertheless, it was certain that the story that once began in Selkelgen would continue in Drytgastadl as well. It could be suggested that the world of Selkelgen was a shared dream world of the elves, which prepared them for a greater journey. All the decisions and deeds of the elves in the world were part of this greater plot, which the people wanted to continue infinitely. One could say that every accomplishment that was done by an elf was just part of the story, an effort to reach the end of the long-living legend.

THE CHILDREN OF THE SKY

Mother Sky, also known as Gailinimoler was one of the children of Arbigolear, the creative power of the sky, and Hegelus, the profound spirit of love. The two were very protective of their daughter, so they decided to create Selkelgen with the assistance of other powers and spirits. In here, Gailinimoler met Qlaskastet and the two fell in love. After many years, the two could not have children, which saddened both deeply. Gailinimoler knew that she had to create her children by herself, making the elves of the sky fall into her arms. This was the dawn of her people, who gave her the name: Mother Sky.

The mother built a glorious home for her elves, who were happy and affluent from the very first day. It seemed that nothing could change the bliss of the situation, as the days passed in this forgotten world. Mother Sky knew that Qlaskastet was envious of her creations, which were going to be the most successful elves in Selkelgen. Mother Sky did not know that Qlaskastet was involved with many other powers of the world, which eventually changed the course of history.

When Stala came to Selkelgen, Mother Sky remained oblivious to his presence and relations with Qlaskastet, the father of the storm elves. Stala had a plan which appealed to him, and this was the first chapter that could lead to a tragedy of blood and lost love. When Mother Sky completed Ylvantail, the greatest of cities in Selkelgen, she decided to build great halls upon the skies to celebrate the achievement. Once again, Father Storm could not stand the sight of Ylvantail and the sky elves, who had gained all the glory and prosperity in the world. The storm elves began to question Father Storm, since he was not improving the situation, and Stala knew that he could easily use the circumstances to his advantage.

Father Storm and Stala began to conspire behind Mother Sky's back. Stala promised that Father Storm could take his elves to Drytgastadl, where they could live with the halmhendens and become more powerful than in Selkelgen. Father Storm could not see through the deceiving eyes of Stala, whose wish was to use the storm elves as simple servants and soldiers.

Ultimately, the sky elves began to look down on the storm elves, who had not achieved the same level of grandiosity. This arrogance caused many confrontations and Mother Sky could sense the coming of troublesome times. The mother sent many spies amongst the storm elves, who found out about the plan that had been brewing between Father Storm and Stala. At first, Mother Sky was not angered about the secret plan, but Stala's hidden presence and shadowy moves alone made her furious.

Mother Sky and Stala met each other in the mountains of Selkelgen, which dwarfed even the largest of mountains in Drytgastadl. In here, Mother Sky declared war on Stala, who she claimed had deceived Father Storm. Unfortunately, the father supported Stala, who had promised him all the riches and power in Drytgastadl, ending the story of Gailinimoler and Qlaskastet.

The battles that commenced between the elves in Selkelgen were bloody and broke many families apart, forging new and unexpected allegiances as well. For ages, Mother Sky stayed in her halls above the firmament, as she was disappointed in the world and the powers who reigned there. Father Storm, who was an active part of the war, realised that the storm elves could not win the war on Selkelgen's soil. Instead, Father Storm created a plan to cast down Mother Sky from her home with a fleet of his finest warriors.

Father Storm raised a bridge of water to the skies during the early days of autumn. The mother did not know that her elves were attempting to prevent this daring creation of Father Storm. Nevertheless, it was too late, as the great fleet of storm elves sailed to the skies waving their spears in a thunderous rhythm.

Mother Sky saw how her home had been filled with water and hundreds of hostile ships. In her final defence, Mother Sky created the silvery birds, which were sent against the storm elves and their fleet. For countless days the elves fought, ultimately forcing Mother Sky to break the sky in half.

The elves commonly believed that this was the beginning of the age of Drytgastadl, when the whole of Selkelgen broke and the great waves took the elves to the world. All the greater powers fell with the world as well, leaving Mother Sky and Father Storm weaker alongside many others. It forced all of them to hide and find a place to gather strength and influence for the coming days.

For many years of silence, Mother Sky and Father Storm met in Drytgastadl, where they both regretted the events of their beloved Selkelgen. Unfortunately, Father Storm, who had been working with the halmhendens, had followed his moves in the shadows. The father unintentionally led an army of halmhendens and Stala to the secret meeting point, escalating another intense clash.

Mother Sky and Father Storm decided that the love they once had was worth saving, making the two confront Stala and his servants. The battle raged all around the lands, eventually leading to the depths of the world, to a place that was familiar to many old powers. The well of Kulus appeared in front of the belligerents, who had been battling for many days. In here, the fight that had taken many lives and destroyed the unity of the elves finally ended.

The crushing force of Stala and his halmhendens were too much for Mother Sky and Father Storm, who decided to jump into the well to save their weakened lives. Stala gazed at the depths, where some of the captured spirits attempted to escape. Swiftly, Stala closed the well and the creative powers of the elves disappeared from the world. However, after enough time had passed, many legends claimed that Mother Sky and Father Storm returned to Drytgastadl, where they moved as nameless wanderers.

LIVING MEMORY NAMED ALVUNAIL

After the events in the shores of the inland sea of Yeldes, Terwas Oldanhalv declared himself as the high king of all sky elves. This was not agreed by more than half of the sky elves, as they were looking at Fyerell Holsgerv, now declared as the high queen. During the day, the unity of the sky elves was broken and High King Terwas took his elves south, where his intention was to establish a kingdom.

Terwas wanted to build a city that would remember the age of Selkelgen and so he gave it the name 'Alvunail', meaning 'Memory'. Terwas dedicated his whole life to building the city, which began as a simple town with wooden cottages and walls. During these years, the high king wrote numerous books, which remained as important sources for the folklore of the sky elves.

Later in time, Queen Vlostnelle Oldanhalv commenced a project to build several libraries to the city of Alvunail to store these books. The buildings had become lavish with decorations and commons, often having a lot of influence over the realm. All the knowledge the sky elves of Alvunail possessed was gathered to these libraries, which caused partial competition between their sages. Every library wanted the best and oldest tomes, as in many cases there were only a few copies existing.

The city of Alvunail had five highly regarded libraries and several smaller ones. The five were named: Prilven, Fovoent, Asmariod, Gimbacte and Hylkoskaus. The rivalry between the libraries and their elders was so fierce that Klostnelle Oldanhalv, Vlostnelle's daughter, commanded her forces to intervene. Ultimately, order was reinstated by experienced mages, who confiscated the most sought-after books. For many seers, this was an unfair intervention, as they felt that their authority was removed.

Vlostnelle Oldanhalv died under suspicious circumstances, which created an uncertain atmosphere in the city. It was believed that the assassins of Ikirias had killed the queen, as the relations with the storm elves were shambolic. However, it was later revealed that the queen had been slain by a member who worked in one of the archives. No one knew which library the assassin came from and who had hired the killer to do the task, but it soaked the internal relations in blood. This also started the era when many of the libraries were harshly distrustful towards each other, and many mysterious events happened around royal and literary circles.

Conflict with Ikirias was inevitable after ages of scheming, eventually commencing the War After the Whispers, which occurred between four different factions and their allies. Alvunail had five armies, of which one abandoned the main task to defeat Ikirias' armies. The storm elves of Ikirias had six armies, but two of them were full of mercenaries. It happened to be so, that Alvunail's army, which abandoned the war quest, was commanded by Fust Kaus, a sworn enemy of the Ikirias' mercenary army's commander.

The clash between commander Kaus and the mercenary Lord Smardas forced the war in an unforeseen direction. It did not help either, that Kaus and Smardas were half-brothers. The family of the two got heavily involved in the war, which was mainly raging between Ikirias and Alvunail. Also, when sky elf commander Chaamos Igunn led his armies to the realm of Ikirias, his family was kidnapped by agents of Ikirias and it was believed that the archive of Prilven helped in this. Chaamos did not hesitate to act and the commander sent a letter to Alvunail. The letter commanded his guard to take hold of Prilven and slay the traitors. The event started another part of the war, which led to many battles within Alvunail's city. As one could see, the situation was one bloody mess.

The War of the Gleaming Bonfires defined a lot of fates in the world of Drytgastadl. The spies of Alvunail had been following and investigating various gabyr clans, which possibly had the long-lost information regarding Kulus. Gabyr warlord Milokg gathered his large armies when the presumed location of Kulus was found in Hevnenkoil. The concerning and distressing information reached Alvunail, and a great army was assembled by Queen Delianke Oldanhalv. The sky elves of Ylvart joined the war hosts of Alvunail in an attempt to finally unite the two realms, which had been separated for too long.

The storm elves of Ikirias joined the war as well, having somewhat different aims compared to the elves of Alvunail and Ylvart. In the eyes of the sky elves this appeared to be a clear intrusion. It was generally believed that when Mother Sky and Father Storm fell into the depths of Kulus, the only way for their complete return was to open the well again. This of course set the stage for the two sides who hoped for the return of their mythic parent.

It was no surprise that halmhendens joined the war, as it was essential for them to capture all the spirits of the well before halmhaers could consume them as energy. The more the halmhendens could seize spirits, the weaker the halmhaers would become in Alasgastadl. The sky elves of Alvunail at first did not realise the scale of the war, but when the halmhendens appeared into the picture, the situation became more serious than ever. Due to the several belligerents, Alvunail and Ylvart decided to send their troops to Hevnenkoil, where the gabyr armies had resided before entering the underground complexes of Kulus.

The first battles of the war happened in the spring, when the sky elves, storm elves, gabyrs and halmhendens with their mercenaries fought on the fields of Hevnenkoil. Later the war moved underground, to the great stone halls of Kulus, where eternal bonfires lit the ancient walls. Ultimately, the sky elf armies found themselves in a distressing situation. The main body of the army had been mostly pushed on the side, leaving some of their smaller sections in the very eye of the ongoing clashes. During one of these fights, the smaller sections were saved by a sudden arrival of the dwarfs of Saunfrud. The dwarfs landed from above, falling from the ceiling of the stone halls, which looked like starry skies. It seemed that the dwarf army had found a way to elude the boundaries of the world, moving through a hidden passageway, between the physical landscapes. This was unseen by everyone in the conflict, and even the halmhendens could not believe their eyes in the heat of the battle.

With the assistance of the dwarfs, the sky elves pushed back the halmhendens, gabyrs and the storm elves, who all were giving each other the good old kicking. In between the clashes, the commander of the Alvunail's army, Lincaltarga Paurta, spoke with the commander of dwarfs, Douste Haskk. The dwarf commander said that according to their folk's legends, an ancient smith forged four ethereal keys, which he accidentally dropped into a furnace that was connected to the same magic as Kulus. The keys were created to open particular doors, which the dwarfs used to find hidden passageways. It seemed that the dwarfs had found at least one of the keys, as the manner of their arrival was unreservedly unexpected.

The keys were also said to help the dwarfs to find a way to Hjardabristallum, the greatest of stars, where their elder protector dwelled. Nevertheless, commander Paurta was very suspicious towards the dwarfs, since they appeared from a place that was beyond the reach of mortal beings. No one knew whether the commander suddenly lost his mind, but he decided to stab the dwarf commander without any decent reason. This action led to the death of the dwarf lord, whose soldiers did not hesitate to attack after the insane act.

For weeks, the battles continued in Kulus, where the atmosphere had turned into a furnace of hate. The halmhendens and their mercenaries had gained control of the well, and commander Paurta, who was now heavily targeted by the dwarfs, decided to break through the lines of the halmhendens. During the charge, the halmhendens opened the door of the well, causing a massive blast. The explosion was so vast, that the whole of Kulus and its halls collapsed, bringing everybody to their untimely deaths.

According to many legends, the soldiers who fought in the war continued the fight somewhere beyond the mortal spheres. The ending of the war was utterly frustrating for all sides, since it did not solve anything, nor had it provided any winners or losers. It seemed that the whole war had been an elaborate ruse by the spirits of Kulus to cause as much destruction as possible. Most likely, the spirits could feed on the deaths of the thousands of soldiers after the collapse. This also possibly meant that this was only a distraction, and the true location of the well was somewhere else. It was an apoplectic disaster for all sides of the war and in the deep darkness the spirits of Kulus rejoiced.

Alvunail lost the armies of Pundentark, Voisenbaste, Maugasplevet and Ciniausfrand. The loss of the four armies was such a tragic setback for the realm that Alvunail had to hire various mercenaries to replace the shortage of soldiers. Eventually, the gabyr army, led by the Lord Nava, attacked Alvunail, using the horrendous situation of the realm to their advantage. The conflict of Alvunposget lasted for two years, and during that time the remaining armies, guards and mercenaries defended the realm. Ylvart joined the mutual front with Alvunail, amalgamating the relationship of the two realms. After the war, Alvunail and Ylvart had a strong alliance, which was the very first time the realms were on good terms. Ultimately, the ending of the devastating war led the two realms to combine their powers, so they could find the way to bring back Mother Sky.

THE FIRST HIGH KING OF THE SKY

The first high king of the sky elves, Terwas Oldanhalv, was the son of Thenwas Oldanhalv, presumably an ancient king in the age of Selkelgen. Terwas was a determined and driven elf, who wanted to preserve the memories of Selkelgen at any cost. This also meant that he could protect his own (and his family's) right to the throne of Alvunail. Terwas saw Fyerell Holsgerv, who was declared as the high queen of the sky elves, as a threat to his family and its power. Terwas thought that many of her supporters were undervaluing the importance of Selkelgen's legacy and it was essential to protect the past from ignorance.

"If you forget the past of your people, your realm will drown in lies."

Terwas travelled south with his loyalists and began to build a town, which later became Alvunail. During these years, the king saw several visions and prophecies whilst he was sleeping. The most important vision Terwas experienced regarded the return of Mother Sky. The king wanted to build a throne for her glory and place it in the same hall where he resided in Alvunail. In his dreams Terwas saw how Mother Sky split the firmament in half and an imposing rain of light struck the earth. Amongst the golden drops of light fell the greatest of birds, which had lived and protected Mother Sky in Selkelgen.

Terwas claimed that he had seen many dreams of Selkelgen where Mother Sky and Father Storm lived and loved each other. He saw the age when Father Storm, known as Qlaskastet, built a glorious bridge of clouds, which he used to walk to the skies. Terwas often spoke about how every step of Qlaskastet caused a great thunder and Mother Sky was amused by the grandeur of his arrival. In here, Qlaskastet proposed to Gailinimoler, who was later known as Mother Sky. Terwas wanted the greatest love story the world had ever seen to be immortalised in the wooden carvings in Alvunail. This was exceptional, since it was common for the sky elves to dislike everything that had anything to do with Father Storm.

Alvunail's name meant 'Memory' and Terwas Oldanhalv built a large wooden hall in the middle of the city to collect all olden tales together. The place was unsurprisingly called the hall of memories, or Alvunaillvalet. The reason behind such an important project was his dreams of an immense hall, where all the mighty elves of Selkelgen stood in a vast crowd, cheering at Terwas. The hall had many important and recognisable faces who once dwelled in Selkelgen and according to the words of the king; wished him good fortune. Some sages of Alvunail later were suspicious of the vision, calling it a self-granted and self-important lie, which Terwas used to justify his legendary status as a king.

However, many of Terwas' books and works were regarded as the most important source of knowledge in the realm of Alvunail. For instance, the king wrote many books about ancient battles that happened in Selkelgen. However, there was a whole book dedicated to the last war, which broke the primordial world of the elven peoples. Terwas described in great detail how Mother Sky had left above the clouds, where she was gathering her powers. Father Storm raged in Selkelgen and made the skies rain for years. The whole land was filled with skirmishes and rain, which destroyed many houses in the process. Whilst the mountain elves were building their large towers and the shore elves were sailing in the surrounding seas, Father Storm raised a bridge of water to the skies. He had gathered all his warriors and was ready to fill the firmament with waves and tempest.

Terwas wrote about the storm elf ships which rose through the bridge, causing the violent winds to blow icy spikes. This was the moment when the great silvery birds appeared and Mother Sky ordered them to descend upon the longboats of the storm elves. Clashes happened on the tides and many pikes were broken, as the creatures attacked the ships. Eventually, Mother Sky had to break the firmament, as the war was calling an end for everyone and everything.

Kulus kept playing an important part in Terwas' visions. His grandest prophecy regarded the return of Mother Sky, who presumably was trapped in the depths of the world. Terwas saw a grand well in his visions, which later was assumed to be Kulus. The king talked about an ancient realm of halmhendens, where the well lay in darkness. The wisest of elves in Alvunail suggested that the place was probably the realm of Moltraugad, an ancient home of halmhenden's folk.

Terwas also saw a dream about the coming of the gabyr wars. In the dream, the king was inside a small cottage in the middle of a misty spruce forest. In here, he looked out of the loft's window and saw a warband of gabyrs marching. He was suddenly approached by an elven king, who resided in the cottage, and he said the following words:

"I am of different people and time; I am your thoughts at your prime. You have seen now the marching fury, for it is not me who will assemble the bury. Behold the dawn and the coming of the five lords, for they bring more than just swords. I am of a different life and fate, was it five lords or perhaps even eight?"

The vision and the prophecy regarding the king in the cottage and the gabyrs were lost background knowledge of the elves. The king of the cottage was Aldkjest Oldanhalv, Terwas' forgotten half-brother, who was partly of storm elf blood. The legend said that Terwas' father had a clandestine relationship with the storm elf, Lady Nievatuulit, and their only child was Aldkjest. When the secret came out, the already convoluted situation in Selkelgen burst into flames. The sky elf family of Holsgerv accused Thenwas Oldanhalv, Terwas' father, of treason.

REGARDING MEMORY AND ITS HOLDERS

The elves who lived and worked in the libraries had their own rules, currency and set of order, which occasionally seemed very odd for an outsider. The majority of these elves were lonely researchers, dedicating themselves to many abstruse and forgotten subjects.

One of these shadowy subjects was held inside the library of Noltval. In the large loft of the library, which was often used by the scholars as a meeting place, was a peculiar mat on the wall. The mat was woven from materials which were said to have disappeared from the world long time ago. The mat was named Kajoste, meaning 'Oblivion of Heroes'. Kajoste was hanging in the northern wall of the loft, where its pictures and textures were gliding slowly. Kajoste seemed to show stories, which lasted for years, gathering a following of elves who wanted to see all its tales. Every now and then, the pictures of beasts and warriors in the mat fought each other and the scholars loved to gamble about their victory. No one could understand the magic behind the object and whether any of its pictures and landscapes were real. The mat was brought to the library by Vlistan Oldanhalv, who was part of the royal family. According to the story, the mat was made in Selkelgen and it displayed tales how they occurred in Oblivion of Heroes. Of course, all of this was just fathoming by several bored sages.

ELVES OF THE NEW DAWN

When the elves departed the shores of the inland sea of Yeldes, Fyerell Holsgerv was declared as the rightful high queen of the sky elves. For Fyerell, this was obvious, since she descended from the ancient royal line of Holsgerv, who dwelled in Selkelgen. There was a confrontation between Fyerell and Terwas Oldanhalv, who claimed half of the support of the sky elves. Fyerell Holsgerv accused Terwas and his family of a betrayal that happened in Selkelgen.

In the old stories of the sky elves, Thenwas Oldanhalv, the father of Terwas, married a storm elf lady named Nievatuulit Vimpar. According to the legend, this broke the unity of the sky elves in Selkelgen, where they had been battling the storm elves and their allies. The storm elf family of Vimpar was a dedicated enemy of the sky elves of Holsgerv, who could not understand the marriage of Oldanhalv and Vimpar.

However, when Terwas departed, Fyerell decided to forget everything about the age of Selkelgen, since it seemed to cause nothing but tears and hate. High Queen Fyerell Holsgerv led her people not too far from the shores of the inland sea and established a town. The town was named Ylvart, meaning 'Tomorrow', and was a reference to Fyerell's intention to focus on the coming days, instead of the past.

For the people of Ylvart it was important to write about their lives and early days of the realm. Queen Holsgerv began to support the writers, since it meant that the years of Drytgastadl were written into their new legacy. The sky elves established many guilds dedicated for writers and the royals of Holsgerv were enthusiastically supporting the cause.

It was common for the sky elves of Ylvart to build stone buildings, which did not have walls, but instead had several pillars supporting them. Beautifully decorated canopies covered these stone halls, and the sky elves built their homes underneath these stone structures. The buildings were named Ylvartal Taigas, meaning 'Tomorrow's Shield'. The royal family of Holsgerv was certain of the wrath of Father Storm, so they decided to build all their homes under the ground. This meant that everyone had their front door by the end of a staircase that descended from the ground level of Ylvartal Taigas. Most of the stone halls included at least eight homes and were delicately hidden. The light could reach these rooms through circular windows, which were installed on the ceilings of the Ylvartian homes.

Two mighty sky elf sisters crafted four crystals to celebrate the years of Ylvart. Loraunad and Edonvelle were two of the most skilful jewel crafters in the young realm and the royal family of Holsgerv was very pleased with their workmanship. The four crystals were left outside for display, which affected them in mysterious ways. The crystals could absorb energy from each season of the year, surprising even their creators. The crystals were simply named summer, autumn, winter and spring, and each stone gained a specific colour.

Fyerell Holsgerv ordered that the four crystals should be preserved and embedded into larger items, so they would not be lost in time. The smiths of Ylvart took the crystals and carefully attached them to great heirlooms of the royal family. Summer crystal found its place in a sword, winter crystal in a dagger, spring crystal in a staff and autumn crystal in a bow. After this, the items with the crystals were given to the four most powerful families in Ylvart.

The family of Uljamiel, who was leading the warriors of Ylvart was given the sword, which glowed strong light from its crystal. Vainn Uljamiel, who was the commander of the soldiers, carried the sword with pride and promised that his family would serve the line of Holsgerv until the end of time.

In the legends of the sky elves, the family of Hestamperlen had always protected the royals of Holsgerv from all sorts of threats. This tradition was continued in Ylvart and Fyerell gave the winter crystal to Cuvelsoi Hestamperlen, the leader of the town's guard. This was a great tribute for the services of Hestamperlen and Cuvelsoi swore eternal allegiance to the family of Holsgerv.

The spokeswoman of the farmers of Ylvart was Yalon Tulos, who was given the staff with the spring crystal. In the old journals of Yalon, the woman mentioned the staff several times, saying that it had powers to make any land productive and bursting with flowers and useful plants. This was the first time Queen Holsgerv began to observe the crystals more closely and their magical powers. It was apparent that these crystals would have an important part in the future of the realm.

Lastly, the autumn crystal was given to Fikaslk Dosperlen, the leader of the hunters. The crystal was attached to a bow, which was made of dark oak with carved decorations. It was said that any arrow with the bow would find its way to the target, and one could see in any forest through the leaves, as if it was eternal autumn. Also, the bearer of the bow could see in in absolute darkness and feel no cold.

Haelgade Hestamperlen commenced the long-lasting tradition of the sky elf guard. The guard was a separate force from the army and it offered its services to the realm of Ylvart and the towns and villages that were outside the city's lands. It was partially a mercenary army, remaining loyal to Ylvart and the family of Holsgerv. The idea behind the guard was a rather bold one, since its purpose was to secretly control areas that did not belong to Ylvart, and make the realm wealthier through their expertise.

In the coming decades, the sky elf guard made many pacts north of the realm. Becoming the guardians of the trading town of Lhorem, the guard brought a lot of stability and riches for Ylvart and its surrounding lands. The sky elf guard built their numerous buildings in Lhorem, which served as their strongholds and vaults of wealth. The guard was popular amongst the folks who lived in Lhorem and surrounding villages, since they kept the lands safe and did not seem to present any threat to the domains of manfolk.

The sky elf guard became so favoured, that even the realm of Ikivial hired many of its soldiers and took them northeast. At the time this move was accepted by the families who supported the sky elf guard, and by its founder, Hestamperlen. For Ikivial, it was a brilliant move, since by the end of the same decade a war was knocking on the door.

When the War of the Dagger Front began, the realm of Ylvart was spared from the worst impact, but it felt obliged to assist the realms of Dyveln and Aetari, as their trade was flourishing. The grand commander of Ylvart's army, Hadainn Tulgerv, sent two armies to aid the manfolk realms, where massive battles took place with gabyrs.

Nonetheless, in the last decades of the war, Ylvart's situation worsened. The realm of Dyveln had been very successful in keeping the gabyr armies away from their realm, which meant that the gabyr hosts tried to attack Ylvart instead. Many of the villages and towns of the realm were burnt and pillaged, due to the lack of guards. The majority of the armies were in Enberahl, and the realm of Ylvart was left with too few fighters. The royals and their supporting families panicked as they realised how the gabyr armies had eluded from the far west, and were now marching in their lands.

Desperate battles occurred in the towns of the realm and soldiers were called back to Ylvart. Ultimately, the realm received its long-needed support from the guard and could finally protect itself from the blight of the gabyrs. When the most ferocious part of the defence was over, the royals realised that one of the guard regiments did not answer the call. This regiment had remained in Ikivial and were later enjoying their time under their queen's service.

The family of Hestamperlen and their supporting families heard outrageous news regarding the regiment, which was called Orden sa emmet, meaning 'From beyond the northern winds'. The regiment had named themselves Brew Guard and their loyalty had changed to the realm of Ikivial. Lady Aikomlas Hestamperlen declared that the guards of the regiment were traitors, who should be punished when the war was over.

The wish of the lady Hestamperlen never happened, as the war was very successful for Brew Guard and they gained the respect of many army and guard commanders who fought in the war. It seemed that it was more important for the family of Hestamperlen to demonstrate their power than win wars, which was noted by many of their friends. Hestamperlen kept control of the sky elf guard, but it became more cautious about where to send their troops.

In the War of the One-Eyed Seer, a mighty gabyr sorcerer tested the lands with his black magic. For many realms, the sorcery was so perplexing and ancient that it left numerous people insane and hollow. This time, Afalanosvolon, the great fifteen wizards of Ylvart, intervened. These individuals claimed to be direct sons and daughters of Selkelgen's greatest spellcasters. They could set their foes ablaze by touching fire and freeze everything around them by simply draining the spirits of ice. This was truly a rare gift, which the sky elves did not quite understand themselves.

The fifteen wizards led the armies of Ylvart, which fought alongside Aetari and Dyveln. In the war, nine of the wizards fell in battle and two disappeared. The remaining four wizards, who saw the end of the war due to their exceptionally long lives, returned to Ylvart where they lived till the end of their days.

One of the wizards who survived the war, Fyn Lauskelen, had a grim secret. During the war, the dark seer, who led the armies of gabyrs cursed the wizard after a battle, which Ylvart's northern army lost. Fyn resisted some of the black magic which was inflicted upon him, but it was not quite enough. Fyn barely escaped the battle and for several days he was lost in the deep forests of Enberahl. In there, he was taken over by a curse, which changed him forever.

When Fyn Lauskelen returned to Ylvart, he came across two wizards who were also part of Afalanosvolon. The spellcasters could sense that something had changed in Fyn, which made them question the elf. However, Fyn had learnt to use his new abilities and he began to talk to the two wizards with persuading words. It did not take long until the two were in control of Fyn Lauskelen, who commanded them to disappear forever and forget that he ever possessed such skills.

Ylvart's families welcomed Lauskelen back, after three other wizards had returned to the realm as well. Fyn did not have any quarrel with the remaining mages and he could continue with his secret ways. Due to the curse, Lauskelen started secretly the lineage of elves who could manipulate people with their words and make them do deeds against their will.

"I knew about his abilities after the war, but I could not act, as no one would have believed me. He was a friend of the royals and their closest families. He was regarded as a hero who won the war. Inside, he was a snake who only loved himself, a black heart of corruption and lies. I do not know what happened to him during the war, but he was not Fyn who I used to know. Half of him had been changed by darkness, which was smiling on his face day and night."

Later in time, the War of the Returning One was a more defining conflict, which shaped many internal relations of the realm. It was also part of an age when many great heroes of Ylvart arose from the shadows to finally end the madness in the world. For instance, one particular sky elf individual showed exceptional strength for his old age in the conflict.

The elf's name was Rylskar Halmverlen, the master herbalist of Ylvart. Rylskar was the second highest of all the seers in the realm and a well-known advisor of the members of the royal family. His bravery and skills helped Crayvar Vostger, Wahlvern Hebelcurnn and Diwion Heliory in their quest. The four had a significant part in the War of the Returning One, which lasted only a year, but was fierce in its spirit. Due to the actions of the four, one could say that the war was won and Lord Vhyolan defeated, who was a halmhenden leading an army of gelders. Rylskar's tale became part of Ylvart's folklore and his knowledge about life, herbs and the world was used by many scholars and students in the realm.

Many sky elves had heard about the mysterious well of Kulus, which lay somewhere under the ground. Kulus was a place where spirits of olden times were imprisoned and their emancipator would be granted great powers. It was also believed that Mother Sky could return through the opening of the well and this was considered as a great opportunity to approach the realm of Alvunail as well.

However, scouts of Ylvart and Alvunail discovered that a powerful gabyr clan had found access to Kulus in the lands of Hevnenkoil. Since Alvunail and Ylvart had the same intentions in the war, the two realms decided to unite their forces to defeat the gabyrs and claim the well. Of course, the war was not going to be a simple one, since the storm elves of Ikirias became interested in Kulus as well. Ylvart's king, Tol Holsgerv, started to doubt the true intentions of Alvunail, because of their ancient relations with the storm elves. According to the king, this could have been an elaborate plan to defeat Ylvart, so Alvunail and Ikirias could reign as two realms.

King Tol Holsgerv decided to use the services of Afanagil Lauskelen, who possessed a dangerous ability. Just like Afanagil's ancestors and several members of her family, she could manipulate people by talking and suggesting different ideas. The family of Lauskelen had been used in various conflicts before, but this time King Holsgerv had an exceptional task for Afanagil. The king wanted to send Afanagil to war with the main army, which was commanded by Mlasas Koultlen. The old story mentioned that King Tol Holsgerv said the following words to Afanagil:

"All of these relations with Alvunail are as fragile as glass sword in a battle. They are most likely plotting against us whilst fraternising with those children of the storm. They have their roots tainted by an old alliance, which we will not forget, despite my family once wanted so. You, my dear, will help me in this war with your undefeatable wit and words.

"You will go forth to war alongside Grand Commander Koultlen and you will observe him. The day when you will face battle, you shall fight with Alvunail like brothers, but be vigilant like a sleepless wolf at all times. Regardless what the grand commander does in the battlefield, Alvunail must not get hold of Kulus. I would rather give the bloody well to Ikirias than see those Alvunail schemers feasting with its glory. Make sure that their plans will go in vain with the poisonous bite of your words."

The war commenced and the armies of Ylvart were sent to Hevnenkoil. The lands of Hevnenkoil turned into fierce battles, where Ylvart, Alvunail, Ikirias and the gabyrs fought. Even the halmhendens had heard about Kulus and their mercenary armies were swarming in the lands. As soon as the main entrance was discovered, the armies began to rush through its small gates. This was one of the few moments in the war when the armies did not focus on fighting, but instead running to the depths, to claim the mythic well.

Just like the rest of the armies, Ylvart's troops found themselves in the great stone halls that had been built under the ground. In these chambers of eternal bonfires, the battles continued, as the search for Kulus raged frantically. In the Battle of Kulesparakke, Ylvart's and Alvunail's armies were pushed to the other side of a narrow bridge, which led to the large halls where the well lay. Unfortunately, the sky elves could not make another charge, since they were waiting for reinforcements to appear from above.

Mlasas Koultlen spoke with the grand commander of Alvunail's army, Lincaltarga Paurta, about the unruly situation. Afanagil kept a close eye on both grand commanders since it was absolutely necessary to make sure that Alvunail would not be victorious. Afanagil's concentration was interrupted frequently, as the archers of gabyrs and Ikirias were occasionally sending waves of arrows to the other side of the bridge.

During the battle, the most unbelievable sight occurred. An army of dwarfs fell down from the ceiling, which looked like a black star sky. The arrival of the dwarfs almost stopped the whole battle, as no one could believe their eyes. The dwarfs joined the Battle of Kulesparakke and their soldiers took over the bridge that had been dividing the sky elves and rest of the belligerents.

With the help of the dwarfs, Ylvart and Ikivial advanced to the northern section of the grand hall. The battle had stopped for a while, since all the armies had to reform their ranks and take a rest. In the grand hall, all the armies waited in silence for the next moves of their foes. Kulus was in the middle of the armies and the grand commanders of the sky elves were planning the much-needed charge.

Afanagil saw how Alvunail's commander, Paurta, became friends with the commander of the dwarfs. The lady became concerned, as she thought that Alvunail would make an alliance with the dwarfs as well. It was time to act and Afanagil spoke to commander Paurta, corrupting the elf with words of malice. No one knows what Afanagil said to Lord Paurta, but his facial expression changed from confident to hollow dullness.

Afanagil's task was done and she saw commander Paurta approaching the dwarf commander, Douste Haskk and stabbing him in the throat. The dwarfs and the elves of Alvunail began to fight, which gave Ylvart's army a cheeky chance to push towards the well of Kulus. An intense sprint commenced towards the well by all the armies, making many of the soldiers fall into the ravines.

When the halmhendens and their mercenaries cracked open the well, an immense blast of air struck the stone halls and the star skies began to tremble. It is believed that this was the last sight the armies saw, when the whole complex of chambers and caves collapsed on their shoulders. It was a certainty that the well they had opened was not the real Kulus. According to some seers who wrote many stories about the war, the well was just a way for the spirits to slay many mortals and drink their fallen spirits from the soil. The actual location of Kulus remained a mystery and the useless battle had cost the lives of several armies.

King Tol Holsgerv lost his faith towards the family of Lauskelen and began to think that perhaps sending Afanagil was the reason why they lost three armies. Since no one survived the battle, it was impossible to know what had happened and whether anyone found Kulus. Nevertheless, King Holsgerv decided to outcast the family of Lauskelen from Ylvart, simultaneously ending the war for the elves.

THE QUEEN AND THE CRYSTAL

High Queen Fyerell Holsgerv was often described as a passionate and wise leader, who hated her enemies and loved deeply her own. She had staunch opinions and many of them regarded Alvunail and Ikirias. In several of Fyerell's journals, the queen stated that she was fulfilling a prophecy of Selkelgen, which would influence something much larger later in time.

In many ancient scriptures of Holsgerv's family, Ylvart was the opposite of Alvunail. The realm's fate was to progress positively in due time and make the lives of the elves brighter, whereas Alvunail dwelled in the shades of the olden days. Fyerell saw the light in Ylvart and its elves, who were willing to accept the new age and its challenges. Fyerell believed that if Ylvart turned into something similar to Alvunail, the story of the elves would have an untimely end and would disappear into the shadows of the past. For the queen, it was important to keep the balance in the world, so the grand story of the elves would see its plot moving forwards in the days of Drytgastadl.

Fyerell built many guilds for writers, who witnessed the growth of the town of Ylvart. The writers were close friends of the royals and they often wrote about their deeds and stories. Several authors hailed the queen as a legendary character of Selkelgen, whose destiny was to lead the people of Ylvart to a path of glorious tomorrow. Fyerell often pretended that she did not care about these writings, but was secretly very flattered about her fabled status. For the queen, it was somewhat controversial, since she wanted the age of Selkelgen to be forgotten and the characters of the legends buried under the soil of time.

Eventually, four mighty crystals were crafted by Loraunad and Edonvelle, the two sky elf sisters. At first the crystals were purely for decoration, but soon their powers got the attention of the elves. The four pieces absorbed power from each season of the year and received a certain colour. Fyerell was excited about the crystals and began to think of how they could be used for the good of the realm. The idea came to the high queen that they should be attached to different valuable items.

For Fyerell Holsgerv, this was also an exceptional opportunity to keep up with the good internal relations of the realm. Four influential families of the realm received a crystal, related to their obligations in the lands of Ylvart. Maunosva Aflen, the realms oldest seer, advised Fyerell not to give the winter crystal to the family of Cuvelsoi Hestamperlen, as it would be the undoing of its bearer. The crystal would be lost and never returned to the realm and the carrier of the crystal would be nothing but a shadow amongst the clouds.

Fyerell disregarded the stories of Maunosva and told the old elf that he sounded like something from Alvunail's ancient books. Later, Fyerell asked the elven sisters to craft one more crystal for herself, since she was very mesmerised by their presence and appearance. Loraunad and Edonvelle made one more crystal and it was the largest of them all. Fyerell gazed deep into the layers of the gem and named it Gailinimolerge unvas, meaning 'Mother Sky's dreams'.

High Queen Fyerell kept looking at the crystal, where she saw visions and landscapes. Occasionally, Fyerell met a person in the visions and spoke with the character. The being claimed to be in a room in Blesk, guarding the doors of the upper rooms of the world. Often the character talked about the folk of halmhenden, whose influence had filled the rooms like stardust-like steam.

Fyerell did not know that she was talking with Bovenkauv, the gatekeeper of the skies. Bovenkauv was Mother Sky's brother, who had been trapped in the worlds between the sky and Hasgastadl, the realm of halmhenden. Fyerell could talk with Bovenkauv, because Father Storm left his crystal heart for the gatekeeper, before disappearing to Hasgastadl to make a pact between the storm elves and halmhendens. Father Storm's heart was still connected to Mother Sky, which led Loraunad and Edonvelle to recreate Mother Sky's heart, so they could prevent the complete separation of the elven story.

The high queen understood that the two elven sisters were spirits sent by Mother Sky, but refused to believe that their role was to bring Father Storm and Mother Sky together. Nonetheless, Fyerell kept listening to Bovenkauv talking about the place where he resided. The gatekeeper of the skies gave a specific description of Blesk, which seemed to be a place of secret lofts and wooden corridors. One could say that Fyerell's later drawings of Blesk were the only existing maps of Loft World in the entirety of Drytgastadl.

It took decades to draw the maps of Blesk, which eventually drained the life out of the high queen. Ultimately, the establisher of Ylvart passed away and a statue was built to commemorate her wisdom and love. Fyerell's grave was decorated with the maps of Blesk, which left many Ylvart's scholars confused, as they mistakenly thought that the maps illustrated Selkelgen.

FROM THE FIELDS OF HERBS ROSE OLD WARRIOR

The family of Halmverlen was known for their services towards the royals of Ylvart. Many of the family's members had been advisors, soldiers, herbalists and teachers, who had given important input into the realm's wealth. Rylskar was born during a winter to Delnende and Vruskar Halmverlen. Unfortunately, Rylskar's father Vruskar disappeared during the same winter, when the realm suffered from harsh snowstorms.

Vruskar had visited the family's cottage in the forests of Liegpyrul, southeast from the realm's main city. Most likely the blizzard had killed Vruskar and young Rylskar was left without a father. The young elf was raised by his mother, Delnende, who was a renowned herbalist in the city of Ylvart. Delnende taught Rylskar many things about plants, mushrooms and all sorts of herbs, which the young elf considered fascinating.

Rylskar spent the majority of his early years in the park of Ylesga, which was inside the city of Ylvart. Ylesga was a wide open and flat grass field, filled with right roads and lines of planted oaks. The park had several small schools and quarters for the soldiers, who trained in the fields. Quite close to the lake, which was in the southwest part of the park, Rylskar met many soldiers. Whilst studying herbalism in the school of Vefalos, Rylskar often made his own wooden swords and sparred with these warriors.

Rylskar decided to become a soldier, which his mother did not approve of. Nevertheless, Rylskar's siblings could understand his choice and Delnende let Rylskar join the ranks of Ylvart's military after long hesitation. Young Rylskar kept studying herbalism, but the majority of his time was consumed by the rigid training of the army.

Rylskar did not mind returning occasionally to the school, since he had met Naswelle whilst studying rare mushrooms. The two bore each other's hearts, which ended up with Rylskar and Naswelle marrying each other. Naswelle also became a good friend of Rylskar's mother and the two wrote several books about herbalism. Simultaneously, Rylskar rose in the ranks and was moved to the army of Merenkuulen taus, meaning 'Spears of Rainy Gate'.

Rylskar rose until he was granted the rank of lieutenant. The elf's intelligence and excellent leading skills were noted by the seers, who inspected the army troops regularly. Rylskar was granted the titles of a military and herbal advisor, which was a notable promotion for the young lieutenant. Around the same time, Rylskar and Naswelle had three children, who were named Anelde, Feldele and Lendenskar.

Rylskar's reputation as a warrior was known around the military circles and he received the title of Calas hyagen, meaning 'Sword Master'. For years, Rylskar enjoyed his success and several titles, which had been given to him due to exceptional services towards the realm. Nonetheless, Rylskar's luck turned during a routine patrol in the lands of Ylvart.

Some years later Rylskar and a handful of his finest soldiers were walking near the villages of Ylvart when they saw bandits attacking traders near the road. Rylskar, now a captain, ran towards the bandits with his soldiers, who had drawn their swords. The fight was not challenging for the experienced warriors, but it changed Rylskar's life forever.

Amongst the bandits was an old man, who stared at Rylskar when the elf swung his sword. When the brigands had been defeated, Rylskar looked at the old man's eyes and felt his whole body becoming feeble. The captain lost consciousness and fell on the ground. The rest of the soldiers tried to catch the old man, but he vanished like a shadow in the night, leaving no trace behind.

After the mysterious encounter, Rylskar had become weaker than he used to be and he had lost all his sword skills. Regardless of how hard Rylskar tried to relearn his lost abilities, he simply could not return to his former shape. Rylskar became miserable, since he could not accept that the old man took away his expertise through dark sorcery. For a long time, Rylskar refused to leave his home, since he was devastated by the unexpected loss.

Some years after the happenstance, Rylskar decided to return to herbalism, which at least had not escaped his mind. Despite losing his sword and fighting skills, Rylskar did not lose his fiery ambition. The elf began to study intensively and became a master of herbalism after ten years. His teaching at the schools of Ylvart gave him hope, since he could spread his wisdom for the young elves of the realm.

The War of Tarnfros' Might commenced when the large armies of gabyrs returned to the lands of Enberahl and Liegpyrul. Ylvart answered the call and sent its armies to the north, where they built a mutual defence with the realms of Dyveln and Aetari. Rylskar was expressively crushed, because he could not join the fighting forces of Ylvart. Instead, he was appointed as a military advisor, who joined the armies in the battlefields without taking part in the actual combat.

It was not what Rylskar had wanted, but was better than staying at home. During these years, Rylskar also met Crayvar Vostger of Aetari and Wahlvern Hebelcurnn of Dyveln. The three had known each other for years through various military related meetings, but this time they were sharing a battlefield. Rylskar was jealous of the two, as they got to paint their weapons and mail-armour in blissful red.

After the war, Rylskar discovered that his son Lendenskar wanted to join the military as well. Rylskar did not accept his son's decision to join the army and told him to forget about swords and shields. The conversation between Rylskar and his son got into a fierce argument, since Lendenskar thought that his father did not want him to succeed in the military, possibly surpassing his achievements.

The War of the Returning One began, when Vhyolan hired an army of gelders and commanded them to attack the city of Honedimn. Rylskar's role as an advisor was needed again and he was invited to a meeting in the citadel of Dyveln. In the city, Rylskar met his old friends, Crayvar and Wahlvern, who had also attained high ranks in their militaries. In the summit, the three also met Diwion Heliory, a storm elf from Ikirias, who was there to ensure that the storm elves were not in alliance with Vhyolan. Diwion joined the three friends, when they were moved to the trading city of Lhorem as a part of the war plan.

In Lhorem, the first defence battle occurred, being ferocious, but victorious for the defenders. Rylskar stayed behind in the battle and helped the wounded with his ancient skills. After the fight, Rylskar, Crayvar, Wahlvern and Diwion were sent on a mission to travel to Ikirias and spy on the realm and its people. From there they later joined the armies who were planning to take back Honedimn.

At first, Rylskar had his doubts towards Diwion, but never decided to openly express them. When the travellers arrived in the realm of Ikirias and the situation unfolded, Rylskar's image of Diwion and the storm elves changed. It seemed that the elves of Ikirias had not joined the war and Diwion was not a spy of the enemy. The discovery came through many days of observation, which included the assassination of the storm elf king and internal battles between the realm's houses.

Much later in the same war, Rylskar fought in the Battle of Honedimn which was a great disaster for the attacking armies. The four and many others barely survived out of the city. Wahlvern was also wounded, but Rylskar helped him to stay alive when he was poisoned by a gelder weapon. The companions travelled to the realm of Podfrud, the home of the dwarfs. In here, Wahlvern was saved, and the four warned the dwarfs about the coming of gelder warbands.

The dwarfs defended their home realm and with the help of the travellers, the resistance was hard as steel. After the successful defence of Podfrud and recovery of Wahlvern, the travellers continued their journey towards the south.

Aetari, Dyveln, Podfrud and Ylvart had planned a massive attack on the lands of Galtreken, where Vhyolan held his fortress. Rylskar and the three others were sent with the armies to the lands, where final battles of the war happened. Rylskar took part in the battles of Jarlidan, Hurlgaltrin and Worlgaltrin, which ended the War of the Returning One. Crayvar and Diwion lost their lives in the final battle, which was a hard loss for Rylskar and his friend Wahlvern. The two had a very special relationship after the war, since Wahlvern married Rylskar's daughter Anelde, who he had met earlier in the war.

FAMILY OF WHISPERS AND WRONG FRIENDS

The family of Lauskelen was full of peculiar sky elves, who had plenty of power and wealth in the realm of Ylvart. Fyn Lauskelen was a particularly gifted sky elf who had magical abilities. He was a quick-witted mage, who was part of Afalanosvolon, a group of wizards of Ylvart.

Fyn took part in the War of the One-Eyed Seer. The elf was blessed with an exceptionally long life, as he possessed magical skills beyond the reach of most mortals. This meant that Fyn witnessed the majority of the war, which was full of black magic and horrid curses. During the war, many of the wizards died in battles and even Fyn Lauskelen was forced to retreat from the conflict.

The story tells that when Fyn was returning to Ylvart, he was cursed by a gabyr sorcerer, whose powers Fyn could not resist entirely. The black sorcery left a mark on Fyn and a part of him changed drastically. The elf did not become evil, but he became fascinated by dark subjects, which were rare in the realm of Ylvart.

Fyn was aware that he had new abilities, which could make other people do anything for him. He only had to talk to the folk around him and they would obey every single command that came out of his mouth. Fyn knew that he had a lot of power in his hands, but decided to keep the curse a secret, as it could be used to his advantage in the future. Fyn retreated to his family quarters, which were one of the biggest and most secretive in the realm.

Lauskelen's family quarters were under the ground, just like any other home in the city of Ylvart. Their home was a large complex of corridors, chambers and small halls, where the family had their riches and various rooms to relax and drink expensive wine and cider. In here, Fyn got the idea that the best way to help his realm was to train spies and other sorts of scouts, who could benefit from his magical abilities.

Ultimately, Fyn spoke about his special ability with the royal family of Ylvart, who happened to admire Fyn's honesty. The elf explained that his skills could be used to train spies, which the royals agreed to be a valuable resource. Ylvart's military began to train their elves in the family quarters of Lauskelen in the same autumn, since the war needed competent scouts and other kinds of shady warriors. Fyn tested the spies with his abilities and taught them to resist anyone who would try to interrogate them.

For ages, the family of Lauskelen and their home served as a training quarters for selected soldiers of Ylvart. Nevertheless, some of the family's members, who had inherited Fyn's magical skills, became power-seeking brutes. These elves of the family established their own guard, which was named Bur Amkria, meaning 'the Rogue Guard'. Under the protection of the guard, Lauskelen's family became an intimidating force for many of Ylvart's folks. Several of the realm's elves said that the family had acquired too much power and should be taken under inspection.

The family of Lauskelen remained rather sovereign from the royals, as their services for the realm were appreciated greatly. Aedom Lauskelen began the search for Alasgastadl, the hidden realm of halmhaers. The elf wrote in his journals how he also envied the storm elves, who had once built good relations with the halmhendens. The elf thought that it would be wise to meet at least the halmhaers and build an alliance with them.

The family had several magical items, which were of halmhenden origin. Aedom claimed that he had a door that led to Hauesk, Cellar World. The place was built by the halmhaers and it served as a resting place, before they could ascend to Drytgastadl. Aedom thought that it would be a great place to meet halmhaers and begin to build relations with the infamous folk.

No one particularly knew what sorts of magical items the family found through their explorations in Hauesk, but many rumours circulated that the family had rooms full of marvellous items, which were crafted by the halmhaers. This could have suggested that the family had built affiliation with the people.

When the royals of Ylvart discovered the door, the guard of the city was alarmed and sent men to the Lauskelen's quarters. Many of the magical items were confiscated from the family, and the door that allegedly led to the place was destroyed. The family of Holsgerv hated the halmhaers and it was unacceptable for the realm to work with the folk. Lauskelen's family lost many of its powers and rights, which made the family poorer than they had ever been. Many of the magical items that once belonged to the family of Lauskelen disappeared and found their way into the homes of the royals and other influential families.

REVERIES OF THE STORM

Qlaskastet was born in Oblivion of Heroes, which existed once in the lost lands. It was a place where ancient warriors had ended after several years of adventures. In here, they fought against many beasts and their glory was eternal. Qlaskastet was amongst the young heroes and his destiny was to leave a mark to the world of Drytgastadl.

In Oblivion of Heroes, which also had the name Kajoste, Qlaskastet met Stala and the two became good friends. Both wanted to leave a mark on the world and achieve something extraordinary. For countless years the two and many others protected Kajoste from various threats. One day, Qlaskastet was approached by his parents, Ustarpag and Leasgesket, who asked Qlaskastet to be the guardian of Selkelgen. It was the greatest honour one could achieve, so Qlaskastet took the task without hesitation and left Kajoste behind.

In here, Qlaskastet resided and eventually met Gailinimoler, who changed the whole life of the guardian of Selkelgen. Their love was so intense that even the most beautiful rose could not do justice to its presence. For many decades, the two attempted to have children, but regardless of their striking love and efforts, no children were born from their bond.

In the shadows, Stala rejoiced under the circumstances, since he had secretly cast a curse upon Qlaskastet and Gailinimoler. The spell was to prevent the two having children and it was the first page to be burnt in their book of love. After the events, Stala appeared in Selkelgen and spoke with Qlaskastet without showing himself to Gailinimoler.

The problems that started in Selkelgen were complicated, and were made of a number of various factors.

Qlaskastet created storm elves after seeing the glory of Mother Sky's makings. Qlaskastet, who was now named Father Storm, could not comprehend the perfection of the sky elves, which held the torch higher than any of his clouds could ever reach.

Father Storm had the desire to leave something grand to the world and decided to build a realm with his enthusiastic elven folk. Despite being behind in the long list of achievements of Mother Sky, Qlaskastet simply could not understand that his elves were not considered as the definition of excellence. Nevertheless, Father Storm thought that if his creations were not born in excellence, they would eventually attain it through mighty deeds.

Stala, who supported Father Storm, suggested that he would take his people and leave for a new world, where the storm elves could reign with all their potency. In this world lived Stala's people, who he had named halmhenden. Father Storm was very charmed by the idea, but he could not abandon his pride, which demanded him to outshine Selkelgen's other houses.

The reasons why the war began in Selkelgen were intricate and were the result of several schemes. Nonetheless, one of the most defining factors was when Mother Sky discovered Stala's presence and influence in Selkelgen. For her, this meant betrayal and inevitable war, which she could not forgive. No longer could the love that once existed soften her steel-like determination and weaponry.

The War of Selkelgen ended when Father Storm raised a great water bridge to the skies, where Mother Sky dwelled during the war. In here, the firmament was filled with waves and the fleet of the storm elves challenged Gailinimoler. Large birds attacked the ships and the battle lasted for several days. At some point, Mother Sky broke the firmament and the whole world of Selkelgen collapsed. This was also the birth of the legend that all the storm elf cities and towns were built around the pieces of ships, which fell from the skies to Drytgastadl.

For uncountable years, Father Storm and Mother Sky were lost and only some tales told that they were moving in Drytgastadl's western parts. For instance, it was said that Father Storm met Mother Sky and the two finally reconciled after realising the madness they had imposed upon themselves and their peoples. However, Stala had been observing Father Storm and numerous halmhendens had been spying on his moves. When Father Storm met Mother Sky, the halmhendens attacked, making it another dreadful event in the long series of their lost love.

Stala expected Father Storm to let his forces slay Mother Sky, but the two began to protect each other. The creator of the halmhendens cursed Father Storm and shouted how he had deceived his only friend. Father Storm ignored the words of Stala and the battle continued towards the east. Eventually the fight was taken under the ground, to a place that was possibly one of the wells of Kulus.

To save their love, Father Storm and Mother Sky fell into the well, which was rapidly shut by Stala. After the events, only silent stories in the shadowy corners of taverns suggested that perhaps Father Storm and Mother Sky were moving in the world as nameless wanderers.

It is unknown when exactly Father Storm returned, but some legends tell that he went through a long journey before his reappearance. Father Storm was said to have ascended to Hasgastadl, where Stala lived amongst some of his halmhendens. Whilst making his journey to Hasgastadl, Father Storm also met Bovenkauv, the guardian of Loft World. In here, Father Storm left his crystal heart to the guardian, as he did not want to compromise the only object that still connected him to Mother Sky.

In Hasgastadl, Father Storm was met by Stala, who was deeply disappointed in his actions. Stala said that he would not only destroy the sky elves, but the storm elves as well, unless Father Storm would set an eternal pact. Left with no choice, Father Storm pledged his alliance to Stala, who could now trust the storm elves in the times of war. The pact was not enough for the creator of the halmhendens, who also wanted that Father Storm would become the guardian of Cellar World.

Father Storm reluctantly accepted the offer and through various visions informed the wisest of the storm elves about the events. Father Storm left his heart for Bovenkauv, who promised to guard the crystal till the end of times. He trusted the gatekeeper, who waved at Qlaskastet, as he commenced his journey to the depths of the world.

His journey continued to Cellar World, a place of endless forests, mystical deifying sites and several villages. In this world lived various spirits, witches and vile creatures, who were said to be the fallen foes of the heroes of Kajoste. Father Storm began to live here to keep the order, occasionally fighting some of the beasts and halmhaers who attempted to ascend to Drytgastadl.

Father Storm did not realise that this had been a plan by Stala to remove him from the world and capture him to Hauesk. Stala hated the halmhaers, but he knew that they possessed a useful unique ability in the world. The halmhaers could absorb magic and powers from all being in the world, which could be the undoing of Father Storm as well.

The halmhaers had heard that Father Storm was in Hauesk, so they sent their mightiest wizards to challenge the father of the storm elves. In the battle, the wizards removed a significant amount of Father Storm's powers, which made him weaker than ever. Father Storm had to escape, which led him to a lakeside village with stables. In here, he hid and hoped that the chasers would lose track of him.

In the village Father Storm covered himself behind one of the houses that belonged to several ancient spirits. Inside one of the small wooden huts lived a family, who were interrogated about the location of Father Storm. Qlaskastet heard how the halmhaers killed the family, by removing their ethereal enchantment. Only the cries of a baby were left behind, as the halmhaer wizards stepped out of the hut, leaving the village.

Father Storm felt sad about the events and sneaked inside the hut, where he found a baby crying next to a peaceful fireplace. Father Storm could not leave the baby alone, who did not understand that his parents were gone forever. Father Storm took the baby and promised that he would protect and take care of him. With tears in his eyes, Father Storm named the baby Haust, meaning Abyss.

For many years Father Storm and Abyss travelled the world of Hauesk, where the young spirit grew into a cunning man. Many times, the two avoided the halmhaers, who were on a hunt to catch the two cads. Abyss and the father of the storm elves had become a small family who supported each other. Since Father Storm was trapped in the world of Hauesk, his only chance was to give the remaining shard of his heart to Abyss. The shard had the power to keep anyone from turning into a spirit in a world, which was outside the reach of mortals. It was regarded as the last touch to the world above, if one ended to a place like Hauesk. Unfortunately, Father Storm could not use it on himself, which meant that Abyss was its natural bearer.

One day, the luck of the travellers ended and they came across Aervalasam, a merciless wizard of the halmhaers. Father Storm decided to face the mage, so Abyss could escape Hauesk by using the heart shard. The sudden happenstance did not give much time for goodbyes, but Abyss promised that he would unite the shard with the rest of the heart, so Father Storm could find his way out of Cellar World. Young Abyss had learnt everything that had happened in Selkelgen and who Stala was, which led him to promise a tale of revenge.

When Abyss escaped to Drytgastadl, Father Storm was alone once again and his avoidance of the halmhaers continued. He barely escaped Aervalasam and was now chased by several mages, who wanted to absorb his remaining powers. The halmhaers had become very interested in Father Storm's shards, since they could provide an alternative route to the world above.

At the same time in Drytgastadl, the storm elves were separated into the ones who were loyal to halmhendens and to the ones who spat in their direction. Stala's scheme to unite the storm elves under his command did not go as planned and his influence was partial between their realms. Especially the ones who opposed the halmhendens hoped the return of Father Storm, who would eventually cast down Stala and his servants.

TOUCHED BY MARBLE GALE

In the early days, Audun Sadetske was declared as the queen of the storm elves, who had suspected Stala's involvement in Selkelgen. Queen Sadetske demonstrated open contempt towards Stala and halmhendens who, according to her, were the reason behind Selkelgen's conflicts.

The storm elf family of Raverek could not understand the choice of Sadetske, who showed strong defiance in front of the halmhendens. Whilst the halmhendens welcomed the family of Raverek and their supporters, Queen Audun Sadetske confronted the leader of the halmhenden group. A story tells that the queen said the following words to the lord of the halmhendens.

"No magic, no spell can deceive us from your true intentions. You and your Stala dragged us here after you obliterated our home and now you want us to serve you. You said we are making a disastrous mistake by not joining you; I say, you made your worst mistake in Selkelgen. Come your wrath and might, at least we are not fools."

The leader of the halmhendens, Vaukonn Aer, could not believe the words of Queen Sadetske, who had thundering fire in her eyes. In response, the king of the loyalists, King Cauelt Raverek, spoke of how the fall of Selkelgen was the fault of the elves who had decided to out-power each other. For Queen Sadetske these were feeble words and she decided to take her family and their supporters away from this pit of poisonous alliances.

When the family of Sadetske left with their loyalists, a spirit appeared to Queen Audun. The spirit was named Mestetaus, who had been a prisoner of the halmhendens for years. Mestetaus used to be inside the well of Kulus before it escaped, but was captured by the halmhendens, who interrogated it about the location of the well. Since the spirit could not return to the well, it was abused by the halmhendens relentlessly.

Mestetaus, who was filled with hatred towards the halmhendens spoke to Audun Sadetske. The spirit said that the halmhendens would destroy everyone who would not join them or their lackeys. Mestetaus proposed that Sadetskes and their families would leave to the east, where certain spirits were gathering in the comforting shades.

In this place, the storm elves of Sadetske would be safe from the halmhendens, who would certainly start hunting the defiant storm elves. The queen agreed that dark times were coming swiftly, unless the folk would begin their journey to the east, towards the land guided by Mestetaus.

The daring journey, which took the whole summer and part of the autumn, led the folk first towards the north, where they travelled until they met the northern end of the inland sea of Yeldes. From here, they continued towards the east and eventually southeast, to a land that was named Drugenn. During the travel, many halmhendens spied on the storm elves and several attempts to disrupt the journey occurred.

When the storm elves arrived to Drugenn, Mestetaus introduced the elves to the rest of the spirits, who lived in the dense spruce forests of the land. Mestetaus told them that the elves were enemies of the halmhendens as well, which brought smiles to the faces of the spirits. Queen Sadetske was aware that Mestetaus had not been the only spirit that was tortured by the halmhendens and their mutual hatred ensured a strong alliance with the spectres.

The storm elves ultimately began to build villages in the spruce forests of Drugenn, which offered an effective hideout for their people. Several forest villages of the storm elves were named Haustrn, meaning 'Marble Gale'. The realm expanded to all directions in the forests and built a vast connection of subtle villages and towns, which all supported Queen Sadetske and her family.

The realm kept growing and its storm elves were hiding from the eyes of the halmhendens, who were very keen on destroying the ones who challenged them. After many careful ages, the realm was reigned by King Afal Sadetske, who was a descendant of many hidden royals of the land. Under his rule, the realm entered a new chapter, which defined many lives in Haustrn.

For several centuries, the storm elves of Sadetske had undertaken various scouting missions in the north and northwest, where a few halmhendens moved and spread their influence. Tinesildun Asatska, who was appointed by King Afal Sadetske, led a group of rangers whose mission was to kill the halmhenden representatives. The task was not easy, as many of the halmhendens knew that the storm elves of Haustrn were hunting them. It was obvious to the halmhendens that the folk of Haustrn were not imprudent, and they indeed gave a formidable resistance.

During these tasks, Tinesildun met a character who introduced himself as Abyss. It was a cold winter evening and the whole landscape was filled with thick layers of snow. A group of rangers were near the town of Syysven, which was far west from Haustrn, and Abyss had been following a halmhenden lord named Hustefkalde Aimonkylmae. The highly regarded halmhenden presumably had the crystal heart of Father Storm and Abyss had shadowed him for half a winter.

Tinesildun heard from Abyss that apparently Stala had killed Bovenkauv, who had the crystal heart of Father Storm and gave it to Hustefkalde, so he could take it to Hillfort Lands. Tinesildun Asatska supported Abyss' mission as it served the interests of the realm as well. For many years, the realm had dreamt about the return of Father Storm and now a man appeared from nothing who claimed to be his adopted son.

The rangers and Tinesildun joined Abyss, who travelled to the southeast areas of Hillfort Lands. In here, they had a great bout with the halmhendens and their band leader

Hustefkalde. Abyss told Tinesildun that the halmhendens were taking Father Storm's heart to an old seer in Hillfort Lands, who could use the crystal to find the exact location of Haustrn. After seeing the passion and fury in Tinesildun and the rangers, Abyss knew that the storm elves of Haustrn would be excellent allies.

At the same time, the halmhendens were aware that if the storm elves discovered the location of the heart, it would provoke them to reveal themselves from the shadows of Drugenn. Tinesildun saw the three influential hillforts, who were friends of the halmhendens, since they had given them riches to overtake rival domains in the nearby lands. It all seemed to be an elaborate plan by the halmhendens, who took the crystal heart near the storm elves and hoped them to make an exposing move.

Tinesildun and Abyss spied on the hillfort of Lopaunkiv, which was one of the strongest holds in the southeast parts of the land. In here, they discovered that the halmhendens wanted to take Father Storm's heart to a man named Tarkas Viimen. The man had the ability to look into any item and see its origin and everyone it was related to. This meant that it could possibly reveal the location of Haustrn.

Halmhendens could create magic, but they often had a problem examining it, which led them to a situation that required the help of several outsiders. Since many of the oldest manfolk peoples lived in Hillfort Lands, it was possible that amongst these folks lived individuals of unnatural ancient knowledge. For Tinesildun and Abyss, these people were targets and were to be eliminated as soon as possible, so the realm of Haustrn and Father Storm would stay out of their reach.

Tinesildun and Abyss assembled a group of rangers whose task was to travel to Hillfort Lands, and recapture the crystal heart and slay the people who presented a threat. Halmhenden Lord Hustefkalde guessed that his very visible presence and movement would catch the attention of their foes, which led him to take the crystal to the northwest.

In the northwest lay Tarnfros, 'Moss Fortress', which was harnessed by the halmhendens as revenge towards the peoples of Hillfort Lands. A majority of the folks of the land did not want to join the halmhendens, which forced the people to find ways to destroy their ignorant resistance. Halmhendens created the fortress and concentrated their darkest magic to its centre, which allowed gabyrs to spread into Hillfort Lands.

Since the gabyrs were grateful of their sudden empowering summoning, the halmhendens decided to use them in their further plans to control Hillfort Lands. Hustefkalde thought that it would be a splendid idea to take the crystal heart to Tarnfros, as it was now guarded by thousands of gabyrs. The other allied hillforts of the halmhendens were fooled and told that they would keep a hold of the heart, leaving them as a false frontier for the storm elves.

At least this plan did not deceive Tinesildun, Abyss and the rangers, who followed Lord Hustefkalde to Tarnfros. The company saw the armies of gabyrs, who had been mustered by halmhenden wizards through their dark magic. The most powerful of the wizards was Vhyolan Rauwos, who had plans to remove all manfolk realms from Drytgastadl. Tinesildun and her companions saw the wizards and their leader going inside Moss Fortress with the crystal.

For several days, Tinesildun, Abyss and the rangers spied on the fort and around its dark corners, avoiding the gabyr guards. Finally, the companionship moved inside Tarnfros, in an attempt to steal the crystal. In the gloomy and murky halls of Tarnfros, the adventurers found the large chamber, where the heart was kept and examined by Tarkas Viimen. With swift moves, Tinesildun and Abyss slew the man, who fell on the stone floor.

In the obscurities of the hall, a halmhenden laughed. Tinesildun and her friends saw a figure who they identified as Vhyolan. It all had been a trap to lure Abyss inside the fort, where the halmhenden could kill Father Storm's only chance to come back. However, the halmhenden did not know that Abyss had a shard in his pocket, which he connected with the crystal heart. To the shock of Vhyolan, the heart began to radiate and a piercing echo howled through the fortress, bringing several winds inside its grim hallways. It was Abyss' turn to laugh, as from the pitch-black corridor appeared Father Storm, punching every gabyr to death with his fists. A battle commenced inside the stone chamber, when Vhyolan took a torch and threw hurls of fire towards the companionship.

The battle was concentrated but fierce and lasted till the night. Father Storm, who had suffered many years in Hauesk, could not stand the magic of Vhyolan and ultimately collapsed on the floor. The halmhenden wizard was also wounded and had to retreat behind his gabyr guardians.

Badly injured, Father Storm spoke to Abyss and Tinesildun, explaining that the key to defeat the halmhendens was the winter crystal, located somewhere in southwest. Father Storm continued his story by telling of how, in a dream, he saw how the love between him and Mother Sky had brought life to two baby girls named Loraunad and Edonvelle. The dream meant that Father Storm and Mother Sky had finally had children of their own, but they were unfortunately missing somewhere in the world.

"My child, be not concerned, as the storm will never perish, it will return with all its screaming thunder."

Tinesildun, Abyss and the surviving rangers fled the fortress, chased by Vhyolan and gabyrs, who had gathered their remaining strength. During the wild pursuit, Abyss headed to southwest, Vhyolan and his servants behind him. Tinesildun and her rangers beheld the horizon, where Abyss ran towards new challenges, leaving many questions unanswered.

"There goes the man with the crystal heart, now seeking the winter's might. I hope they do not lead to your demise in the coming days of uncertainty. Until then, I shall look forward seeing you, son of the storm."

One could say that one of the reasons behind the three gabyr wars that struck the realms in southwest, were ignited due to the events in Tarnfros. Presumably Abyss found his way to the southwest, where later the halmhendens sent several gabyr armies, creating an involvement of numerous realms and legends.

Eventually, Haustrn was saved from the horrors of the gabyr wars, which raged many centuries on the other side of the inland sea of Yeldes. Yet, Haustrn was not spared from difficult times, which began in the ages to come. While Queen Sendla Sadetske ruled the realm that was in peace and most of the problems with the halmhendens were absent, a peculiar folk from the south came to Drugenn, in search of a new home.

The people were from Undene, an expanse that had vast fields of swamps without forests or bushes. The folk dwelled underneath the swamps, which took them to a world that only they could access. Something had happened in the swamp domain and the folk flooded out of their homes. The elder of the people explained to Queen Sendla that they could not enter their ancient homes any longer and they would need to find a new swamp to live in.

The queen discussed with her family about the situation, which did not seem to threaten Haustrn or its folks. The swamp folk did not appear to be malevolent with a desire to wage evil. The queen agreed that the swamp people could reside in their lands until Undene would return to its primordial condition. The leader of the swamp folk, Kjolfko, was deeply humbled by the queen's words. Nevertheless, the decision did not please everyone and soon subtle confrontation started in the realm.

The spirits who lived in Drugenn were foes with the swamp folk, which the storm elves of Haustrn had been oblivious about. The spirits of Haustrn told Queen Sendla that they would refuse to accept the swamp folk and threatened to leave the forest, possibly exposing the realm to halmhendens. Suddenly, some storm elves of Haustrn began to contemplate whether the great flood was done by the halmhendens to cause disorder and disunity amongst the people. It was obvious that the relations in the realm were changing and soon many families stood up and spoke their mind. In the front of the families was the house of Nehalsk, who were known to be exceptionally loyal towards the forest's spirits.

The leader of the spirits was Tabaurken, a mighty warrior, who had once been in Undene's uncharted sub-worlds, where he defeated the four moss lords. Many centuries ago Tabaurken had seen the halmhendens exploring the swamps, as they attempted to find secret passages to Hauesk. The halmhendens asked whether Tabaurken would have joined their quest, but the warrior spirit told them to go Plesket, which cannot be translated, being a too vulgar expression.

Tabaurken was certain that the halmhendens were not behind the flood, as the swamp lords were their enemies as well. One could say that their history was not friendly and they all had ended up fighting each other. In fact, it was common belief that the swamp lords attempted to flood the world themselves, so they could have more space for their grander monstrous creations.

Nevertheless, Sendla Sadetske, the family of Nehalsk and Tabaurken did not come to an agreement and the realm was on the verge of falling apart. This was exactly what the halmhendens wanted and the queen knew that they could not lose the spirits, who protected the forests of Drugenn. However, Queen Sendla came up with a proposition, which could save the situation.

The queen asked whether Tabaurken could travel to the swamp domains and defeat the lords once more, but the warrior spirit refused abruptly, as he almost vanished during the battles of the past. Instead, Tabaurken left to the west with the family of Nehalsk and their loyalists. The royal family of Sadetske became concerned about the future of the realm, since too many spirits were swiftly relocating outside Drugenn.

Kjolfko and his people begged Tabaurken to stay, but the spirit had made up his mind. The storm elves of Haustrn came to realise that perhaps the spirits of Drugenn and the swamp folk had a more intricate past than they would lead people to understand.

For centuries, Nehalsks, Tabaurken and the spirits built a beautiful town by the shores of the inland sea of Yeldes, directly west from Haustrn. In here, many gardens were created, as the family of Nehalsk had grown tired of the murky spruce forests of Drugenn. Ultimately, garden of Rora was flourishing with several stone buildings, a harbour and large gardens, which hid many of its homes behind colourful bushes of flowers.

The town was led by Lady Felpaelen Nehalsk who with the help of Tabaurken made the gardens of Rora a wondrous place of trading and crafting. The storm elves of Rora did particularly a lot of trading with the town of Syysven, which lay northwest of the gardens, enabling various travellers to their lands.

Felpaelen was aware that the halmhendens knew about the gardens of Rora and could face a conflict in the future. Tabaurken promised to protect the land with the help of an army that was established to guard its integrity. The King of Haustrn, Neldkalla Sadetske, arrived in the gardens of Rora to open a conversation. For many days, Lady Nehalsk and the king discussed mutual defences, should halmhendens threaten their lives.

Lady Felpaelen agreed with the king, that the time of disunity was over and gardens of Rora would become part of the realm of Haustrn. However, it was crucial that the family of Nehalsk ruled the town and the storm elves of Rora would not be controlled by the royals of Haustrn. The king had no objections and an alliance was finally established after centuries of silence.

The situation in Haustrn had also changed as Undene's lands had returned to their usual condition, and majority of the swamp folk had returned to their homes in the expanse. Kjolfko, who had lived hundreds of years, told that the swamp lords had been defeated by someone else. Unfortunately, this wonderful and mysterious hero had soon disappeared to the depths of the world.

As expected, the halmhendens had planned an attack on the gardens of Rora, so they could reveal the armies of Haustrn from their ancient forest home. Ineahal Gavaml, a powerful halmhenden lady, had hired several regiments of mercenaries from Hillfort Lands, who had violent desire to attack the storm elves of Rora. Some of the mercenaries were people of the hillforts, which had been raided by Haustrn's rangers in the past ages. These warriors were paid impressively and they could finally avenge their fallen ancestors.

The War of the Crying Garden began, as the cavalry of the hired swords attempted to break the tight defences of Rora, full of skilful archers and spearmen. For a year, the siege did not move, but eventually there was a change for all on a certain winter morning. A ferocious wave of annihilation arrived from the north, which struck the backs of the halmhendens and their mercenaries. A band of halmhaer wizards had followed Lady Gavaml's moves and decided to make their assault during the bright winter morning. The siege fell into chaos and first the defenders of the gardens thought that they had won on the marble walls of Rora. Soon the situation turned grim, as the army of the mercenaries had no choice but to run towards Rora, to escape the horrific magic of the halmhaers.

Amongst the escapees was Lady Gavaml, whose spells gave a chance to create a gap for the attacking army to run inside the garden. During the assault, many of the attackers fell and this would have been a disastrous tactic in any other situation. However, this time, the army was fleeing in panic and Lady Gavaml entered the gardens with her battered forces.

An odd and short stalemate took place in the town, when the two sides were confused about the halmhaers, who had now become the largest threat. In their bafflement, the halmhaers had the opportunity to enter the town where they challenged the distressed Lady Gavaml. The storm elves of the town and their leaders were powerless, as they watched the great mages fighting each other in the snowy Rora's streets. Lord Berl Nehalsk ordered his soldiers to abandon the town, as it seemed useless to challenge the wizards, who were having a disastrous and exclusive fight of their own.

In the process, many of the mercenaries hired by Lady Gavaml died when they attempted to defeat the wizards, who simply froze them to glittering statues of ice. Even Tabaurken had difficulties fighting the halmhaers, who seemed to possess undefeatable powers. In the end of the battle, Lady Gavaml fell and most of her mercenaries fled out of the town in horror. Tabaurken was no match for the wizards, who could drain his presence, and in Rora the warrior spirit faded into nothingness for all eternity.

The soldiers of Haustrn retreated to the forest of Drugenn in the east, which had been a magnificent time for the observing halmhendens to attack the forest. However, the sudden arrival of the halmhaers had ruined their plans and Haustrn remained safe in the forests. Being oblivious of halmhenden's view of the situation, Lord Berl Nehalsk escaped with some of his storm elves to the south, as they were too scared to return to Haustrn.

When the thousands of storm elves fled to the south following the coastline of Yeldes, Lord Nehalsk promised that he would build a new town to commemorate the glory of Rora and Haustrn. Lord Berl did not know at the time that his promise would give birth to a new storm elf realm of Pranhilhas that would indeed remember the times of Rora.

After being an abandoned town for many centuries, Rora was adapted by Haustrn's army and turned into a garrison. In here, the realm deployed three regiments, which were named Vealten, Haust and Eanemyst. Rora, which was now a stronghold, kept trading with the town of Syysven in the northwest.

One day, a mysterious traveller with concerning news from Syysven arrived to Rora. The trader had witnessed a strange change in the atmosphere of Syysven, making its welcoming habitants weary and suspicious. In the forest, north from the town, several members of a secretive elven order had been seen and it was believed that they had now infiltrated the population of Syysven as well. However, it was difficult to spot outsiders in the town, since it was located in a busy crossroads with several visitors each day.

A rumour had begun to spread that the order was after a man named Wiliasc Torbel, owner of a stone key that could possibly open the gates to the shrine of Lemmesujelten. It was unknown what the order wanted from the shrine and why they had arrived now, but their presence had caused a series of disappearances. Some of the townspeople had been found dead and the town's guard was in need of help and serious sword power. The guard had tried to find the members of the order and drive them out, failing in this task miserably. The folk of Syysven had become afraid and only a few people walked in the streets after sunset. The trade had also suffered, which affected the lives of the ordinary people of the local land.

Eventually, a messenger arrived from Syysven to Haustrn, who brought a letter asking for help. The whole town had fallen into times of uncertainty and the trade was suffering every day. Haustrn's commanders decided to act, as it was in their own personal interests to protect their most important trading partner. Haustrn's Grand Commander Ajejulmas Forvin ordered the regiment of Haust, deployed in Rora, to be moved to Syysven.

The assignment was to provide safety for the city and its inhabitants, simultaneously attempting to capture the members of the clandestine order. Amongst the regiment was a storm elf lieutenant named Cylof Laqetske, well known for his excellent skill to investigate and interrogate. Only some days after the arrival of the messenger, the regiment began to march in the autumnal fields and forests of the land towards Syysven.

After a long travel, the regiment arrived in the trading town, which ambiance glowed with motionless melancholy. The guard of the city invited the regiment in, which was greeted with miscellaneous reactions. Some of the townsfolk were relieved, but a few were concerned that this would ignite further violence. Sadly, the few were right as the series of disappearances increased, and the town had to halt their trade for good.

The scouts who worked for the city's guard had found that the order called itself Duolanva Dimentaiten, meaning 'Gathering of the Sky'. The order, which was led by an elf, Kemvas Kumnal, was looking for the shrine of Lemmesujelten, where their leader was held as a prisoner. However, the motivation and the cruel methods of the order had remained a mystery for the townsfolk.

The autumn was exceptionally rainy and the town's streets were filled with water and colourful leaves, which had fallen from the numerous oak and maple trees of Syysven. The regiment had started to patrol the town and tried to prevent as many acts by the order as possible. The possessor of the stone key, Wiliasc Torbel, had been hidden by the regiment and was protected day and night.

Lieutenant Laqetske and his closest soldiers received a special assignment to track down the members of the order in the town. Many nights, the group investigated and observed the damp gravel streets of Syysven that could hide many secrets behind every corner. Several raids were done by the regiment and numerous people fell doing so. The members of the order broke into the houses of the townspeople and slew them if they could not tell them the location of Wiliasc Torbel. When this did not work, the order declared through letters, that the killings would continue unless the city would hand them the stone key and its holder.

For many days, the situation remained stagnant and Lieutenant Laqetske suggested an elaborate deception, which would include several risks. According to Laqetske, the only way to get the enemy out of Syysven, would let them believe that Torbel escaped from the safekeeping and disappeared into the night. In the cover of the night, the guard would leave a body in the forest north of Syysven, including a false stone key. After the deed, the guards would begin to spread a rumour amongst the people regarding Torbel.

Laqetske hoped that the deceptive rumour would reach the ears of the order and they would begin to search for the man. At the same time, the guard would send their troops near the shrine where they would wait until all the members would try to open the gates. An effective ambush would take a place after many days of wait, making the soldiers' blades drool blood.

Firstly, the guard sent men into the forest in small groups, disguised as woodcutters and other sorts of workers. It was crucial that the false rumour sounded as plausible as possible and the guard pretended to be in utter chaos after the disappearance of Torbel. As expected, this of course caused disarray amongst the townsfolk who were oblivious of the secret scheme.

The plan took many days and nights and shadowy characters moved in the foggy roads and lands of Syysven, preparing the ambush. The scouts of Syysven reported that they had seen unknown people by the body, bearing the false stone key. After the observation, several hooded people had been seen leaving the town towards the north.

Lieutenant Laqetske knew that his plan was working, as the slayings stopped after a few days of spreading the rumour. The troops were sent in the areas near the shrine, where they waited for the appearance of the servants of the order. Ultimately, a proud group of hooded elves approached the gates of the shrine, which was well hidden in the deepest parts of the forest.

Laqetske and some of his men had joined the guards, who had been waiting for the redemptive ambush for several days. The band had taken risks and they had no idea how many foes they would be facing. When the great gathering happened in front of the rugged stone gate, an arrow wave struck the servants of the order. A crushing charge commenced and the storm elves, alongside the manfolk guards, attacked the cloak-covered mystics. During the battle, Laqetske faced the elf, who had been in front of the gathering, fighting with him until successfully piercing his sword through the elf's chest.

By early morning, the battle was over and the forest was filled with silence. The bodies of the servants were searched and peculiar items and books found. Whilst doing the elaborate search, the stone walls moved aside and opened the shrine of Lemmesujelten. Stunned by the sight, the lieutenant saw a tall and bearded figure coming from the early morning mist. The manfolk guard bowed in front of the figure, who stared at the quietened battlefield.

Lieutenant Laqetske knew that the figure was Lemmesujelten, king of the forest spirits, and his booming voice filled the forests walls. The spirit spoke of how he had seen the coming of the storm and breaking of the firmament, making brothers and sisters kill each other. Lemmesujelten pointed at Laqetske, who did not know that he had defeated Kemvas Kumnal. Confused, Laqetske spoke to the forest king and asked about the leader, who the order wanted to free from his hidden sanctuary.

Laqetske wrote in his memoirs that Lemmesujelten laughed and said that the leader was a withered woman, a somewhat mother-like character with incapacitated powers. Laqetske could think of no one else than Mother Sky who, according to Lemmesujelten, was handed to a group of halmhaers. All the words of the ancient forest spirit made sense and Cylof was disgusted by his unexplainable actions.

WANDERING MIND FLOURISHED

Tinesildun was the fifth child of the family of Asatska, who were famous for their distillery, where they had lived for many centuries. The distillery looked like a wooden fort, with several rooms for malt spirits. Whisky was the family's expertise and they were well known for their quality, maturation and good taste. Tinesildun's mother was Aveasildun, who often sent her to the forests, to find all sort of plants and berries for their new experiments with beverages. Tinesildun learnt to move in the wilderness from a young age and she fell in love with adventure, peril and stories of old. One time, Aveasildun asked Tinesildun to go to the forest in the north, where a particular berry was growing. The berry was called sunbright and it was so delicious in taste that it could improve many of the family's well-known recipes.

Tinesildun travelled to the north where she had been many times. However, one night she was ambushed by mercenaries from Hillfort Lands, who worked for the halmhendens. The men decided to take the storm elf to their hillfort, where they could keep her as a prisoner and command the storm elves to reveal themselves.

Tinesildun was put inside a cart, which was pulled by two horses. The mercenaries became comfortable and began to drink their suspicious brews after many days of travel. The drinking distracted them from the gabyrs, who had been following them for some time in the glooms. However, Tinesildun had kept looking at the dark forest in the sunset and had prepared her escape.

When the surprise attack happened, Tinesildun swiftly jumped off the cart and hid underneath it. The mercenaries were busy fighting the gabyrs and the young storm elf ran to the forest unharmed. Tinesildun knew how to navigate through the woods, despite the uncomfortable darkness.

The events of the previous day did not bother Tinesildun, who had actually enjoyed the peril. Being many miles from home, the elf did not hesitate to explore and look for the sunbrights. The young storm elf girl was aware that her family was worried, but a little additional adventure would not change anything. After a few days gathering the berries, Tinesildun returned home, where her parents hugged and kissed her out of joy. Tinesildun spoke of what had happened and the story of the young storm elf began to circulate the realm, eventually reaching the ears of King Afal Sadetske. The king wanted to meet the family and their daughter, who had so bravely acted in the situation.

The king was excited to meet Tinesildun and suggested that she should become a scout for the realm. The family of Tinesildun did not want this to happen, but it seemed to be impossible to stop the young storm elf. Tinesildun, who was driven by adventures and danger, joined Haustrn's army and began her exercises. For a decade, she learnt many things she had not quite mastered during her earlier years. Eventually she entered the service of Haustrn's rangers, completing her training.

For many years, Tinesildun worked with the rangers, hunting enemies of their realm in Hillfort Lands. She learnt much of the halmhendens, who had been trying to put their sorcerous fingers in every plot in the world. During one of her journeys, Tinesildun met an old lady, who lived in a small cottage and offered the rangers a place to stay inside her home for the wintry night. Inside the cottage, Tinesildun found out that the lady was a soothsayer, and she was very keen at looking into Tinesildun's life.

At midnight, the lady took Tinesildun's hands and stared deep into her eyes. The rest of the rangers followed the intensive moment near the fireplace that crackled serenely. The old lady said that she saw a man, someone she had seen a long time ago. Tinesildun would meet the man and there would be a task to be fulfilled. The old lady suggested that Tinesildun should follow the man, until thunder would howl in dark halls. In here, she should give a piece of shard to the man and tell him regards from Iemel.

For many years Tinesildun thought about the vision the lady had seen and the shard she had given her. During one of her journeys, Tinesildun and her rangers were near Syysven, where they met a man, who introduced himself as Abyss. The man told that he had been following a halmhenden named Hustefkalde, who possibly had Father Storm's heart.

Tinesildun began to put the pieces together and realised that possibly Abyss was the man the old lady had mentioned. Tinesildun did not reference anything about the vision to Abyss, as she could not trust the man fully. Their quest took Tinesildun, Abyss and the rangers near a hillfort, where they spied on the actions of the halmhendens and their hired swords.

During this time, the company learnt that a man named Tarkas Viimen could examine Father Storm's heart and possibly reveal the location of the storm elves in Drugenn. After some time, the halmhenden Lord Hustefkalde decided to take the crystal heart deeper into Hillfort Lands, where it could be protected by gabyrs.

"When we ran over the hills and through thick forests, I could not prevent myself thinking that I was charging towards my own doom. Who was this man and why did I join him? He claimed that this was about our father's heart, but were his words worth the storm? I was mystified by the inscrutabilities of the journey."

When Tinesildun, Abyss and the rangers arrived near the infamous Tarnfros, the elf woman could recognise some of the surroundings. She claimed that she had seen the place in her dreams, guided by the old soothsayer Iemel. The returning memories forged faith in Tinesildun, who had at first been wrestling with heavy thoughts in her mind.

Eventually the storm elf woman and Abyss confronted the thieves of Father Storm's heart, who unfortunately had been waiting for Abyss to appear. The man laughed at the ambush and connected the heart with a piece of shard he had taken from his pocket. Suddenly, Father Storm returned out of the dark, and helped the companionship in the fight.

Nevertheless, Father Storm was too weak after years of absence and he fell to the ground injured. Swiftly, Tinesildun learnt about the winter crystal and how it could be the key to defeat the halmhendens. The elf woman took out the piece of shard she had carried for years and Father Storm smiled whilst bleeding on the stone floor.

Tinesildun told him about Iemel, and Father Storm laughed loudly in the hall where the battle had calmed for a moment. The storm elf woman gave the piece of shard to Father Storm, who explained that Iemel was Bovenkauv's wife, who had escaped to Drytgastadl after her husband was slain by Stala. With the shard, Father Storm could find Bovenkauv and bring him back to fight the creator of halmhendens.

Tinesildun escaped Tarnfros with her rangers and saw Abyss changing his course towards the southwest. Somewhere there, allegedly, the winter crystal was waiting for Abyss and Tinesildun barely managed to bid her farewell to the man. The lady of the rangers had obligations in her realm and she returned to Haustrn with her warriors. However, Tinesildun was certain that this was not the last time she would meet Abyss.

Tinesildun kept seeing dreams of Iemel, who took her to places she could not recognise, but had a strangely familiar atmosphere. Often the visions included landscapes above the mighty forests of Hillfort Lands, where a large bird was ridden by a man in black clothes. Tinesildun did not want to forget the sights of the dreams and decided to make several tapestries in her home. The decorations were named Heje Kjaldum, meaning 'Reverie Tapestry' and they decorated the walls of the family's houses for centuries.

THE TEMPEST STRENGTHENS

"Beyond all the winds and thoughts, a force brewed. With its hurling might it echoed in the forests and pierced through the mountains. The birds fell from the sky, and with them, the storm that was here to remain."

Cauelt Raverek declared himself as the direct heir of the royals of Selkelgen and quickly gained immense support. On the shores of the inland sea of Yeldes, the storm elves began to gather under the banner of King Raverek. The determination of the new king caught the attention of the halmhendens, who had observed the early steps of the elves closely.

King Raverek discussed with the approaching halmhendens about the future and how the peoples could build their relations. The leader of the halmhendens, Vaukon Aer, was very keen to establish an alliance with the storm elves, if they could provide military presence and assistance for their people. In return, the storm elves could acquire a share of all the wonders of halmhenden magic.

King Cauelt Raverek visualised kingdoms and eternal glory, which he could achieve with the help of the halmhendens. After some days of negotiations, the king made a pact with the halmhendens, who were now challenged by Audun Sadetske, declared as the queen of the storm elves. The fierce defiance of Audun Sadetske surprised King Raverek, who considered Audun and her supporters to be sheer dullards and downright blind to a great opportunity. According to King Raverek, the elves brought the fall of Selkelgen by themselves and neither Stala, nor the halmhendens, had anything to do with the downfall. Neither did Raverek show much respect towards Father Storm, as he did not believe in his return or earthly influence.

"I have risen above our Father, for I am the sovereign and supreme, the thundering fire!"

Lord Vaukon Aer guided King Raverek and his storm elves away from the shores, towards the western lands of Cilegkham. The halmhendens had a stronghold there and King Raverek had a hard time believing how familiar the hold looked with its wooden parts, as if they were from a large ship. Lord Vaukon gave the land of Cilegkham to the storm elves and proposed that a mighty city would be built around the sanctuary of Lkauem Nyrs, meaning 'Tempest Pillar'. King Cauelt Raverek was deeply honoured and named the city Ikirias, meaning 'Beauty'. With the magical help of the halmhendens, the storm elves began to build the city, which rose faster than any other elven establishment in the world.

The friendship between the storm elves of Ikirias and the halmhendens flourished and the royal family of Raverek took the lead in the ever-growing competition of the elven tale. However, the elves of Ikirias did not know that by allying with halmhendens, they had made a very dangerous enemy; halmhaers, who had obtained powers from the black nadirs of the cosmos.

For centuries, the storm elves of Ikirias kept expanding their prospering realm and it acquired many strategically important locations. The halmhendens, who did not live amongst the storm elves any longer, returned to Ikirias to discuss a task, which required attention urgently. The queen of the era, Noilv Raverek, met the halmhenden Lady Civostenes Arpitel, who brought concerning news with her.

The news told of how the halmhaers, sworn enemies of the halmhenden, were planning to wage a grand upheaval on the world. To achieve this, a few halmhaers who had managed to slip into Drytgastadl, had found the hidden places named the beacons of day. These mountain halls had great stone pillars, which were a crucial part of the cosmos' structure according to halmhenden lore.

The three beacons of day were in different locations around the world, where their magical presence was said to prevent the world collapsing into the depths. The halmhaers attempted to capture and drain the magic from these beacons, causing the dislocation of the astronomical order. This could have swallowed Drytgastadl into the realm of night and pushed Alasgastadl, the home of halmhaers near the halls of the halmhendens. The halmhaers thought that this was one of the only ways for them to challenge their counterparts, since it was purely impossible to defy the cosmic order with traditional means.

"Listen to me, whilst I do not understand the words you say. War is a word and it means fear and abandonment. Perhaps I do not understand the meaning of those two, as I have never experienced love in the way it should be. For many of us it is unforgivable and beautiful, the last words of our ancestors carved into stone. Maybe love is in the past and the days to come will bring something better, at least something trustworthy. Why should anyone cry for love, as it is mortal and predictable?"

To prevent the baleful tragedy, the halmhendens and their storm elf allies of Ikirias set a company of warriors, whose task was to relocate the beacons of day and prevent the horrid plan. The force, which was led by storm elf captain Vlios Foltad and halmhenden mage Sauenge Partal, consisted of over hundred travellers. The company included warriors, hunters and crafters of magic and it was supported by twenty-one halmhenden wizards.

The first beacon of day was said to be in the mountains of Hulumnoar, which looked like a great wall, dividing Drytgastadl into west and east. The halmhendens had once built there a beacon of day, when their power was still flourishing and the realm of Moltraugad was on its peak. Hulumnoar had many mountain halls, which could be entered through small doors, crafted on the mountain sides. In the halls, the halmhendens lived until the place was abandoned, leaving a beacon of day hidden in the caves of the mountain.

Captain Foltad and Mage Partal commenced their ambitious journey towards the west alongside their fierce force of warriors. Ultimately the band of travellers arrived at the mountains of Hulumnoar, which was glimmering with its green tint and bright snow. Captain Foltad met a mountain elf near a door that looked like an entrance to the mountain. Partal and Foltad spoke to the elf, who said that their people had lived here since White Hat had shown the path for their kin. Captain Foltad wrote in his journal about the following events:

Partal kept asking about the beacon of day and whether they had seen any halmhaers in the area. The elf's face was astonished since he said that they had guests, who looked very much like the halmhendens in our brave band of warriors. Partal's eyes changed swiftly and she asked about the whereabouts of these guests. The elf, being confused, told that they were in the dining halls enjoying a well-earned soup, as they had been very helpful to their people. Partal pushed the elf aside and ran inside the mountain, us following the lady with heart-throbbing haste.

In the mountain halls, we heard distant sounds of conversation. Partal kicked a door in, which opened a sight to a crowded dining chamber. I could see the halmhaers staring at Partal, dropping their cutlery on the table. A silence reigned in the chamber for a short while, which was broken by one of the halmhaers standing up and throwing a blazing burst of fire towards us. The fire caught some of the mountain elves, who sat in the way of the spell, incinerating cruelly its victims.

The battle began in the dining hall and the group of halmhaers cast spells in an impossible manner and pace. Our noble warriors engaged with our foes, despite them being significantly more powerful. The folks of the mountain seemed to stay out of the sudden encounter and I could quickly read fear from their faces. For their fortune, the battle moved towards the west, through various smaller chambers.

We chased the enemy into the marble quarters of the royals, where the fight was put into a halt. Both of us were tired after the shambles we had gone through so far. The blighter halmhaers had to gather their strength and had retreated to the western end of the hall. During the hiatus, something unexpected happened.

In the northern parts of the hall was a door, which was suddenly kicked open, revealing a man with fully black clothes. It all seemed very unconventional and distracting, yet we were intrigued by this unexpected act of arrogance. The man looked at both sides with questioning eyebrows. I could hear the leader of the halmhaers enquiring his name.

'Abyss.' A name that stuck to my mind for many years was given by the character. The man calling himself Abyss said that he was trying to find a way to Hasgastadl, so he could slay Stala, the mighty friend of my kin. Those rotter halmhaers were pleased to hear this and asked whether the man would join their cause. My initial anger turned into mocking amusement, as the man refused, by saying, "Bugger off, you halmhaer bollock, you are even worse than halmhendens." Faint laughter was heard in the hall's resounding stone walls, as Abyss took several steps forwards into the chamber.

Lady Partal asked the man about his allegiance. Abyss' face did not hesitate to keep anything as a secret in the moment, and he proudly praised the name of Father Storm. I could not believe it, nor could my warriors, who were confused whilst continuously swearing and spitting on the floor. The man's announcement was somewhat uncomfortable for us and for our halmhenden friends, and it seemed that this time it was the halmhaers' turn to be entertained.

The man also mentioned that Stala had slain Bovenkauv and imprisoned Father Storm in Hauesk. It was his mission to bring justice and according to him, the halmhaers did not deserve the chance to challenge Stala either. Of course, I was baffled by the words and could not decide whether I hated or liked the man.

What eventually escalated the situation was the realisation by the halmhaers, that Abyss possessed a piece of Father Storm's heart. It was said that Father Storm visited Moltraugad, the realm of halmhendens to see Stala. In order to travel, he had to pay with his heart by sacrificing small parts of it. Father Storm was not the mightiest or the oldest spirit, and he could eventually become mortal, if he lost all his heart.

The halmhaers knew that Father Storm's heartbreak over the loss of Mother Sky prevented him using the shards by himself. Abyss decided to act quickly and escape to Hasgastadl, before the halmhaers realised his hidden piece of heart. Unfortunately, the sharp-eyed halmhaers sensed the company of strong magical presence in the man and began to approach him.

I have never seen anyone running that fast. The man charged through the halmhaers, making him look like a precisely gliding bat. The halmhaers started to run behind the mysterious character and we followed the abnormal meeting. The events proceeded deeper and deeper to the mountain halls, where the light was dimmer and mustier.

In the last great hall, located somewhere in the northwest part of Hulumnoar, we saw a decorated stone formation. The chamber's northern end had a door, which was open to unfathomable darkness. As we kept running, I felt the moment slowing down and all the people in front of me looking hazy. My sight became darker and the people around began to fall on the floor. With my last steps, I leapt inside the door, where the halmhaers had disappeared along with Abyss.

Abyss, Captain Foltad and the chasing halmhaers managed to get through the beacon of day, which took them to the other side of the gate. Apart from Captain Foltad, the rest of his company were entirely left outside, leaving the conclusion of the situation in the hands of the captain and Abyss. All the same, the first beacon of day was found and secured by Ikirias' troops with the help of the halmhendens. This also meant that the beacon of day was guarded by influential mages, should the halmhaers return behind the magical door.

A few years after the capture of the first beacon of day, the halmhendens who had been residing in Worlgaltrin told that they had found and secured the second beacon near their home. This meant that there was only one beacon left undiscovered in the world. The storm elves and their halmhenden friends did not know whether halmhaers could damage the world by controlling a single beacon. Lieutenant Menelg Hustad wrote in his diary the following story:

In the lands of Galtreken stood Worlgaltrin and Hurlgaltrin, the demonstrations of halmhenden's wondrous mind. Outside Worlgaltrin's gate we met a few halmhendens who told that they had found the second beacon of day in the mountains northwest from the city. The city was awfully quiet and I presumed that the halmhendens had been panicking about the possible destruction of the world.

We did not have any time to waste, as our scouts informed us that the last and the third beacon of day had been found. Apparently, the place was found in the Hillfort land's northern mountain line. For uncountable days, we travelled through the lands and arrived at the northern regions of Hillfort Lands' mountains, creating a border with the sea. In the middle of the mountain line was a gate and cave, which went through the mountain, revealing the ocean on the other end.

As we pushed deeper to the cave with haste, we were ambushed by halmhaers, who were apparently absorbing the energy from the last beacon of day with their grim sorcery. The battle began and its gale of blades and spells was fierce and merciless. The cave hall reminded me of the place we had taken some years ago in Hulumnoar, but this time its decorated stones were spoiled with unrelenting redness.

In the cave of Aiskuelv, we suffered many casualties and the fight was not moving as planned. Yet, we kept charging at the halmhaers like a wounded wild boar, with a dark glow in its eyes. We were running out of time, as the beacon of day began to crackle. The grand mage of the halmhaers stood in front of the door that reminded me of Hulumnoar's equivalent.

In the most desperate moment, a wonder happened. Out of nowhere a man and an elf appeared and punched the grand halmhaer wizard in his face with such a force that he became unconscious. I could recognise the faces; it was Foltad and Abyss, blood on their faces and hands. The sudden loss of the grand mage gave us hope and we pushed into a new attack, which turned the battle into our advantage. With the sudden help of the two, the battle was won, making the halmhaers retreat to the north, where the icy sea waited. There, many of the escapees fell into the freezing water and drowned.

We returned to the cave where we saw the captured grand mage, surrounded by our troops. Abyss ran to the halmhaer grand mage and hit him again, removing some of his teeth. The moment was interrupted by a halmhenden warrior who asked of Abyss whether he had taken a proper battering from Stala as well, making the company laugh and smirk.

The halmhaer grand mage, who was known as Silmost Phaer joined the laughter and told what gullible simpletons we had been. Worlgaltrin had been taken over by halmhaers and the second beacon day was already drained by their wizards. Apparently, the halmhendens who we met in Worlgaltrin, were actually halmhaers is disguise. Bugger!

Abyss killed Silmost Phaer and began to run towards southwest, shouting how everyone should follow him before it was too late. Captain Foltad and Lady Partal ordered some of their warriors to remain with the third of beacon of day, causing an involuntary murmur. Once again, the mighty band was on the move, running as if there were flames under their arses.

These were the events which began the War of Hulstakn, a desperate conflict between the Ikirias–halmhenden alliance and the halmhaers, who had secretly taken over Worlgaltrin. When the halmhaers began to understand their inevitable defeat and failure controlling all beacons of day, it left them no option than avenge their loss and destroy as much as possible in the process.

Captain Foltad served in the first army of Ikirias, which was called Amrakaurt, meaning 'Ancestor'. During this period, the second beacon of day was entirely absorbed by the halmhaers, making their army commander Mund Phaer immensely arrogant and contemptuous in spirit. The halmhendens who once lived in Worlgaltrin had been killed by their conquerors, which made the war an edict of eternal hatred between the two sides of Stala's people.

The mighty champion from Kajoste, Hurastil, son of Burstastil, appeared on the battlefield. The actions of the halmhaers had also threatened his home, making him join the war with the intention to help the storm elves. Hurastil did not like the halmhendens either, as he had been a close friend of Father Storm in Kajoste. However, the situation forced him to join the lesser enemy, as the halmhaer threat could have brought the defining end to all life.

With the help of Hurastil, the halmhaers were defeated. In the final battle, Hurastil slew Mund Phaer in the royal halls of Worlgaltrin, causing a grand release of magic. All the power captured by the halmhaer commander was freed to the land of Galtreken, making the land flourish with magic forever. After the long campaign, Captain Foltad returned to Ikirias with the army and the halmhendens began to restore their primordial home.

Ikirias' location was an advantage for the storm elves when the gabyr wars occurred in the east. Only the War of

Tarnfros' Might touched Ikirias, but even then, the realm did not suffer major losses. During these years, the friendship with the halmhendens had faded and the general presence of their people was absent. It was often believed that the halmhendens had disappeared entirely from the world after many years of sadness and destruction.

Yet, there was one more war to come, which would put the forgotten loyalty of Ikirias to the test. Ikirias was approached by a halmhenden named Vhyolan Rauwos, one of the most influential wizards amongst their folk. He had managed to live for hundreds of years, despite suffering from the loss of his waning kin. Vhyolan appealed to an ancient unity, which their peoples shared, and spoke words of glamorous past.

Vhyolan, who had been involved in the convoluted story of the elves, had fought against Abyss and Father Storm in his past. However, Vhyolan did not have grudges towards the two characters or Haustrn's storm elves. Instead, he wanted to see the manfolks and many others burn under his vengeance.

These realms had once been one of the several reasons why the might of halmhendens faded in Worlgaltrin. Nevertheless, the current king of Ikirias saw behind the insane gleam of Vhyolan's eyes and declined the blood-soaking proposal. Vhyolan was deeply disappointed in King Raverek's decision and decided to turn on the side of the gelders, who resided in the north.

During the War of the Returning One, Ikirias went through several internal troubles. The families of Lyshim, Alaverek and Oldfolhim were influential in the realm and were the only families still willing to join Vhyolan's cause. Their idea was to bring back the glorious alliance, which the storm elves of Ikirias and the halmhendens once had.

The three families schemed against the Ravereks during the war and their aim was to overthrow the royals and to rule in unity. King Raverek and his family could sense that something nefarious was brewing against their health, and decided to retreat to their holds in the city. It did not take long until Lady Ylva and Lord Inabyr Alaverek decided to assassinate King Raverek in the most imposing way possible.

The opportunity came when the king held a meeting in the royal house. It was common for the families of Ikirias to discuss recent matters in the chambers and suggest new ideas for the reigning royal. Usually the discussions were light hearted, meaning that the storm elves ended up talking about the sourness of their cider.

This time Lord Inabyr had hired an assassin, who was disguised as one of the so-called house announcers. Their task was to approach the king or queen and read the proposition on the behalf of a family. After reading numerous propositions, King Raverek was approached by the assassin, whose steady hands thrusted a blade to the king's heart. The slaying of the king was successful, as the knife sunk deep and killed him rapidly. The whole chamber erupted into disorder and the assassin escaped, whilst Lord Inabyr watched the situation with a grin on his face.

For several days, the royal warriors of Ikirias besieged the families, who had been part of the inordinate betrayal. In these clashes also fought four famous heroes named Crayvar, Wahlvern, Rylskar and Diwion. The four had been fighting in the ongoing war and they originally had no intention to stay for long. However, Lord Inabyr eventually lost the battle in Ikirias and was forced to escape the city. The scheming elf was ultimately slain by Wahlvern Hebelcurnn, whose archery skills made the elf join the long list of his victims with the final words, *"Where on earth did that come from?"*

Ikirias also took part in the War of the Gleaming Bonfires. Around these times, the majority of the storm elves of the realm did not consider halmhendens as their allies. In fact, a new rising of loyalists towards Father Storm appeared after many ages of neglecting his presence. One could even suggest that many of Ikirias' families thought that it was essential to defeat the halmhendens, and ensure Father Storm's return to Drytgastadl.

Some of Haustrn's storm elves joined Ikirias, when the word regarding Kulus began to roam the lands. Kulus had immense powers and its opener could be rewarded by the spirits who were trapped in the well. The storm elves of Ikirias began to contemplate whether these spirits could aid the realm in their mission to bring down Hasgastadl and locate Father Storm in the process.

Nelleffe Atmoryn, a famous bard, joined the armies so she could witness the battles herself and write stories about the majestic endeavours. When the troops of Ikirias began to march towards the presumed location of Kulus, Nelleffe heard many rumours about soldiers' sundered opinions. Some of the warriors supported families that were still loyal to halmhendens and they were not keen to fight for the well, if its purpose was to bring down their formidable and ancient ally. Nelleffe saw a dark seed of discord growing amongst the soldiers and their leaders.

What Nelleffe and many others feared was that the army of Ikirias would divide during the war. To distract and soothe the atmosphere around the commanders and soldiers, Nelleffe performed some of her songs in the halls between the clashes. Many of these songs penetrated the storm elf warriors and created an imprint of legends, which flew in the wind to the world.

"May these songs of mine fly in the air and remember the world how our warriors saw it. Every day and night is the same, every blood and sword is different. It does not matter in which battle you fall, since you will not see the end of the war either way. Let this music be worth it, let it be free unlike the ones who suffered for a better tomorrow."

The fate of Nelleffe and many others remained a mystery, when Kulus blasted and the cave halls collapsed upon the armies. Only the wind which carried the songs from the battle to Ikirias, remembered the names of the fallen soldiers. In their memory, several boats sailed to the north through the river of Cilegkham. The boats were greeted by the honour guard, who took the commemorative items to the stone mansion of the fallen heroes.

"It was a rainy and windy morning when the boats were set to sail north. Against the grey sky a faint music played, as if someone had composed a beautiful song for our heroes, whose bodies we could never see."

Even the mightiest forces in the world had to bend time to time and this time it had been Father Storm's turn. Halmhaers had imprisoned Mother Sky and threatened to absorb her life, if Father Storm would not obey their commands. The halmhaer Queen Alka Founea had ordered Father Storm to use his abilities to find passages between the worlds and wait underneath the well of Kulus.

For several days, Father Storm shouted and raged, as he could not commit such a foul deed, nor kill his own people. Yet, the love towards Mother Sky was greater and with teary eyes Father Storm opened the well from the other side, causing an unbearable imbalance between the places. Father Storm was left in the dark as he saw the screaming ghosts of the warriors, slain by the sudden fall of the chambers. Amongst the ghosts was Nelleffe sitting on a stone, gazing at nothingness.

Father Storm, being tired of the eternal struggle, looked at Nelleffe and sat next to her. The exhausted face of Father Storm was full of hate, which was no longer covered in tears. Father Storm spoke to Nelleffe about the annulling end of their lives. The bard listened to Father Storm, who held his wounded chest. With his last energy, Qlaskastet, Father of the storm looked at his crystal heart that looked beaten by hate and love.

With trembling hands, Qlaskastet gave his heart to Nelleffe and told her to find a man named Abyss. The man would be able to use it and bring merciless death upon their enemies. Nelleffe took the heart and beheld the reducing breath of Father Storm. Qlaskastet's eyes became pale and his final words were, *"For love, this storm quietens above."*

It took decades before Nelleffe found Abyss, since the man was not too far away from being a ghost himself. The spectral bard gave the heart to the man, who was now carrying two broken hearts on his earthly journeys. Abyss was usually a cold and mild-mannered wanderer, but this time his presence set into revengeful flame. After a moment of constricting silence, the man explained that with the heart, he could finally find a way to Kajoste, an ancient home of heroes. In here, he would gather a group of the finest of warriors and set the world of halmhaers on fire. Many of the fallen storm elf heroes of Selkelgen would gladly join the quest, as they once served Father Storm in the battles of the past.

ANCESTORS OF DISTANT TIMES

An old legend tells how the ancestors of Vlios Foltad bore the name of Foltaanvielta in Selkelgen. The storm elves of the family were particularly gifted at planning structures like towers and fortresses. They had a unique talent to see something extraordinary in the world, something which other elves and mortals could not.

The ability was called syfangaetson and it allowed the elves of the family to see energies which, like strings, held the world together. These patterns were used by the family to find magical points for the buildings they created in Selkelgen. Several families wanted their homes to be built on these concentrations of magic and it was a common belief that if the world collapsed, these strong points of magic would protect their inhabitants.

Despite being talented wizards, halmhendens lacked the ability to see certain raw energies of the cosmos. This made the elves of Foltaanvielta folks of interest. Stala approached the family and asked their people to build three beacons of day, which could build arcane bridges between distant places. Taipaleita Foltaanvielta accepted the offer, since the beacons of day gave the elves the opportunity to connect themselves to the lands of Drytgastadl faster than before. Taipaleita and her family travelled to Drytgastadl and began to use their mysterious aptitude. After three decades, the imposing beacons of day rose in three different locations in the lands.

Aivigilmoli, the sky spirit of Kajoste, befriended the storm elves of Foltaanvielta and gave them four gifts. These were Bostentelpylv, the four black owls, who gave birth to the long line of large birds and their mission was to protect the storm elves. The mightiest of the birds was Caulfog and it was believed that its energy and presence was so strong, that it was coupled with the western beacon of day, making Caulfog an ever-moving part of the beacon. Aivigilmoli, who could sew the cosmic fabric and places together, let the sewing shine as belts of stars above the firmament. Caulfog was said to be her hands and its beak was the needle that pierced the skies, attaching primordial strings to the aether's structure.

Vlios Foltad was part of the same story and inheritance, only much later in time. The elf was born in Ikirias and possessed the very same abilities as his ancestors did in Selkelgen. He could see and feel winds and strings of energy moving in the world, guiding the way to the sources of enchantment and mystery. Vlios joined the army of Ikirias at a young age and mostly ignored his astonishing skills. The elf did not know the importance of his aptitude for halmhendens, who eventually had major plans for him.

After a dull military life, Captain Foltad finally received a mission that he thought was spiffing enough to make his soldier life worth living. Halmhenden Lady Sauenge Partal had approached the storm elves when they had discovered the frightening news about the halmhaers and their involvement in the beacons of day. Lady Partal knew that Captain Foltad could see something which other elves could not, making him the leader of the coming expedition.

Vlios was surprised by his assignment, as he had not expected to obtain such a significant task and responsibility. Soon enough, a powerful band of warriors set their way towards west, from where Foltad sensed strong energies. One could say that it was natural for him to follow certain patterns, which seemed to be there for a purpose. Lady Partal observed the captain's reactions and behaviour, as the band came closer to the mountains of Hulumnoar. The captain wrote in his memoires about the journey he faced, after chasing Abyss through the door of the beacon:

I came to realise that I was the only one from our company to get through the impossible door. After this moment, my memories of the two years I was gone cannot be described sensibly. The journey I took felt like a day of lives and fates, which one mortal could not experience in a hundred years. It all felt like a dream, me being a legendary hero, whose story was told by someone in a different time.

I became friends with this Abyss, with whom I fought the halmhaers several times and helped the peoples we met on our journey. I remember an island, small in size, its people warm in heart, who delivered letters to cities and towns. I even wrote a letter myself, hoping that it would once reach the lips of my wife.

I remember another land which I recognised from the myths of our people. No one ever said the name, but I was certain it was Selkelgen, the home of our ancestors. They were living there as if the world had never been broken, no tears fallen. Perhaps I was living someone's memory of the place; perhaps it was just a dream of the old ages.

Much later, Abyss led me to a place which was nothing but endless lofts with rooms and narrow corridors. I had no idea where I was, but it seemed to be the place where I belonged. In these faintly lit corridors, we met a man named Waine, a regular face in those parts of the world. The man had a small room, where he had kept writing books for himself. He told me that no one had ever read any of his writings, nor did he care if they were ever shared with anyone.

We spent several days with Waine and one day he suggested that we would accompany him to a tavern named Bohjanahjossa, meaning 'Star Cauldron'. After following the man for quarter of a day, we arrived in a chamber, where everything was made of wood.

The tavern was full of people I could not recognise, nor did they seem to care about our arrival. The room was split into four sections, which all had round and long tables, surrounded by joyful people drinking ale and whisky, whilst eating roasted pork and vegetables. The corner, which was named as the northern peak, had a fireplace with three men sitting and enjoying rare malts in their small decorated cups. One of the men was called Varnan Bort, a wizard with a detached nature.

Varnan Bort claimed that he knew how to access Hasgastadl. According to the man, there was a room, which had not been touched by anyone for decades, full of dust and old items. In this room, one could find a hatch that could take a traveller to a path of forbidden road. Abyss and I were charmed by the information and asked whether Varnan could show us this murky room.

Alas! Our lovely night of ale, mead and food was interrupted by a halmhaer raid, catching us off-guard. Varnan had been talking something about an ill feeling in the atmosphere, and his gaze into the fireplace ended with the words: 'They are here.' The halmhaers broke every door and thundered in, like a winter night with a thousand needles of ice. They climbed out of the cellar and even the fireplace, they were everywhere and they were undoubtedly looking for us. I would have rather been cleaning the garrison's floor with my buttocks than have been there, but I had no choice in this world of unpredictability.

I remember Abyss shouting, "Reserves of Selkelgen, rise!" A heave of fire and blood took over the tavern, as the turmoil commenced with all its mayhem. The halmhaers drew their weapons and fought the warriors of Selkelgen with swings that could have cut a bear in half. The swordsmen, Abyss and I retreated from the tavern to a room, which was next to the fireplace. Behind the door, we were led by the commander of the warriors further into a series of lofts. I was not happy at all.

The commander was Hoskenn Turmnkaar, who told us that we would be sailing today to the shores of Hasgastadl if it was our bidding. I was abashed by his words, as I did not see any water in this world of wooden rooms and lofts. Regardless of my hesitance, we followed him to a chamber, which began to tremble as if we were floating on a cloud. Soon the room turned into a ship that was on sail towards the room which Varnan described earlier. I screamed as the *bowsprit hit the hatch of the loft, breaking the world around me. I was greeted by mighty waves and I held onto a rope in the rain.*

Captain Foltad's memoirs ended before the ship reached the shores of Hasgastadl. The storm elf made a note that his memories were too fragile and the only recollection of the place was a disorder that covered him in blood. Vlios did not know what had happened and whether any part of the journey he took was real. The captain and Abyss appeared from a door, which was located at the northern beacon of day and was greeted by an unfamiliar face. The face belonged to the halmhaer mage Silmost Phaer and without any hesitation Abyss and Foltad punched the mage. This sudden act of ferocity gave Captain Foltad finally that little smile he had been missing too long.

THE SORROW BEARER

"It was a night of hard rain. The water was flooding the soil and the essence of heroes rose from its old cold-bitten layers. On that same night, Diwion was born into the family of immemorial tales. The fireplace in the house was sparkling and howling, when Diwion came to the world, facing its fresh breeze. In his eyes glimmered much more than ordinary life, a striking intensity that our ancestors once had."

Diwion was born into a wealthy family of Heliory, who had acquired most of their riches from trading. Since Diwion was the only child, his parents were remarkably protective towards him. Young Diwion did not get to venture and most of his childhood included being in the house, reading books about realms and lore. Bored Diwion was dreaming of adventures beyond the walls of the city and often gazed at the landscapes standing in the distance. Unfortunately, Diwion's parents passed away before the elf reached his adulthood. The family of Velioryst, who were good friends of Heliory's, decided to help the young elf and invited him to join their house.

After the untimely death of Diwion's parents, the family of Velioryst gave him a freedom that he had never had. Loised and Kiesvona Velioryst introduced Diwion to the family and the relations were warm in the beginning. Diwion's daring attitude towards life impressed Loised Velioryst, a veteran of many battles. Loised had always dreamt of having a child who would join the military, but none of his children wanted to carry the heavy heart in the warrior's road.

Loised and Diwion became close friends, making Vaised, Loised's son envious. Eventually, the father considered Diwion as his son, which turned Vaised's envy into contempt. The young elf could not tolerate that his status as the golden son was derogated, causing many conflicts between the two. No one knows whether Vaised eventually lost his mind during these years, as he kept disappearing for days after fighting with Diwion.

Loised did not want to lose his son and he suggested that Diwion would join the military. Diwion was more than willing to accept the idea and left the house of resentment and scorn. However, for Loised the departure of Diwion was grim, as he was everything he had wanted to see in Vaised. The mother, Kiesvona, hated the thoughts of Loised and blamed him for pushing his own son away with his dreams.

Diwion's time in the military was not easy, as he had trouble obeying his superiors. The elf was excellent at using swords and shooting with bows, but he expressed no desire to follow the chain of command in the army. Yet, the commander of his regiment did not want to expel the storm elf, since he was a remarkable runner and could deliver messages faster and more quietly than anyone else.

Diwion's captain moved the elf to the royal messengers, who worked under the representatives of Ikirias. Diwion's noble background and knowledge gave him an easy access to the role that suited his cunning and charming character. During the years in the royal messengers, Diwion rose in ranks and he became a respected member of the order, rapidly building a reputation of a well-mannered maverick.

Ultimately, Diwion became one of the representatives and was sent to the east several times. Ikirias attempted to keep relations with the manfolk and the sky elves, who with Ikirias shared an intricate and convoluted past. In the same year's spring, when Diwion returned from Dyveln, the storm elf met Cilumel, a beautiful lady of Ikirias' families. During the journey to the realm, the two spent many days talking and admiring the shine in each other's eyes.

When Diwion and Cilumel returned to Ikirias they were inspected by Vaised, who was apparently deeply in love with Cilumel. Diwion could not believe this, as it seemed that every setback in his life led back to the same plonker. Vaised saw the play of eyes between the two and sunk deeper into his dark dwellings of jealousy.

During the same summer, Vaised could not take another defeat and decided to kill Diwion. The elf felt that he had been stripped from all of his achievements and only shame smiled upon him. Vaised, being completely inexperienced in fighting, decided to attack Diwion in a tavern, which held a midsummer celebration. Whilst Diwion was battering Vaised's face into a wooden table, the following words were heard:

"I do not owe you anything! I lost my family a long time ago and your father helped me to become the warrior I am today. I will not apologise for my own success, and if it draws such a long shadow upon you, then perhaps you ought to look to lands far enough where it cannot reach."

The third gabyr war was named the War of Tarnfros' Might and its remorseless coldness smothered part of Diwion's life away. During the war, Cilumel was travelling to Ikirias for her personal matters. The cavalcade she was part of was ambushed by a band of gabyrs, who were looking for storm elf transports between the towns. Cilumel and rest of the travellers were slain by the gabyrs, and once again Diwion's heart was pierced by the cruel knife of grief.

"With the necklace I bought for Cilumel, I shall strangle every gabyr in the world and the land will be filled with ash."

For years, Diwion battled his sorrows and lived alone in the great house of Heliory. The elf occasionally took tasks from the royal house and visited other realms to take a break from the endless sea of thoughts that so deeply dwelled in his head. Little did he know that he would take his final task, as the War of the Returning One began. Diwion happened to be in Dyveln, when the war broke and the elf became friends with Crayvar, Rylskar and Wahlvern. During the war and unexpected friendship, the four travelled first to Lhorem, where a battle took place against an army of gelders.

The halmhenden Lord Vhyolan, who had asked Ikirias to join the war to honour their ancient alliance, was disappointed as King Raverek declined the proposition. This was not enough for the other realms and they decided to send Crayvar, Rylskar, Wahlvern and Diwion to Ikirias, to make sure no preparations were put in place for such alliances.

Diwion experienced frequent waves of desolation and in many ways hoped that the war would bring meaning to his life. Ultimately, the elf took his three companions to Ikirias, where the situation had become as brittle as his own life. The city had remained out of the war, but there was a resistance brewing. The situation escalated when King Raverek was assassinated by several rival families, commencing an outrageous revolt.

Diwion and his companions helped the city guard and the royal loyalists defeat the traitors, who had planned to join Lord Vhyolan and his gelder armies. The journey continued from here to Honedimn, which was a disaster for the alliance that consisted of armies from Aetari, Dyveln, Ylvart and a smaller warband from Podfrud. In the battle against the gelders, the four travellers managed to flee the city, commencing a journey towards the home of the dwarfs.

Wahlvern was badly wounded during the battle, but was eventually saved in Podfrud, which offered the travellers a resting place. However, the rest was not long, as the gelders had the intention to attack the dwarf realms as well. Diwion began to enjoy the fighting, as he could combat for other peoples and care less about the troubles of his homeland. In a very strange way, the unceasing presence of death revived him from his long torpor.

After the successful defence of the dwarven realm and the recovery of Wahlvern, the four returned to the lands of Aetari and Dyveln. The regrouped and reinforced armies were planning a grand war quest to Galtreken, to challenge Vhyolan and his armies directly. The four became part of these armies, as they began to march towards the northwest. In his journal, Diwion wrote:

"This land shines in the dawn, it chants to me like your smile. I will follow your steps and play with the blade, singing along to the songs of blood and steel. You will see me ending this dance without footsteps in the snow."

Diwion took part in the Battle of Jarlidan and Worlgaltrin, which pushed the dawning victory forward. Vhyolan's mercenary army of gelders had received concerning news from their homeland regarding raiding gabyrs. This made most of their warriors return to the north, which was a defining reason behind Vhyolan's defeat. In the end of the Battle of Worlgaltrin, Vhyolan escaped in an attempt to disappear and travel to Hurlgaltrin.

The final battle of the war took place in Hurlgaltrin, where Diwion, Crayvar, Wahlvern and Rylskar fought alongside the legendary Lord Commander Faerkroll and his guards. During the battle, Crayvar was mortally wounded by Vhyolan, which made Diwion charge carelessly at the halmhenden lord. This was the final mistake of the storm elf, who had suffered much in his peculiar life. The battle was over, but so was Diwion's life. Wahlvern wrote in his memoirs how Diwion spoke to Rylskar after defeating Vhyolan:

"Do not start to lie in your old age, someone may even think you have become completely brittle. I am going home, you could not save me and nor would I want it. Crayvar is dead, like we all are going to be eventually. You were like brothers to me, after the fading of my family and the death of my love, I have not wanted anything but to leave here.

"Do not mourn for me, as I have never been happier than now. I do not know whether anyone is going to remember me, but does it even matter? When we all are gone, who even remains to remember? However, I do have one request. Take my gold necklace and put it around my

neck before you burn my body. Through it, shall my love burn one last time.

Then again, who would forget me? Impossible!"

Diwion, Wahlvern, Crayvar and Rylskar.

LADY OF THE HOME ROADS

The family of Nelleffe Atmoryn was one of the peoples who protected the stone mansion of Laulaskaiun. The mansion was also known as the halls of the fallen and it was believed that Ikirias' dead heroes resided in these chambers and its great apple tree gardens. Nelleffe's family was not prosperous or well known, but were good in heart and respected by the storm elves of the domain.

Nelleffe was a talented singer and she always remained in the minds of the storm elves, who had heard her songs in the village. Nelleffe had a tradition to sing before she went to sleep and often the whole village came to see her in the small market square. Regardless of the season, Nelleffe sang and the village admired her striking, but soft voice. The young storm elf grew up performing and helping her mother with the garden, which inspired her to come up with several vegetable related songs. These chants were amusing and many nobles came to see Nelleffe, when she was singing in the larger nearby towns.

Many of the storm elves of Ikirias who had lost track on their journeys, claimed that every evening they heard a faint singing in the distance. By following the voice, many of the lost found their way back home, possibly saving their lives. Nelleffe did not know that her singing had powers and they could be heard far away from her village.

Many of Ikirias' storm elves began to talk about the voice of a young girl, who was chanting about the past of the storm elves and vegetables, which seemed to be an odd combination. Nelleffe's talent remained a secret until her father disappeared in a gabyr ambush. Nelleffe's mother, Helevelle, became desperate and wanted to see the place where her husband was apparently killed. Against all advice, Helevelle told her sister to take care of the family until she would return from her journey.

Helevelle went to seek her husband's body, since the military could only find some traces of the ambush, but not any corpses. After a short while, the family became concerned about Helevelle, who had not returned from her travel. Nelleffe began to write songs to her mother and sing them in the market square as usual. Heartbroken, the storm elves of the village listened to the young girl, who wished that her mother would find her way home.

The unexpected happened when the mother returned to the village, looking withered by nature. The village celebrated and wondered how Helevelle found back home, after being astray for such a long time. The mother told that she had heard Nelleffe singing every evening and she kept following the voice of her own daughter. Soon, the story about Nelleffe's talent began to circulate the realm and many elves of Ikirias came to ask the young elf girl whether she could help them to find their lost relatives as well.

Lieutenant Stonlpolt asked whether Nelleffe could join his company of warriors to revoke the old memories of fallen heroes with her beautiful songs. The bard began to follow the army around the lands, where they fought raiding gabyr warbands. Soon, Nelleffe became hugely respected and her stories and chants became a crucial part of the northwest army section's presence.

Her ability to bring delight to where it was dark uplifted the spirits of the soldiers. It also gave Nelleffe the opportunity to immortalise numerous fates of life, otherwise forgotten by time. The northwest army was deployed to the south after the realm found information regarding the well of Kulus. Nelleffe's company was highly demanded amongst the ones who wanted to bring back Father Storm after many years of silence. However, Nelleffe was deeply worried about the divided ranks of their soldiers. Most of the warriors of Ikirias wanted to bring back Father Storm, but there was still a good share of storm elves, whose plan was to make an alliance with halmhendens.

When it was clear that the storm elves of Ikirias would be marching to war, Nelleffe was assigned to join Stonlpolt's regiment. During this journey to the presumed location of Kulus, Nelleffe took an old instrument with her, which was called a lendellonen. Hundreds of years ago it had belonged to a gelder, who had called it Lendelloin and it was a piece of flat wood, with strings attached to it.

Nelleffe wrote songs about each soldier who she met in the company and the songs became fables, eventually floating to the skies. Some stories suggested that these chants became clouds that brought down the melodies and words when it rained. In one way, Nelleffe eternalised the warriors of the army through her abilities. The journey to Kulus was full of hard rains and storms, which made Nelleffe believe that the divide between the soldiers made the clouds furious. Every sung story sent to the sky, caused a thunder strike and Nelleffe could see the minds and spirits of the army in the firmament's grey presence. Nelleffe wrote her thoughts about the atmosphere in to her small book of travels;

I could see old songs floating in the air, as if they had been kept there for thousands of years. They told me tales of old regarding people and places that no longer were. There were so many of them and they all seemed to fight each other, as if the stories were battling for their right to exist. They could not escape their past and they were spilled on the walls and they were frightened by the light.

I could see the songs dancing on the walls and on the ceiling, performing battles and landscapes of the times when my ancestors were young. They all followed certain patterns that told a story, repeating particular parts again and again.

The halls of Kulus were divided into many sections, full of large bonfires that had been enlightening the rooms for thousands of years. Everything around us seemed depthless and full of opportunities and inscrutabilities, which we could not interpret with our mortal knowledge. The battle between the armies had taken a halt. Our warriors remained in a hall close to the well, where we were keeping the hordes of gabyrs in the southern end of the chamber.

The northern and western ends of the hall expanded, where the ceiling looked like an open bare sky full of stars and distant events. Every part of the ceiling was telling a story of curious characters, as if they were still living their lives above our eyes. I did not know whether I was the only one seeing the visions, but certainly, they were as beautiful as untouched diamonds of snow. All the ceilings waved like the lights in the northern sky in green and faint blue, meshing with the ancient tales of the world.

One of the ceilings told a story of what I could understand as the tale of the dwarfs, folk who I had met only twice in my life. It showed me a mountain range and fields of grass that swayed in the cold slithering winds of the night. A great star shone its light upon the fields and a chant began to echo in the chamber. Suddenly these dwarfs began to fall from the star skies, every glimmer bringing a bearded warrior to the battle. It seemed that the whole chamber had taken a halt amidst this baffling encounter.

As the fight continued, I also heard songs, which seemed to be louder and coming directly at me. It took me some time to understand that the first chant was from Mother Sky, who had been imprisoned in Alasgastadl. The mother was looking for Father Storm and she told how the emotions she felt could not be described with words, as they would pierce any man's heart. She once treasured Father Storm, but the curses of halmhaers had destroyed her ability to feel love. Her feelings were burning away like a rose bludgeoned by fists of immovable death. I did not want to believe the words of the chants, as it crushed my heart in the middle of the horrors of the war.

The song of Mother Sky also included a secret message that was supposed to reach Father Storm. It told the gateway to Alasgastadl and about its weakest points, so Father Storm could wake absolute bereavement within its sphere. Nelleffe was too confused to understand many of the song's complicated parts, since she was in a hurdle of steel, iron and wrath. Nonetheless, the elf memorised the message and hoped that one day she could meet Father Storm and see the downfall of Alasgastadl. Ultimately, Nelleffe had to stop her pondering, as the storm elf army was called to charge towards the well, now witnessing the clash of all armies. During this attack, Nelleffe could hear deep rumbles from the depths telling her to leave the halls, as her life should not be lost on this day.

However, it was too late by the time the young storm elf woman received the message, as the halls began to collapse, murdering the gorgeous ceiling of visions. The armies kept pushing towards the opening well, which released bursts of light, sounding like deep humming flutes. It was the final moment, as the vast magical sky of the hall fell, abolishing every life into fragments.

I thought I was dead, swallowed by the great warmth and the unknown. I was there looking at an empty place, where some familiar faces roamed. I could see the hall where we used to stand and fight with thousands of people. I could not but stare at the wonders of the moment, coming to me like a dream. I could see some movement near me, a strong character that stood out from the rest. I knew that he was Father Storm, as he sat next to me.

The father was badly wounded and I gazed at him with sorrowful eyes as he gave me his heart. I was too weak to speak of what had happened to Mother Sky, and how the evil had feasted on her sadness. Father Storm gave me a task to find a man named Abyss, who would help me to end Alasgastadl. I saw Father Storm's eyes fading and his eternal pose imploding to the unearthly soil of the place. He said that it was him who had collapsed the well and destroyed all the armies, including me. Halmhaers had forced him to do the deed, otherwise taking Mother Sky's life.

I had to find Abyss and make sure that the halmhaers would feel the rage of our father through our blades and arrows. I would do anything to prepare the last chapter of the arrogant enemies of our old world. Their very names felt like fire on my tongue and soon their lives would feel cold as ice.

I travelled outside and saw the world, which was different and desolate from the warmth I once used to feel. I had to find Abyss and I had the ever-glowing heart of our father helping me. The heart made very specific sounds that reminded me of the shine of frosty crystals, twinkling and glittering in the sunlight. Outside I was greeted by several spectres who all claimed that they knew me.

They were people who had died decades ago, but they had been listening to my songs. Hundreds of these people surrounded me and hugged me, as if I had saved their lives. Amongst them was a familiar face, which smiled at me and looked me deep into the eyes. It was my father. He told me how he had heard my songs, and of how he had run aside my mother when she returned from the journey long time ago. He had always been there for us; we just could not see him.

The spectres promised to help me and wanted to find Abyss, so we could finally end the chapter of the halmhaers in the world. Abyss presumably had a piece of our Father's heart and with it, we could find his location somewhere in the lands far away. The spectres and I began a daring journey to find the man and I wrote many songs to call his presence. The melodies pierced the forests, lakes, hills and mountains and the words flew in the spheres between the light and dark.

It took many years, but eventually Abyss received the songs that had been roaming the world. The man did not believe the messages at first, since he thought that they were nefarious plans of halmhaers to lure him to the light.

However, Abyss could hear a familiar sound in the background of the songs, reminding him of the presence of Father Storm's heart. It was a deep beat that sounded like grinding ice and a whistling cold shine, touching the structures of the sky.

Abyss knew that it was Father Storm and he travelled to Hurlgaltrin and stood by the well. Its endless bottom hummed, and the sound of the heart grew stronger, whilst Nelleffe's singing could be heard as distant echoes. Abyss fell into the well, embracing the recognised and indefinite, seeing the countless layers of life hurtling next to his austere eyes. For an undefined period of time, Abyss fell and heard all the songs Nelleffe had ever written, telling stories of men and women whom he had never known. The man saw seeds growing into trees and people growing old, remembering all their faint words and deeds.

It was a cold wintery night. We stood on a stone bridge between two mountains. From the northern end of the bridge, behind a gate, appeared a man in black clothes and hair. The air was waving his determined stance, which did not break from its frozen foundation. When the man approached me and the rest, the heart of Father Storm commenced a great glow, bringing light to the dim winter afternoon. The man smiled and told me how he had heard me singing. I knew that it was Abyss, his stubbly face was covered in white layer of frost and his tired green eyes gazed at the west, where a slight blue light was barely seen.

I told Abyss that Father Storm was dead and he had asked me to return his heart. I did not know the man, but I could tell that rarely his face showed any emotions, allowing the situation to break him into little shards. On his knees, Abyss took the heart on his lap, revealing his scarred hands and face. I could tell that he was too sad to cry, too tired to shout and his hands trembled, dropping the heart on the snow.

So began the end of Alasgastadl.

The legend continued with Nelleffe and Abyss going to Kajoste, also known as Oblivion of Heroes. In here, Nelleffe sang several songs to gain the attention of the heroes who dwelled in this ancient land. Abyss knew some of these storm elf warriors, who had once served Father Storm in the times of Selkelgen. One could say that these soldiers were part of an elite force trained by Father Storm himself and they had been waiting for a day like this for uncountable years.

The heart that could bring destruction to Alasgastadl, was made by Bethelbas Skaiwon, an ancient force before the world. She gave it as a gift to Father Storm, who was humbled by the great gesture. Stala, the creator of halmhendens was deeply in love with Bethelbas and was envious of the gift. The unrevealed love towards Skaiwon was Stala's weakness and made the heart of Father Storm a weapon against what eventually became halmhaers. It is believed that Bethelbas saw behind Stala and could see that from his creations destruction was brewing.

Nelleffe, Abyss and the legendary storm elf warriors travelled to Hauesk. Despite the place was called Cellar World, it was full of eternal spruce woods, shadowy villages and stones, which were worshipped by witches and suchlike. Abyss told Nelleffe that the heart of Father Storm spoke to him and told him that a way to Alasgastadl was waiting for him in Hauesk. The heart would not only be a weapon, but a key that would reveal something unbelievable to its holder.

When the companionship arrived by the lake of Unolanwirt, Abyss gave the heart to Nelleffe and asked her to hold it in the air, illuminating the silent waves of the dark watered lake. Soon, a large ship emerged from the depths, bringing whitecaps to the shores. The ship was named Fosvmurka and it had belonged to Father Storm and his crew. It appeared that not all the ancient ships had been broken after the fall of Selkelgen.

"We boarded the ship and we made it move by lowering the canvas as usual. In the cold evening, we sailed towards the west and the golden sunset revealed a steam rising from the spruce forests that surrounded the great lake. I could see some of the stone shrines in the northern shores, and characters who waved their torches and shouted something inaudible to us. In the middle of the lake was a curtain of water, which kept falling from the air, revealing the rest of the lake behind its transparent drape. The sunset revealed some sort of scriptum in the thin water curtain, but I did not have time to look at it as our ship charged through it.

"A splash of water woke me and we were in absolute darkness, sailing towards the only light in the distance. I could hear Abyss mumbling something about the realm of night, which I had never heard about. The sight in front of us was hard to describe with words of sense. It looked like a glass bottle the size of a mountain in the middle of black waves. Abyss laughed and yelled how we were arriving soon to Alasgastadl and it would be time to fulfil our destinies. I did not know what to expect from this journey, which appeared to me as a dark daydream.

"We came closer to the enormous glass bottle, which revealed to me a sight below, with forests, rivers and several buildings of stone and wood. We are going to ram into the glass, I shouted to Abyss who kept smiling and telling me how I should not worry. I presume we had reached at least five knots when our bowsprit crushed through the glass, causing a mighty shattering. Our ship was flying in the air, falling to the world of Alasgastadl, creating a waterfall behind its hull. We had arrived!"

The story tells us that the great ship Fosvmurka fell with its crew, whilst the astounded halmhaers could not believe the sight. The ship hit the ancient house of Celtenvalan, breaking through its roof. The water began to flood into the world and a major disorder commenced. Stories of later times described the water as Father Storm's tears, drowning the enemy's world with unforgiving hate.

The battle began and a hurl of steel and spells meshed together. The experienced storm elf warriors of Father Storm barricaded the house and made sure no halmhaers could easily enter the buildings, whilst the water was flooding in the streets and gardens. Nelleffe and Abyss hurried, as they saw the water level rising rapidly, soon getting over the walls that surrounded Celtenvalan.

However, there was one they could not escape and her name was Cojantur Leveget, the grand lady of all spells in Alasgastadl. Cojantur started to pursue Nelleffe, Abyss and the storm elf warriors who began to climb up the stairs to the high tower and its chamber. Abyss could detect Mother Sky's presence, but getting to the tower was not easy, since Leveget could catch some of the warriors, slaying them with her sword and magic. Whilst the storm elf warriors were stalling the sorceress, Nelleffe and Abyss kept running up the stairs and saw how the water was taking over most of the tall buildings.

Nelleffe and Abyss opened the door to the chamber and saw Mother Sky, whose shackles dropped from the indescribable force of the crystal heart. The mother was aware that the object releasing her was also a sign of Father Storm's death. However, the mother did not have time to mourn as she took a better look at Nelleffe. The mother stared at the elf woman, who at first remained silent. Soon, Mother Sky smiled and said how wonderful it was to see Abyss' wife again.

"This all has a meaning and for sure there is a reason why you, Nelleffe, daughter of Helevelle are here today to end the circle of halmhaers."

Abyss looked at Nelleffe whose face began to look more and more familiar. Both felt that dust and time was finally scraped of their shoulders and memories were returning to them. After a brief moment, Nelleffe asked about her origin and place in the world from Mother Sky, who simply replied:

"The love that remains after all this."

The water was getting very high and Mother Sky asked to have the winter crystal from Abyss, who had been carrying it for several centuries. Abyss trusted Mother Sky, who turned the magical weapon into an icy spear and told Nelleffe and Abyss to escape to the roof of the tower. Leveget had managed to slay all the storm elf warriors and kept running up the stairs, where she was greeted by the spear of Mother Sky.

Piercing Cojantur Leveget's chest, the sorceress fell down the stairs, cursing Mother Sky on every possible step. The mother ran back to the chamber and climbed on the roof of the tower, where Nelleffe and Abyss were waiting impatiently. Alasgastadl was now underwater and only a few buildings remained above the surface. Soon, Mother Sky took some water in her hand, threw it into the sky and touched it with the winter crystal, creating spiral stairs to the sky. Without hesitation, Nelleffe, Abyss and Mother Sky ran to the icy stairs, whilst the water kept chasing their feet. When the three reached the top of the world, Mother Sky asked one more favour from Abyss, who was still holding the heart of Father Storm. Abyss knew what Mother Sky meant, when she was reaching her arm. The man looked one more time into the core of the heart and smiled to its beauty and marvel.

Mother Sky kissed the heart and dropped it to the world below, now occupied by waves and corpses of halmhaers. When the heart hit the water, the whole of Alasgastadl froze after a thunderous rumble was heard. The very heart glowed below the three, who saw lightning inside the ice and heard how the sound was becoming louder and fiercer. Briskly, the whole glass bottle world shattered, swallowing all the light and letting the realm of night take over. In the dark fell Nelleffe, Abyss and Mother Sky, hitting the sea of pure black waves. In the cold water, the three lost their consciousness, taken by the numbing and dreamy care of the darkness. Being oblivious, Nelleffe, Abyss and Mother Sky were saved by the guardians of the realm of night, taking them away. Never was the world the same above or below.

REGARDING SHORE AND MOUNTAIN ELVES

According to early myths, when sky elves and storm elves had their several conflicts during the times of Selkelgen, many of the mountain and shore elves left to Drytgastadl. In fact, the very western part of Drytgastadl was an important theatre of events for these elven peoples. The two elven folks found one large realm, which was divided into the northern kingdom and southwest domain.

In the primordial lore of the shore and mountain elves, the western part of Drytgastadl was called Välkehtgen and it was inhabited by many forgotten peoples. It is impossible to place this age within the history of the world, as it was often perceived as an era of early legends. Nevertheless, its stories seemed to continue later in time, when the rest of the elves came to Drytgastadl.

The mountain elves and shore elves called themselves the first ones and they built a vast kingdom, spreading from the north of Välkehtgen to the southwest. The realm was ruled first by the family of Urvenför and later by the elves of Siiwilsoiven. At the time, Drytgastadl had several other domains, which were not pleased by the overwhelming presence of the elves. For instance, the mountains of Valesvelsenen were in the eastern parts of the land, being a home for many malevolent creatures. The peaks were called Odomnan and they were ruled by several old evils of the world.

Many battles were fought between the first elves and the nefarious powers of Odomnan, forging an extensive base for their folklore. However, life in Välkehtgen was not completely about war. The age had numerous long periods of peace, full of light-hearted adventures, usually outliving the times of hardships. Many travellers wrote several books about Välkehtgen, but the most famous one was Floauris Haaengruwerl. The elf's story was a central part of Välkehtiesse, mostly focusing on the adversities between him and Lord Hadjorf Tulunwimmas. These legends helped people of later times to understand what it was like to live in Välkehtgen's lost lands.

THE TREES THAT FLOATED IN AIR

The realm of Whartausa was founded by the sailing family of Ferstas. During their early years, the family had acquired a strong following of other shore elves, who loved adventures and the challenges of the sea. It took about two decades for the elves to build the harbour town of Whartausa, which remained unmapped for exceptionally long. Hilta Nostam Revetruantry, who was the head of the family at the time, ordered that the homes of the peoples should resemble ships, starting the tradition of Whartausa's so-called boat-homes.

The shore elves of the town grew in population and several expeditions were done in the seas. Frahil Nostam Revetruantry, who was Hilta's daughter, did several trips in the seas, discovering several peculiar islands. However, only one of the islands left an unexplainable feeling, echoing limpid hymns through the grey skies. Frahil and the sailors named the island Wistaar, and its discovery began a curious series of events.

The island had sparse spruce tree forests and only one small wooden hut, which lay next to a river. The expedition entered the house, finding their way just underneath the hut. The cellar of the cottage was enchanting, its dark and musty air floating like stardust. The sound of the river streamed its soothing chant, coming together with cooling echoes. Suddenly, Frahil saw several jars full of seeds, making them the only noteworthy items in the cellar. As soon as Frahil touched the jars, the river spoke and its words recalled the lost lands. The voice encouraged Frahil to save the seeds and take them to the east. In the murky sparkles of light, the elf gathered the jars and began her way back home.

The journey went well, but as soon as Frahil saw the shores, a fierce storm hit the sea. Some of the jars, which contained the seeds from the island, fell into the water with their heads open. The crew did not have time to save the jars, as they were getting closer to the harbour town. Ultimately, Frahil and her sailors got home safely and the remaining seeds were taken to the storages of the town.

At first, the guards who observed the ocean did not see anything unusual, but after a few days, an odd sight was observed. It looked as if there was something on the water, far away in the open sea. The sight did not seem to move and Frahil with her crew were sent to investigate the covert sighting. The situation became extraordinary when Frahil's ship approached the area and saw several trees above the water. They were not touching the sea; instead they were growing in the air, their roots just barely above the waves.

Soon, many stories began to circulate about the strange happenstance, which made the shore elves study the seeds. When thrown into the sea, a seed eventually turned into a tree above the waves, by emerging from the depths of the ocean. The plants and the trees kept floating in the air, their roots hanging freely. The family of Revetruantry wrote numerous books about the magical plants and trees, which seemed to point out the location of a place, where there once used to be land.

THE OLD LIGHT OF VÄLKEHTGEN

According to the primordial lore of the mountain elves, Levienet was the northern kingdom of the first elves in Drytgastadl. The realm was ruled first by Urvenförs and later by the family of Siiwilsoiven, who built large mountain halls in the north of Välkehtgen.

The mountain elves of the area were interested in mining, so they decided to dig deep to the depths of the world. King Menassel Urvenförs had heard rumours that in the depths resided an ore named sun root. With the powerful ore, the king wanted to bring eternal light upon his realm, so he could banish the beasts of Odomnan. After a few centuries, the sun root was found, but it was very unstable in the young hands of the first elves, frequently causing a great shine. The brightness was so prodigious, that it eventually made the elves of the mountains blind.

The legend tells how Levienet came to be and why its mountain elves could not bear sunlight, even after numerous generations. Nevertheless, in the folklore of Levienet, the elves believed that all of the four moons under Drytgastadl were their mothers. Their nightly light could bless beverages, making the elves of Levienet tolerate sunlight temporarily. To fulfil the rite, the mountain elves of the realm brewed a specific drink, which was left in the middle of the moon hall of Emimd. The place had four ceiling windows and mirrors, which could direct the light from the four moons. The elves placed their beverages to be blessed in the light, as they hailed the four eternal pieces of the sky.

The primary force behind these constructs was White Hat, also known as Viimelumo in Selkelgen. Viimelumo's departure to Drytgastadl was one of the initial reasons why so many mountain elves found themselves in the lands of Välkehtgen. White Hat also built the tower of Loistegenid, which alongside Emimd, helped the elves to cope with their curse of light.

Loistegenid was the sun tower and Viimelumo went to the land of Loistesse in the west, to find the sun that shone upon it. The force wanted to harness its power and help it reach the northern mountain realm in Välkehtgen. The sun tower in the elven realm was aligned with the sun of Loistesse and a large window let its mighty shine fall down, blessing everyone who was touched by its gleams. The sun of another land had to be used as the sun above Drytgastadl was not friendly towards the elves of Levienet. No one knows what White Hat did in the lands of Loistesse, but its sun removed the dreadful curse from the elves and made them tolerate light once again.

Viimelumo began to reside with the elves of the mountain, bringing them many gifts from Selkelgen and Loistesse. With the gifts, White Hat consecrated the lake of Asella, where he built the shrines of Asalvel. The lakes had water from Selkelgen, Loistesse and Drytgastadl and it was flowing with magic. The three waters and three nameless heroes gained power from this very lake and with its aid the demonic beings of Odomnan could be defeated. Eventually Odomnan fell, but the wars were so devastating that it broke Välkehtgen, giving birth to several smaller elven realms.

After many centuries, the stories of Välkehtgen became part of myths, but the tales kept living amongst the folk throughout the ages. Levienet remained as relatively untouched realm in Drytgastadl and it could peacefully prosper inside its massive mountain hall city. In the later times, the city also expanded to the eastern shores of Welenvel where the mountain elves came to practice sailing and exploration, something which they had not been able to do for uncountable centuries.

MANFOLK

Didly Didly Wazz

OF HOW MORNING FORGED TALES

A great storm was testing the ships that were approaching the shores of the inland sea of Yeldes. The sky was dark grey and thunder was singing its deep hum. The captain of the ships was called Solhamer, and the man kept staring at the beaches in the distance. It seemed to be inevitable that this storm, which was caused by the sea monster named Haug, would make the ships hit the coastline. When the ships got close to the shore, many of them turned sideways, and at this moment, Captain Solhamer saw a great black bear standing on grass fields near the beach. The bear had a rider in a black cape, who looked at the ships with a dark and wild posture.

During the early morning, the majority of the ships had hit the soil, and some of them had broken into multiple pieces, leaving many injured or dead. The sky was still grey, but the rain had become lighter and only a distant thunder could be heard in the background. Captain Solhamer ordered a swift gathering, as he started to receive reports of the bear rider and other black caped strangers. The people armed themselves and assembled all the resources they could salvage from the wrecked ships.

The folk decided to head towards the north, where they found an enormous hill that rose very close to the shoreline. Its eastern and western ends met at ground level, but mostly the flat hill was well above the sea. On the top the hill, the people began to build their village. The place offered the folk a safe location and an opportunity to use the resources provided by the sea.

For decades the people, who eventually became Aetarians, built their houses using wood from the forests that lay in the west. In these woods lived the people who were led by the black bear rider. Eventually, this situation developed into a struggle between the two sides. The old captain Solhamer, now reigning as king, had to face a war that was ignited by the western forest folk.

The mighty black bear rider was known as Mustern. He was the king of the people who he called 'yvvos afso folvaos pra Dyvelnessen', meaning 'Sons and daughters of Dyveln' and a war broke between the two peoples. King Solhamer kept building his realm as he fought alongside his loyal sea soldiers, who had been following him for years. The battles were fierce, but the conflict was missing a true purpose. No one really knew the reasons why the hostilities between Aetari and Dyveln kept going. These were, however, ultimately forgotten, as a new threat came from the north.

After the death of Solhamer, his son Hlusvamer faced a difficult situation, as the armies of gabyrs arrived to the region of Enberahl. This was in an age when Aetari had grown, and its army was able to defend its lands without any trouble. Still, the gabyr warbands started to become too large, and often the people of Aetari ended up defending mutual lands with the people who called themselves the Dyvelnessen. Later in time, Aetari and Mustern made peace as they realised the crushing force of the gabyr armies. Allied, the two realms fought against the forces of the gabyr lords of Hjilos Asgors. After the first war was over with the gabyrs, Mustern and his people decided to leave towards the south and build their realm on the same shores as Aetari. The relationship that had started with blood and fury had now turned into a steel-hard friendship.

"So many of my friends were forgotten. Now, I just see a world of worthless songs that try to bring them back to life. All those words fade into the darkness, just like the day that we buried them in the snowfall. We shall see the dawn one day, when the senselessness will not take us apart. When the home door will glimmer like the tears that once fell to the frozen ground. Mother, I am coming home."

In its early centuries, Aetari became very successful and its towns had become prosperous, inviting a lot of new trade. This was also the time when some of the traders in the city went to the town of Lhorem in search of new businesses. This was an enormous benefit, as all the realms that knew about Lhorem, became acquainted with each other, often forging influential relationships.

However, peace was not everlasting, as many wars were lying ahead. Multiple travelling gabyr armies came from the north and kept attacking the realms of Aetari, Dyveln, Ikivial and Ylvart. Even the trading town of Lhorem received its share of the menacing throngs of gabyrs. The very first gabyr war was often referred as the War of the Dagger Front and it put the young armies to a test. During the war, which lasted for almost two hundred years, many important Aetarians were killed by gabyr assassins. Multiple large-scale battles were fought in the region of Enberahl, eventually ending the exhausting war.

Sometime later commenced the second gabyr war; the War of the One-Eyed Seer. The name referred to the leader of the gabyr war host, who was a great sorcerer from the east. In the war, plenty of dark magic was cast by the gabyrs, which led to numerous curses and other nefarious acts. The war was very different for the Aetarians, who botched to understand the altered manners of their sworn enemy. Some of the old wizards of Ylvart came to aid Aetari, as it was struggling with the one-eyed seer's spells. The help of Afalanosvolon, a group of powerful spell casters, reinforced Aetari's attempts to unleash a grand bollocking on the gabyrs. Following the end of the war, many of the peoples near Aetari began to discuss more amalgamated defences.

"You have these young men freezing in the cold winter night. How many of them are willing to go and see their family after the warm night takes them? Are they not too young? I am also in great pain. In great despair, the feeling of hopelessness surrounds me and I feel ill. I wish this all

was gone, like the embers that are dead in my long-gone fireplace."

The last gabyr war started with reports of several war hosts moving towards Enberahl. It is commonly believed that the gabyrs met in the mountains of Haberlion, to build a massive army to wipe out all the realms in the east. The hordes of gabyrs began to march towards the realms of Aetari, Dyveln and Ylvart, starting the War of Tarnfros' Might.

The gabyrs had decided to wage war somewhere else after the folks of Hillfort Lands had resisted their armies successfully. This time, the large gabyr warbands did not have any leaders, which guaranteed even more disordered results. When the gabyr armies reached the lands of Enberahl, the army of Aetari drew their thirsty weapons of iron and steel.

King Fulhamer was a strong leader, favoured by Aetari's folk and he was ready to defend his people. However, during the war he made many reckless decisions. One of his major blunders was to deploy some of the armies' soldiers to the valleys of Liegpyrul. The Battle of Blood Turmoil happened in one of the passes, in the eastern parts of the region, ending the lives of many young warriors. During the cold winter night, the armies of Aetari faced one of their worst defeats. The majority of their troops were slain by the gabyr army, which ambushed the Aetarians during the night with a hail of arrows. Only a handful of soldiers survived to reunite with rest of the armies in Enberahl.

Crayvar wrote; *"I remember how a massive hail of arrows could be heard in the distance, but none of us could see any of it against the cold and pitch-black winter sky. When the arrows fell on our men, the screams and agony began. The gabyrs commenced their attack and our soldiers panicked. We did not know how many of them were coming and retreating in the deep snow was difficult. I tried to remove some of the arrows from my wounded battle brothers in the snowy fields. The snow was turning dark red. It was too late and we had to escape, many of us drowning in the ice-cold rivers of the pass. I could see how some of the soldiers even jumped on their drowned mates, who were lifelessly floating in the river's icy water. The name 'Blood Turmoil' still haunts me in my dreams"*

Despite being the most furious of all the gabyr wars, the third and final war took only five years. The War of Tarnfros' Might ended in the victory of Aetari and its allies. King Fulhamer was hailed as the saviour of Aetari, but there were also many who were disappointed in the king. Some of his closest servants left the realm because they believed the king had betrayed them during the war. Fulhamer dreamt of a warrior king's title and his dream forced him to apply certain tactics in the war, inevitably leaving plenty of unnecessary casualties.

Nevertheless, it was not long before Aetari got involved in a new conflict that was approaching from the northwest. It was called the War of the Returning One, referring to the halmhenden Lord Vhyolan. The halmhenden and his army of gelders had attacked the city of Honedimn. The news of this arrived from the city, and was delivered to Lhorem, before finally reaching Aetari. The risk of a siege around Lhorem was concerning, so the realm decided to act immediately. Ultimately, a meeting took place in the city of Dyveln. It was a great gathering, hosting the leaders and the wise people of Aetari, Dyveln, Ikivial and Ylvart in the royal halls of the city. The meeting also had a storm elf from Ikirias named Diwion Heliory, who was there to ensure the good relations between the realms and Ikirias. It was rumoured that the storm elves of Ikirias had done a deal with Vhyolan, so it was important for Diwion to prove that the claim was incorrect.

The first touch of the war happened in Lhorem. The city was protected by the sky elf guard, and with the help of the armies of Aetari and Dyveln, the gelders were eventually defeated. The attackers managed to breach inside Lhorem, but after a hard battle, the gelders had to retreat out of the ancient trading city. For King Fulhamer this was a major victory, as he was gaining back the trust of the people who were disappointed in him after the glorified brawls with the gabyrs.

"These soldiers dream of war, they see it as glorious and simple. When I have seen them returning from the battles, they are all silent, all the glory and honour gone. The only thing they have left is the feeling of a bond of appreciation, which they do not want to lose. After returning home they are faced with a life where these traits are not required. They are alone. It is the long and lonely road of a warrior. Only we can understand the pain, the feelings that went through our very bodies. The only words we could say about the war were the words they already knew."

After the defence of Lhorem, the armies of Aetari fought in the Battle of Honedimn, which was an utter disaster for everybody but the gelders. Only a small number of the defeated armies escaped the city, commencing a long and gruelling retreat. When the beaten army returned to Aetari, a true concern arose in the realm. Yet, this led to an even greater alliance between Aetari, Dyveln, Ylvart and even the dwarfs of Podfrud.

The last battles in the War of the Returning One were fought in the region of Galtreken, taking the armies to Jarlidan and Worlgaltrin. These battles ended the war and the army of Aetari returned to their homeland triumphantly. Lord Vhyolan was slain in the Battle of Hurlgaltrin, which was fought by a smaller amount of men. For instance, the famous Crayvar the Unfallen and the storm elf Diwion fought in the battle, when the rest of the armies were finalising the fight in Worlgaltrin. Both heroes fell in the fight, but their stories were told forward by many warriors, including Wahlvern Hebelcurnn of Dyveln and Rylskar Halmverlen of Ylvart. The four men had shared a long journey, but now the end had taken two of their dearest friends.

"I cannot envisage myself as old. I was supposed to die a long time ago."

CROWNED BY THE WAVES

Solhamer was born under the waves and horns of the great fleets that once sailed in the seas of Yeldes. The fleet had wandered for years and no one remembered their origin. Every day the ships travelled the ocean of storms and dark waters, where they gazed at the sky, hoping to find a new home.

The fleet's commander was Losten Hyaales Vostger, and he was regarded as the greatest sailor ever to exist. Young Solhamer admired the man who challenged the sea and its dangers fearlessly. One stormy evening the fleet met a mighty sea monster, which attacked the ships. The monster looked like a pike fish, and had dark blue scales that shined in the murky water of Yeldes. For countless days the fleet fought the beast that had sank many of their ships. Solhamer was willing to do his part in the fight against the monster of the depths.

On the final day of the battle, Losten was mortally wounded by the sea monster Haug, the guardian of the doors of water. A large fin of the pike monster cut Losten's chest as he was fighting it on the top deck of his ship. Solhamer threw a spear through Haug's eye and the creature returned to the abyss. Losten told Solhamer that he would return one day from the seas to protect the realm that would be named Aetari. Until then, Solhamer would lead the fleet towards west, where finally the dawn would break the fog that once blinded their people.

Ultimately, Solhamer, the new commander of the fleet, saw a shoreline in the west. Once again, the weather was stormy and unpredictable. After its defeat, the sea monster Haug had followed the ships and was seeking revenge. As the relentless waves of Haug pushed the ships towards the shores, Solhamer saw a man riding a great black bear. It seemed that the commander was the only one to pay attention to the bear rider, whose stare and pose emanated wilderness.

Solhamer had also seen a large hill near the shores of Yeldes and his mind was already drawing pictures of might on its shapes. The man already knew that the hill was the place where the realm of Aetari would be established. After the ships hit the shores, Solhamer gathered his folks and began their journey towards the heights of their dawn. Eventually, in the north, the folk found the hill and Solhamer gazed at the great hillsides that were green with grass. The hill had a flat top that lay in silence with a peaceful grey and rainy sky behind it. Solhamer beheld the pillars of light that came through the clouds and hit the western side of the hill. The man directed his people towards the northwest, to the roots of the hill where the hillside was located. From here, the first steps of the realm of Aetari were taken.

The early Aetarians began to move towards west, as they needed more wood for their buildings, exposing many new villages to Dyvelnian raids. Solhamer was outraged by the attacks, usually initiated by Mustern, the leader of Dyvelnian warriors. Solhamer sent his sea soldiers to protect the logging villages and challenge the way of the forests. To mark his domain, Solhamer built the first road to the west, which was often tainted by iron, blood and death of the Dyvelnian wild.

King Solhamer was remembered as the one who built the foundations of a great legacy that defined the lives of all Aetarians. His friendship with Losten Hyaales Vostger raised him amongst the mythic characters, whose return was predicted in legends and whispers of the day. These tales would be written down with Losten's sword as the new dawn would shine on the heights and shapes of their home.

THE UNFALLEN

Crayvar, often referred as The Unfallen, was born to the highly regarded family of Vostger. Most of the people of the family had served the royals of the realm for hundreds of years and Crayvar was continuing the tradition. Since his early age, Crayvar worked a lot with swords, as he was a helper in the royal armoury. This was the beginning of a journey that ultimately made him a member of the royal guard.

At the age of nineteen, Crayvar joined the army of Aetari, where he quickly rose in ranks as he was exceptionally skilled with his leadership and fighting abilities. One day, when the man was visiting the royal armoury to refresh his childhood memories, Crayvar happened to meet King Fulhamer, who was doing his weekly inspection. The king approached Crayvar who bowed in front of the man. For Crayvar's astonishment, King Fulhamer remembered Crayvar and recalled some details from the past. Many times, the king and his royal guards had been observing the young lad, who was very excited about the swords and spears. This had made some of them smile and laugh, as the boy had tried to lift some of the heavier equipment.

The meeting made Crayvar and Fulhamer good friends and eventually the king invited Crayvar to join the royal guard, as his skills had been acknowledged. On the same year, Crayvar also married his deepest love, Vivialym, an heir of a successful trading family. Everything seemed to be flawless in Crayvar's life until the War of Tarnfros' Might began.

Crayvar fought against the menacing gabyrs all around the region of Enberahl, but the Battle of Blood Turmoil was the worst out of them. The fight was a major defeat for the

Aetarians and Crayvar was one of the few ones to survive, giving him the name, The Unfallen. The horrors of the battle dwelled in Crayvar's mind for a long time and he had numerous discussions about the matter with the king. Fulhamer was very taken by Crayvar's loyalty, as many had started to despise the king after the defeat.

Crayvar became one of the most trusted royal guards and he often assisted the king in his decisions. Crayvar also had to face some reckless bad mouthing, as some of his friends did not like the king after the war. For years, Crayvar served the king and the royal family of Aetari, which made him wealthy and respected. For the man's misfortune, there was still one war to be fought. This was the War of the Returning One and it commenced the last chapter in Crayvar's life, as he was assigned by the king for a special task.

Crayvar travelled from his homeland to the west with his companions: Wahlvern, Rylskar and the storm elf Diwion. Their task was to travel to the storm elf city of Ikirias and spy its lands. The companions had to make sure that the storm elves were not in an alliance with the halmhenden Lord Vhyolan. Especially for Diwion the mission was a matter of honour as he had been suspected of being an infiltrator by some people.

In Ikirias, Crayvar and his companions witnessed the disarray in the city. It was certain that the storm elves had not joined the forces of Vhyolan, nor had they had any interest in doing so. However, a tragic incident happened as King Raverek was assassinated during a meeting by opposing families of Ikirias. This ensured that the whole realm was too busy sorting out their internal problems.

From Ikirias, Crayvar and his friends journeyed to the northeast, where they took part in the Battle of Honedimn, being the second chapter of the war. During the last exhausting moments of the fight, the tide turned and a vast gelder army attacked the city, breaking the force that had come to unshackle Honedimn. During the battle, Wahlvern was wounded and an escape had to begin to the east, towards the lands of Podfrud. Crayvar remained calm during the difficult journey, despite being uncertain about Wahlvern's survival.

Fortunately in the dwarven realm of Podfrud, Wahlvern was saved with the power of a rare flower named 'Lord of the Ice Mirror Mountains'. The four companions stayed with the dwarfs, since they also brought crucial news with them. The four had seen some gelder warbands heading towards the east, presumably approaching Podfrud. The dwarfs started to prepare for battle, which turned out to be the right decision, since the gelders attacked soon after.

After the successful defence of the realm, Crayvar and the companions decided to return to Aetari. There the kings of Ylvart, Dyveln and Aetari agreed that a massive army would be sent to Galtreken to end the war for good. Crayvar and his friends did not have too much time to rest, as they became part of an enormous army, marching towards the northwest.

Crayvar took part in the battles of Jarlidan, Worlgaltrin and Hurlgaltrin. The man became part of a group, who commenced a pursuit to catch the escaping halmhenden Lord Vhyolan. In the cave of Hurlgaltrin, Crayvar and his peers challenged the halmhenden lord, who had escaped the city of Worlgaltrin from its inevitable defeat. The four friends and a group of others had chased Vhyolan all the way to Hurlgaltrin, where the weapons were drawn one more time. During the battle, Crayvar was mortally wounded and he never saw the death of Vhyolan, who was slain by Grand Lord Commander Faerkroll. In the battle, Diwion fell as well, which broke the hearts of their dear friends Wahlvern and Rylskar. The events were since known as the story of The Unfallen and made Crayvar and Diwion legends in their home realms.

Battle of Jarlidan

UNDER THE EYES OF THE BEAR AND THE SNAKE

The early Dyvelnians called themselves Dyvelnessen and they dwelled in the mountains of Suryel. Alongside the people lived a bear named Velnenpar, which the folk of Dyveln feared and revered. The bear was exceptionally large and it had pitch-black fur and claws like icy daggers. Often, the Dyvelnians saw the bear fighting against a pack of wolves that had appeared from the northeast. The leader of the Dyvelnessen, Celanvern, decided to help the bear to win its trust. During these fights, the early Dyvelnians began to spot groups of people observing the wolves from a distance. These folks were called Silver Capes and they were wolf enchanters.

One early morning the Silver Capes attacked Celanvern's village, simultaneously luring the great bear in the middle of it. The wolf enchanters wanted to slay Dyvelnians and the bear concurrently. Celanvern and her people were outnumbered and they had to escape the mountain. The mighty bear Velnenpar joined the Dyvelnians when the frantic retreat commenced.

For many days and nights, the Silver Capes chased the escaping people and the bear that once ruled the mountains of Suryel. Celanvern and her folks hid in the forests of Enberahl, but the bear was not as lucky due to its large size. From the bushes, the people observed how hordes of wolves fought the fierce bear, filling the air with blood soaked fur. When the battle reached a large lake and Velnenpar looked badly wounded, Celanvern decided to act, as she felt ashamed for abandoning the bear. The Dyvelnians charged from the shrubberies and faced the Silver Capes and their masses of beasts. The fight was named the Battle of Night and Silver and it lasted for two days. The fight was destructive on both sides, making the Silver Capes abandon their attempt to slay the bear.

Days after the battle was over, Velnenpar died from its wounds and the people of Dyveln wept. The water of the lake had turned dark red from the blood that was spilt by its glimmering hem. The folk decided to bury the mighty bear under the large stones that were complimenting the lake's western end. The idea of this was that the bear could now eternally feast on the blood that flew under the water. After the event the people settled in the forest and began to build a village for hunters. The village was named Velnenkolen, meaning 'the Home of the Bear'. For years, Celanvern led the people and the village grew bigger and stronger. Arguably this was also the beginning of Dyveln's hunting tradition.

During a dark winter night, some of the village guards swore that they had heard an eerie growl of a bear in the forest. Old Celanvern ran outside as fast as she could with her weak legs. The whole village stormed out their homes and the people stood in the dark wintery forest, seeing how the lake near them was shining with a deep blue and green light. The light waved like a snake in the black sky with its adamant stars. From underneath the lake appeared a black bear that growled once more and the people of Dyveln stood still. Soon the bear charged towards the forest, the great blue and green light following its wind. It is said that the last words of Celanvern were as follows: *"Night Bear will bring back the greatest of all of hunters in the world - the first king of Dyveln. Velnenpar will bring back my son."*

During an early morning of a late spring day, a bear rider appeared from the northwest. The rider was a tall man with dark hair and a strong jaw. This was the day when Mustern, the son of Celanvern returned. Mustern was hailed as the first king of Dyveln and the lord of the hunt. Quickly the man took control of the village and the people followed the words of their new leader.

One day, when Mustern was on his weekly patrol around the lands of Enberahl, near the coast of the inland sea of Yeldes, the man saw a life-changing sight. A great fleet of ships had been caught by a storm and were now approaching the shores sideways. This was the day when the story between Dyveln and Aetari began and Mustern's heart was beating the rhythm of the forests.

The early relationship between Dyveln and Aetari was full of battles, as Aetari tried to expand to the forest where the Dyvelnians were residing. However, the relationship between the two folks changed yet again upon the arrival of gabyrs. When the gabyr warbands of Hjilos Asgors marched to Enberahl, it caused major trouble for Dyvelnians and the people of Aetari. The struggle made both people realise that it would be better to live in peace and work together, so the threat of the gabyrs would be destroyed. Eventually, a mighty alliance was forged and the war against the gabyr hosts was successful. The bond between Dyveln and Aetari became steel-hard and all the old grudges were left behind. Mustern, who was now a warrior king, decided to lead his people south, where a new realm would be established by the shores of Yeldes.

Velnenkolen was not abandoned, as some of the people remained there for the rest of their lives. This was also the same year Mustern and Night Bear bid their farewell, as the man headed southeast with rest of his people. Later in time, the realm of Dyveln was founded by Mustern and his folk who settled near the shores of the inland sea of Yeldes. It is believed that Night Bear remained in the forests of Enberahl to protect the village and its hunters of the night.

The realm grew and its people became wealthier and more stable. It is said that some of the old seers of the realm had seen a prophecy in the waters, implying that immense warbands of gabyrs were approaching. The prophecy came true, as once more the armies of gabyrs came to the region of Enberahl. The War of the Dagger Front was shared by Dyveln and many other realms, which resided in the nearby lands. There were many attempts to slay the leaders of the realms to cause inner turmoil. However, when it comes to Dyveln, the gabyrs failed, as Dyvelnians had seen the destruction in Aetari, giving them time to prepare appropriately. After numerous battles with the gabyrs for two hundred years, the war was over and the realm of Dyveln returned to its hunting-orientated life.

The second gabyr conflict was the War of the One-Eyed Seer, which was another attempt by the gabyrs to take over the realms in Enberahl and the surrounding regions. The battles were full of magic, as the armies of gabyrs were led by a powerful sorcerer from the east. The war was a difficult one, as Dyvelnians were new to magic and especially to black sorcery, which did not obey the rules of the mortal world. This was the reason, which made the realm of Dyveln dedicate a specific group of hunters to find the nameless sorcerer. The missions were successful, as many of the dark mages were slain by the brave rangers and hunters of Dyveln. With the aid of many other realms, the war was won and the nameless seer was killed by a hunter of Dyveln in the Battle of Asgors.

The third and the last gabyr conflict was named the War of Tarnfros' Might and it lasted for five years. During these years, the greatest of gabyr armies attacked Enberahl and many other regions around it. The war was the shortest of all the gabyr wars, but at the same time the most destructive. During the war, Ieathel Kremm, the king of Dyveln, led his realm to glorious victory, as their armies rolled over gabyrs in all battlefields.

Dyveln was one of the realms that also took part in the War of the Returning One, being a tremendously defining confrontation in the world. The conflict started when Lord Vhyolan sent his gelder mercenaries to pillage Honedimn. Sometime after, Dyveln held a major meeting in their city, where the leaders of Dyveln, Aetari, Ikivial and Ylvart met. The armies of Dyveln joined the rest of the realms to defeat Vhyolan and his gelder warriors. For instance, the army of

Dyveln fought in the battles of Lhorem, where the gelders attacked the famous trading town. The second major offensive was in the city of Honedimn, which was a sheer defeat for the armies. King Ieathel Kremm knew that their time would come after the horrible defeat, but it would require careful planning with their allies. Later that year the armies of Dyveln, Aetari and Ylvart sent their armies to Galtreken to end the war for good. The warriors of Dyveln took part in the battles of Jarlidan and Worlgaltrin, which ended the War of the Returning One.

WARRIOR'S LOVE

Celanvern was born during a stormy night in the mountains of Suryel. During the same night, she was bitten by creature named Horned Snake, which almost killed her. According to many old seers of Dyveln, this was the first trial of the folk, as she was to become the one who would set the people on an inevitable path to glory. Many tales told that Celanvern saw many nightly visions during her early years. Many of these visions became written legends and they explained details about Horned Snake and Night Bear with remarkable detail.

Celanvern possessed unique sorcerous abilities and she could interact with animals in an exceptional way. It is said that when she was walking around the mountains, all the animals liked to follow her. Yet, the greatest of bears, Velnenpar, was suspicious of her powers. The reason why Velnenpar did not like her presence was that Celanvern could also communicate through the corpses of animals.

When the Silver Capes appeared in the mountains with their wolf hordes, the atmosphere turned ferocious and decrepit. Many animals were killed by the wolves and by their enchanters, which made Velnenpar's fur stand up in hate. Celanvern had always respected the great bear, so the woman decided to help the bear to win its trust on the side of the Dyvelnessen. Battles were fought in the mountains, but the number of wolves proved too much for Celanvern's people. Velnenpar and the people fled from the mountains towards southwest. According to some ancient journals, Celanvern knew what was going to happen, as she had seen a vision in her dreams. She could recognise the lake that was glowing under the sun and the pine trees that were slowly whispering in the wind.

The wolves and their masters struck the escaping bear as soon as the people lost track of their path. Celanvern and her people had to change their course as their endurance was running low. From the bushes, the people observed Velnenpar, who was now alone fighting the wolves and the Silver Capes. After a short while, Celanvern could not take the sight and decided to return to the battle with her people. Celanvern ordered the people to gather anything that could be used as a weapon in the forest and to attack audaciously.

The battle ended in a draw and the Silver Capes and their wolves returned to Suryel. Sometime after the battle, Celanvern met a spirit of the forest named Hebel, who had been in the forest all alone for hundreds of years. The two talked for a hundred nights and eventually fell in love. This was the time, when Hebel showed the forest to Celanvern with all its beauty and mystery. However, Hebel's time was over, since its powers and connection to the forest of Enberahl were fading. Before the end, the love of Celanvern and Hebel gave birth to Mustern, the son of Dyveln.

"She danced so delicately on the snow and the people of Dyveln were watching her moving through the white forest. It was a moment where no one could engage with her, she was an untouchable force upon earth enjoying her last moment. Her arms were pointing towards the sky, where the blue and green lights were calling, and she collapsed on the snowy ground. For some time, no one dared to approach her, since the light took her body and moved her towards the lake. The guards ran to her body and held her in their arms looking at her mouth, which was moving slowly. In the snowfall, she said her last words, the prophecy of a storm and a man who would return. The eternity for Dyveln had begun."

End of the chapter, the white forest mourns.

THE HUNTER'S WAR

Wahlvern was born to a family of hunters, a group of elite soldiers serving in the armies of Dyveln. As a young lad, Wahlvern showed remarkable strength and survival skills. This was noticed by his father, who was also holding the title of a hunter. When Wahlvern was only seven years old, he lost his father in a forest after chasing a deer. For two days, Wahlvern wandered in the woods by himself and the family thought that the boy would never be found. Wahlvern's father assembled a search, but even the skilled hunters could not find a trace of the boy. One day, one of the men who was with the hunters stepped on a deer trap. The man's foot was badly injured and when he began to scream, Wahlvern appeared from the shrubberies. The company found Wahlvern's little camp, with a fireplace and a dead deer, which he had been preparing for food. Wahlvern's father Holfern realised that his son had extraordinary resilience, wit and endurance.

Due to his skills, Wahlvern was granted the title of a hunter at a very young age. He was only sixteen years old when he became part of Dyveln's elite troops. This was exceptional, since most of the hunters were almost thirty years old. There were even some opposing the idea, since Holfern was captain in the Dyvelnian army, and his son benefitted from that.

For years Wahlvern trained in the woods of Enberahl and became a well-known character amongst the folk of the realm. The man led many successful missions against bandits, who dwelled there and threatened travelling people in the nearby lands. It was common for him to disappear for weeks with his selected hunters, and come back just to report about another effective quest.

Wahlvern's first greater conflict was the War of Tarnfros' Might, where he and other hunters hit numerous gabyr armies in Enberahl. The nightly strikes were very effective and usually paved the forest floors with carpets of gabyr corpses. Due to Wahlvern's actions, one of the most feared gabyr armies, Foer Triljos, had to change the direction of their march, which led them to a crushing ambush by the army of Dyveln.

During the five-year war, Wahlvern met Crayvar the Unfallen of Aetari. The two became good friends after sharing stories and strong ale around a campfire in the deep woods of Enberahl. Around the same time, the two also met Rylskar, a royal herbalist from Ylvart. Through these unlikely meetings, the three became close friends and they met regularly after the war.

Wahlvern fought as well in the War of the Returning One, which put him and many others against well trained gelder warriors. Wahlvern rarely expressed his thoughts about the war, since he considered himself a true warrior, whose purpose was to live and die in battle. After Diwion of Ikirias joined the three friends, some of his insights of life reformed. Diwion's story was a mournful one, since he had lost his wife to gabyrs and the burning hatred inside him impressed and saddened Wahlvern.

Wahlvern, Crayvar, Rylskar and Diwion were given a special task to work as scouts and messengers during the war, which made the companions even closer friends. The initial seal for their friendship was the Battle of Lhorem, where Wahlvern performed particularly well. This was the first time he was fighting against gelders, who were known to be tall and robust warriors. Wahlvern indeed had a deep respect towards the gelders, even though they were swinging their axes at him.

Wahlvern's most difficult part of the war happened during the defeat at Honedimn. The man was wounded and apparently poisoned by a gelder blade. The companionship managed to escape to Podfrud, the realm of the dwarfs.

After the agonising journey, the man was finally able to receive some medicine. The potion was an ancient brew that could remove even the deadliest of poisons. However, the man's slow recovery prevented him from taking part in the defence of Podfrud, when a gelder warband attacked its lands.

As the war proceeded to Galtreken, Wahlvern and his friends joined several larger armies. During the final battle in Hurlgaltrin, Wahlvern lost two of his good friends, Crayvar and Diwion. Wahlvern made sure that both of his friends received proper burials, as their bodies were burnt outside Hurlgaltrin. Wahlvern was known as a warrior with icy emotions, but this time the loss of his friends cut him deep.

For the rest of Wahlvern's life, the man kept training more hunters, keepers of the Dyvelnian warrior tradition. Interestingly so, all the Wahlvern's hunters were asked to travel to Hurlgaltrin and back, as a final march before fully becoming worthy of the title. Wahlvern also married Anelde, the daughter of Rylskar, who he met during the war. Their bond saved Wahlvern's life, as he had felt hollow and empty for many years and Anelde's love banished the grey stillness away.

DWARFS

Didly Didly Wazz

The legend of the dwarfs began in Loistefruden, which was presumably another name for Loistesse. In the land lived a force named Hjardabristallum, who dwelled in a stone mansion by a lake. West from his home were forests and the mountain of Ulr, and Hjardabristallum liked to gaze at them during the nights, when the calm air glimmered on its snowy sides. Hjardabristallum liked to watch the mountain and draw spells into the air, which rose to the skies creating beautiful formations.

The most important illustration was the great star, which he placed on the top of the western sky and called 'the silvery candle of our father's projection'. Below the western sky Hjardabristallum drew many other pictures, which were strong spells of creation and wealth. By the end of the age of Loistesse, Hjardabristallum was not the only force affecting the world, which caused clashes, making some of his illustrations fall from the western sky. The spells fell to the depths of the world and made the force behind them sad and angry. Hjardabristallum was too large to travel to the depths and reclaim the spells back, so he decided ask help from his own creation, the dwarfs.

Hjardabristallum wanted to ensure that his creations could fit into the smallest of tunnels in the depths, thus he made the dwarfs short but very resilient. He taught the dwarfs to see the world how he saw it and showed the western sky and its pictures, making the dwarfs understand many invisible mysteries. Every picture in the sky was a spell or a guide to a certain place, and the dwarfs began to give names to the illustrations in the western sky, strictly framing it from rest of the firmament.

Hjardabristallum sent his brave dwarfs to the depths of the world after his homeland was attacked by his foes. Many secret spiral staircases of stone were found, which led to the bottom spheres of Loistefruden. In the dark tunnels, chambers and halls lodged the cruellest and most wicked creatures: gaberleks, the ancient ancestors of the gabyrs. These creatures had acquired some of the spells and put them into their murky halls. It was up to the dwarfs to claim back the magical pictures, which had been shattered into clusters of faint grey light.

It was the age when the dwarfs learnt how to fight hard, despite their small stature. In the heat of many battles with the gaberkels, the dwarfs understood the importance of well-made armours and weapons which could last for generations. The dwarfs managed to acquire almost all the fallen spells, except one, which eventually changed the course of their folk forever.

Hjardabristallum sent all his dwarfs to the depths to fight for the last fallen picture, so the western sky could be complete. Only a small group of dwarfs remained with their creator, in case something happened in the underground world. This was a wise choice, since the gaberleks had been waiting for the dwarf invaders. After the armed dwarfs entered the domains of the gaberleks, the tunnels were collapsed, making the dwarfs trapped. Once again, their kin had to learn how to fight in the dark against the beasts that were two feet taller.

Hjardabristallum, who was very protective over his creations, could not abandon his dwarfs and began to contemplate a daring endeavour. The creator of the dwarfs had to ascend to the sky and live amongst the silvery candle light, which he was able to direct at places that had never seen light. With its power, the dwarfs could survive and find a way out from the perilous world of the gaberleks. Hjardabristallum bid his farewell to the remaining dwarfs and told them to travel to the east, where he would guide them with his light.

Hjardabristallum rose to the western skies and became the silvery candle, the brightest of sky torches, and projected his hope to several places in the world. With the light, he wrote several messages in the air which the dwarfs could read, even in the depths. Everyone knew their mission and what had to be done. During these days, the bravery and unforgivable starkness of the dwarfs were crafted with blood and tears.

"Here are the words of might. You shall wait and see. You shall see a door, but no key. From the fury and strength of the three, the dwarfs shall march to a world that's free."

A daring journey began to the east, but the dwarfs above the ground did not know whether they would ever see the rest of their kin again. For many years the journey moved towards the east, where Hjardabristallum had presented a land he called Podfruden. In the thick spruce and pine tree forests of Podfruden, the dwarfs built a forge, as Hjardabristallum had a way to bring back the separated dwarfs.

"It was a small chamber full of anvils and all sorts of tools that the smiths used in their work. The dwarfs' eyes were glimmering in the dark chamber, as they hit their hammers on the anvils. There was a thick smoke in the room, which hurled around the swiftly working dwarfs, who every now and then gazed at the starlit sky, which could be seen through small holes on the ceiling of the forge. It seemed that every time the smiths hit the anvils, the stars twinkled at them. When the night reached its darkest hour, the greatest of stars, Hjardabristallum, created a pillar of light on the small stone gate inside the forge. The light came through the ceiling, which now revealed an open gate, and so the dwarfs marched out of the forge and into the world."

The three elder dwarfs were Kolengas, Mlaurfen and Hurenmullas, who had become the leaders of the dwarfs and were saved by the forge. However, many of the dwarfs had not been saved yet, as the years in the depths separated the folk, and some were still seeking a way out. Hjardabristallum could still see his creations in the underground domains and gave a task for the dwarfs to follow his light and find old stone cliffs, which had caves and simple chambers inside them. In places like these, the remaining dwarfs found themselves in the lands of Podfruden.

After many decades, all the dwarfs were found except one group, whose fate was not revealed for many centuries. Regardless, Hjardabristallum was relatively happy, as so many dwarfs had been found. The dwarfs arrived at the mountains of Folu and with the light of Hjardabristallum a home was carved inside it. This was the birth of a great story of the dwarfs, who later also expanded into the forests around the mountains.

BY EVERYTHING THAT IS BEING HELD

The oldest of the three leading dwarfs was Kolengas, who was declared as the first king of the dwarfs in the years of the gathering. It was a delightful situation for the dwarfs, since Mlaurfen and Hurenmullas were too young and greedy to be kings at the time. Dörsmiten and his father Tuldbydar, who were legendary warriors and respected by the folks agreed on Kolengas' kingship, gathering him unquestionable support. At the very beginning of his reign, Kolengas ordered the dwarfs to inhabit the mountains of Folu, which Hjardabristallum had blessed for their kin.

Not all the dwarfs wanted to live in the mountains, which made them build forest towns near the cities of Podtyr and Podmyr, providing them stable trade and protection against perils of the world. The dwarfs in the cities and towns became very dedicated to their crafts and their prosperity began to flourish. The dwarven perseverance towards their professions was seen everywhere, regardless of whether it was farming, cooking, fishing, forging or fighting. Fishing became an especially popular occupation amongst the dwarfs of Podfrud, who were enthusiastic about the river of Folu and its fish.

In the early years of the realm, brewing ale and distilling stronger spirits gained a strong foothold in the traditions of the dwarfs. Many breweries were founded during these years, and famous beers such as Pod's Fist and Steel Pork were created. Numerous festivals entertained the dwarven year and the villages in the realm took part in these festivities, reinforcing the folk's unity.

After Kolengas' death, Mlaurfen Porenhal and Hurenmullas Ikiwulket both wanted to become the high king of the dwarfs which, as expected, caused a fight between the two. The only way to decide the true king was to set a competition, which included the two competitors going through various tasks. These challenges involved wrestling, beer drinking, fishing and boot throwing. For several days Hurenmullas and Mlaurfen contested, but happened to be awfully intoxicated from the ale they had enjoyed in the past days.

To compromise, Tuldbydar, the old and wise warrior, suggested that the realm was to be split between the Porenhal and Ikiwulket families. A great bridge would be built between the mountain lines, which would connect the cities of Podtyr and Podmyr in the southern end of Folu. The drunken rivals agreed on the idea and hugged each other, as some sort of hazy demonstration of peace. Tuldbydar and his son Dörsmiten promised to guide both kings with their decisions, since in their blood ran the will of Hjardabristallum.

Centuries passed and the eternal blooded Tuldbydar and Dörsmiten aided the dwarfs to a greater expansion. The town of Falonladu was built south from Podtyr and Tammarkaus west from the mountains of Folu. Dörsmiten became the leader of Tammarkaus and established the first garrison outside of Podtyr's or Podmyr's direct influence. One could say that this was a much-needed addition, as the western parts of Podfrud's lands had received unwanted folks in the past century. The gaberleks had found a way outside from their buried domains and had established a realm of their own to the northwest border of the region. Their strongholds had taken over the northern parts of the mountains, which bordered the region of Galtreken.

From the grim depths of their world, the gaberleks had brought vicious monsters with them: Urmaulvs, enormous cave bears, which served under the wicked hand of the gaberlek Lord Fesvulc. It did not take many decades for the two peoples to meet each other, and when they did, familiar battles continued. However, this time the dwarfs were in a different situation, which gave them a chance to avenge all their losses of the past. Dörsmiten gathered his army and challenged Fesvulc and his beasts in the deep forests of Podfrud. The War of Ancestor's North lasted for several decades and it ended after the halmhendens had noted the long-lasting fight between the dwarfs and the gaberleks. Soon after the halmhenden's involvement, the gaberleks disappeared, which started a rumour that the halmhendens had captured them and used them in their clandestine magical experiments. This is one the stories which made people believe that halmhendens created the gabyrs.

After the war, several dwarfs reported a distant shine in the horizon, catching the attention of Tuldbydar. The dwarf warrior came to believe that the glow was perhaps part of the western sky. Tuldbydar and his warriors commenced a courageous journey towards the west, where the presumed works of Hjardabristallum were. Dörsmiten remained with the dwarfs of Podfrud, who had now built a good relationship with manfolk in the south. The realm was in peace, but its tranquillity was broken when Tuldbydar's warriors returned from their journey. Dörsmiten's father had fallen against a malicious mountain snake, which dwelled in Haberlion. For half a year, the warriors had tried to avenge the death of their dear leader, but the beast had been too mighty a foe.

Nevertheless, Tuldbydar's warriors had good news as well. They had travelled all the way to a distant land in the west, where they had seen the familiar shine of Hjardabristallum's work. In the land, they had met dwarfs, who had been lost for hundreds of years and they had built a realm, which they called Saunfrud. The separated dwarfs had been finally found and despite the sorrowful news, Dörsmiten celebrated the discovery of their kin. The warriors claimed that the dwarfs in Saunfrud possessed ancient knowledge about Hjardabristallum's powers, which were beyond mortal comprehension. Dörsmiten became interested and sent a band of soldiers, with whom he travelled to Saunfrud, to see its glory.

While Dörsmiten was away, the realm of Podtyr and Podmyr completed the bridge of Folusjo, which connected both domains in the southern ends of Folu. These were also the years when gabyrs began to appear in the area, causing troubles in the forest villages and farms. For instance, the mines of the Ice Mirror mountains were lost to gabyrs, who had raided them after appearing from the northeast.

Dörsmiten and his soldiers returned to Podfrud after two years and brought an immense energy with them. Dörsmiten claimed that he had seen how Saunfrud's smiths had risen to the skies and set the fallen pieces on the firmament, when they had seen Dörsmiten's sword. After several centuries, the old warrior had realised that the very weapon he had been carrying was one of Hjardabristallum's illustrations and was part of the western sky. With a smile on his bearded face, Dörsmiten gave his sword for the smiths, who sent it to the sky to guard its projection till the end of ages. Upon Dörsmiten's return to Podfrud, the sky blessed all the dwarven realms with its protection and made their foes fear the mountains they were living in. After that day, gabyrs had faded from the mountains, being terribly scared, and only targeted the forest villages and towns. This started to change the nature of the convoluted relations which the dwarfs and gabyrs had in the land.

North from Podtyr and Podmyr, near the northwest parts of the mountains of Folu, was a piece of land named Hulofrud. The region was between the mountain ranges and it had a vast lake, which had gathered a lot of mysterious folks since the early times. Hulofrud was also the land where the mighty dwarfs Tuldbydar and Dörsmiten had once resided. Gabyrs had found a way to access the secretive land of Hulofrud after they found information regarding the garden of Holdilalj. The garden was guarded by a series of large oak trees. Their canopies were named 'the northern sky'. It was a place where Hjardabristallum's magic had remained intact and was a location of interest for the malicious gabyrs.

The spear of Tuldbydar disappeared after his fall in Haberlion, but was later found by wandering gabyr warbands. Gabyr Lord Gullof found the weapon, which received the name 'the Great War Spear of the North', and it was taken to Hillfort Lands. Later in time, Gullof took the spear to the garden of Holdilalj so he could destabilise Podfrud's dwarfs and their western sky's protection. When the spear finally met the northern sky in Hulofrud, it overpowered Dörsmiten's sword in the western sky, removing the fear the gabyrs had felt towards the mountains of Folu. Being excited about the northern sky's blessing, Lord Gullof mustered his armies and attacked the dwarfs of Podfrud with all his strength.

The War of Hulofrud commenced between the dwarfs and the gabyrs, who had conquered large parts of the mountains of Folu. Dörsmiten and the dwarven armies set a bold task to take back all the lost lands. The war was very destructive for both belligerents and no celebrations were seen on either side. The glory had been tainted with sorrow and blood and honour had sunken too deep. After three years, Dörsmiten's army took the southern parts of Hulofrud, which set the final phase of the strenuous war. In the last battle of the war, Dörsmiten and Lord Gullof met in the deep oak forests of Hulofrud, where the two duelled under several moon lights. The battle was even, but Dörsmiten, being blessed by Hjardabristallum, fought his way to absolute victory.

During the years the spear had spent in Hillfort Lands, it had received carvings on its blade, which looked like symbols of hurthallans. Dörsmiten knew that it was his father's spear and the engravings were added later. It was obvious for the dwarven warrior to set his foot on another path of revenge. Dörsmiten gathered his most experienced warriors, took the spear and his sword and left to the north. In here, the mighty warrior challenged Hejesvim, the chaotic dragon leader of the hurthallans. With the two weapons unified, Dörsmiten could defeat Hejesvim

Gwlinvinvor's guardians and fight the dragon. The battle was quick, and Dörsmiten threw his father's spear at the large beast, which was devastated by its force and grandeur. The great dragon fell to darkness, leaving its fate unknown. At least for Dörsmiten, the conflict with the hurthallans was over, as he barely staggered out of the cave of Hejesvim Gwlinvinvor. The dwarf was mortally wounded in the fight and asked his warriors to take him to Hulofrud, where he could eat rye-bread and adore forests one more time.

Hulofrud became part of Podfrud's realm and it served as an important piece of land, where the forest folks of the area welcomed back the dwarfs after many years of absence. The mansion of Dusp, which was in the western parts of Hulofrud, became the burial site for Dörsmiten. The warriors chanted in the stone halls of the manor to remember the dwarf, who had brought good upon his people in the times of dark and dread. Ultimately, Furldem Oiossas, the commander of the army, organised a regiment named Duspfrud, making the mansion their first garrison.

In the early days, the problems between dwarfs, halmhendens, hurthallans and gabyrs embellished. Stala, the force behind the halmhendens, had a tricky past with the western land of Loistesse, which the dwarfs called Loistefruden. In the land, many ancient forces had built stars on its sky, being manifestations of powers like jewels on a crown. There was a particular belt of stars which was called Ikiaasudenwyrral, meaning 'Armour and the eyes, blossom fallen behind the skies'. The light, which Hjardabristallum had captured, was one of these stars, and it could possibly aid Stala to defeat one his sworn enemies; the hurthallans.

Stala's desire to claim the light of Hjardabristallum grew immense, as he wanted to use its energy to defeat not just the hurthallans, but to break Alasgastadl, the place he had created for the doomed halmhaers. When the halmhaers' potential and threat was discovered by Stala, he had to destroy their existence by using the light of

Hjardabristallum. The light alone had the ability to reach Alasgastadl and deflect from there to the realm of night, causing it to escape due to the sudden brightness. The light could inflict a vast protrusion and even larger contraction, causing the possible fracture of Alasgastadl, killing all the halmhaers in the process.

After Stala inquired about the light, Hjardabristallum told him to sod off, which obviously did not make him particularly pleased. However, Stala did not give up, as he knew that the western and northern skies included ancient illustrations which could give access to the powers of Hjardabristallum. Both skies had been written with the symbols of the dwarven past and Stala decided to capture their presence with force. Stala ordered the halmhenden captains to move their gabyr armies, who were gullible enough to serve as their bulk of an army.

"Someone who desires too much power, deserves many foes."

Amongst the commanders of the halmhendens was Lord Vhyolan Rauwos, whose gabyr army's task was to conquer the northern sky. The garrison of Duspfrud answered to the threat and its superior, Launmald Oherlut, ordered the dwarven forces to fiercely defend Hulofrud. The gabyr armies were severely outnumbering the dwarfs and Launmald came up with a courageous plan. The dwarf commander was aware that Stala and hurthallans hated each other, but had been practicing some sort of truce for some years. To save dwarven lives, it was essential to make the two sides fight each other again, so the halmhendens would have too many fronts to battle. Launmald decided to gather a band of his most trusted warriors and travel to Hillfort Lands, where they would slay influential hurthallans and make them appear like the doing of the halmhendens.

Launmald had acquired some ancient halmhenden weapons in the past and decided to leave certain items to be found by hurthallans after the elaborate ambushes. Astoundingly, the plot worked and after twenty days, the hurthallan forces were attacking the halmhendens, who had no idea why the truce had been broken. One could say that the wit of Launmald saved the dwarfs and their beloved Hulofrud, as the gabyrs were too busy fighting hurthallan warriors elsewhere.

The frenzied leaders of hurthallans let the gabyr armies move to Hillfort Lands, where their armies crushed the gabyr ranks and morale, causing many of their lords to abandon the battlefield. The gabyrs lost faith in their halmhenden leaders and campaigns, which did not benefit them at all. The dwarfs of Podfrud celebrated the news and Commander Launmald Oherlut was rewarded by the royals of the realm. Nevertheless, the people of Podfrud heard rumours that the enigmatic halmhenden lord had escaped to Hillfort Lands, and was already sowing the conspiring seeds of mystery.

Surprisingly so, the dwarfs did not have to take much part in the three gabyr wars, which happened during the span of many later years. The alliance between gabyrs and halmhendens was not strong, so only a few towns and villages were targeted by independent gabyr warriors. Dwarfs were left alone, as the protecting spell of Hjardabristallum was still looking over their peaks and forests. Since the battles were happening in the south, some dwarfs became mercenaries, who helped in the conflicts that occurred in the lands of manfolks and the sky elves of Ylvart.

The War of the Returning One brought back one familiar character to the dwarfs. Lord Vhyolan Rauwos had returned after a long silence and had hired an army of gelders. For the dwarfs, the threat was not imminent, since Vhyolan was more interested in attacking the realms south from Podfrud, including; Aetari, Dyveln and Ylvart. Being cautious in nature, the dwarfs prepared themselves for a war, as it was obvious that the halmhendens regarded their kin as allies of their foes.

The Battle of Honedimn was the first encounter where the dwarfs of Podfrud joined the efforts of Ylvart, Dyveln and Aetari to defeat Vhyolan and his gelders. Captain Mödvald was responsible, aiding the attacking army to recapture Honedimn, which had been lost in the early stages of the war. Unfortunately, after a fierce battle, an elaborate plan by the gelders worked and the exhausted attacking army was defeated by gelders. When the dwarfs learnt about the defeat in Honedimn, the entire realm began to arm themselves.

The preparations were indeed the right choice, since gelders attacked Podtyr and Podmyr. The defence was successful, but many casualties were taken, when the experienced and large gelders broke into the mountain city of Podtyr. The gelder army surprised the dwarfs from the river, where their plan was to take the harbour side and its trading hall, which gave an access to the city proper. Nevertheless, all the disorder in Podtyr inflicted by the gelders, was just a way to distract the dwarfs from the true intentions of Vhyolan. The old halmhenden lord still wanted to get his hands on Hulofrud and the northern sky.

A vast warband of gelders invaded deep into the land of Hulofrud, where the garrison of Duspfrud was alarmed. The folks of Hulofrud and the dwarfs organised a defence around the lake, which had now silenced from its lively activities. Turmfalt Glimmtuld, who was Mödvald's brother, assembled his regiment and fought the elite gelders. The dwarfs had a struggle against the army and Turmfalt ordered his soldiers to retreat to the mansion of Dusp. When the dwarfs thought that the northern sky was lost, an army of storm elves flanked the gelders and fought them with dark burning fury.

Turmfalt and his remaining soldiers were astonished by the surprising coming of the storm elves, who pushed the gelders out from Hulofrud, saving the dwarfs from certain defeat. Turmfalt met the commander of the storm elf army, who went by the name of Tiliasn Windesules. The storm elf was a general of the army he called Summen houg, meaning 'Emerald Gold'. Windesules told Turmfalt how he was adopted by a woman who lived in Hulofrud. His entire childhood Windesules had lived in Hulofrud and occasionally came to meet the old woman he called Amna. This time, by a pure luck, the army had spotted the gelders and decided to ensure that the people of Hulofrud would not get raided by their host.

As difficult as it was for Turmfalt and his soldiers to admit, the elves had saved the battle and they were so grateful, that the army was invited to the mansion of Dusp, where ale and food was served. During this time, Turmfalt came up with a plan to reduce the threat of the gelders by using their mutual enemy: gabyrs. When the wandering storm elf army from Haustrn began their journey towards their homes, the dwarf commander sent some of his rangers to Hillfort Lands, where vast gabyr lodge camps had been observed. The lodge camps had small wooden forts and cottages, where the gabyrs lived and prepared their malicious raids. The dwarven force's task was to find some of the travelling hermits, who had won the trust of the gabyrs on their side, and bribe them. The money encouraged the hermits to inform the gabyrs how the gelder armies had joined a war in the south and how they have left their realm open for an invasion.

A large gathering was arranged by the gabyr lords, and so, their grim planning of incursion began. In the end of the War of the Returning One, this move by the dwarfs helped Aetari, Dyveln, Ylvart and the dwarfs to defeat Vhyolan and his gelders. Many gelder warriors in the army had to return to north, since the gabyr armies had attacked their homes, causing crushing losses. Not perhaps being the main reason for victory, but surely a helpful addition to the war, as Ylvart, Aetari, Dyveln and Podfrud celebrated their triumph over Vhyolan in the same winter.

Dwarfs also went through the War of the Gleaming Bonfires. The dwarfs were unintentionally dragged into the war, which had invited many belligerents under its bloody shadow. Podfrud's involvement began a half a year earlier when the hurthallan's leader, Hejesvim Gwlinvinvor planned to return to the mythical land of Loistesse in the west. It was believed at the time that the western sky, built by Hjardabristallum, had an illustration of a golden key, just under the silvery candle, which could open a bridge of light to the west. Hurthallans were suffering in Drytgastadl and their desire to leave the land grew after every century. The discovery of the golden key made Hejesvim Gwlinvinvor charge at the western sky, breaking its elements to glimmering dust. The golden key of the bearded folk fell accidentally from the sky and supposedly was absorbed by the well of Kulus' presence in the depths.

Queen Fydja Porenhal assembled an army, whose purpose was to reclaim the golden key from Kulus at any cost. It was the only time in the recorded history of the dwarfs, when the royal house ordered the army to march to the legendary forge, which was claimed to be the first place where dwarfs appeared in Drytgastadl. With the blessing of Hjardabristallum's light, the army marched to the forge and the ancient stone door opened, leading to a place that had been untouched for innumerable years.

Meanwhile the hurthallans were scheming to wake Morvgraza, the lava serpent of the underworld. The monster was a weapon of olden times and it moved in the deep layers of the world, leaving a stream of molten stones behind it. It had the potential to destroy Alasgastadl and the halmhaers, who were also enemies of hurthallans. The hurthallans thought that the end of Alasgastadl would break the construct of the world and would keel it until Loistesse would reappear in the west.

Whilst the fire serpent was moving, the dwarf army advanced in dream-like domains, between ethereal horizons. The soldiers did not know if any of the places were real after they had entered through the forge, due to their distant quality. According to the old prophecy of the dwarfs, an army would eventually face the great fire serpent of the depths and slay it in the chambers buried by dust and time, and places like these indeed relit that prophecy.

The deep-rooted tale included Hjardabristallum, Tuldbydar and Dörsmiten travelling in the world. The struggles between gaberleks and hurthallans were set during these times, as the dwarfs travelled in the cavernous layers of the world and made their presence loud and clear. The so-called separated dwarfs, who disappeared after the ages of Loistefruden, met Morvgraza and had numerous battles with the beast, whilst facing the endless dismays of gaberleks. The legend speaks of how the dwarfs sopped their weapons in the burning stones of the underworld to fight Morvgraza, who had been Hjardabristallum's enemy before the world came to exist.

The separated dwarfs could not slay the mighty beast and it disappeared into the unreachable layers of Drytvaarte. Ever since, Morvgraza was hunted by the dwarven spirits. To answer the threat, an underground stronghold was established in the depths of Jelfruden and its purpose was to give a proper bollocking to the gaberleks and hurthallans. Many tunnels were built to hunt the beast and gaberleks, but ultimately, their devastation was too much for the dwarfs and Jelfruden was lost.

Ultimately, the army of dwarfs faced Morvgraza who they encountered after entering the mysterious forge, west from Podtyr. In the underground tunnels, chambers and rooms of Drytgastadl, the dwarven army challenged the lava serpent, whose slaying was a difficult task. The sudden appearance of the beast was a surprise for the dwarfs, but with the dwarven calm mentality, the long battle was won against the monstrosity. After the slaying of Morvgraza, the army of dwarfs found a way to Kulus, which they did not hesitate to use. The whole army leapt into the Battle of Kulus through a vast hole in the ground, which looked like a sky full of stars.

The commander of the dwarven army was Douste Haskk, who was part of the family that had a direct lineage to Tuldbydar and the elders of Hulofrud. For example, the lady who raised the storm elf commander Tiliasn Windesules was also Douste's relative. There were a few journals left by Douste, which suggested that he knew how the Battle of Kulus would be the undoing of everyone in the fight. However, after their death, the fallen dwarfs could once again enter the land of Loistefruden, where they could meet Hjardabristallum and become his elite soldiers. The details of the story were disputable and Commander Douste Haskk's motivation remained in shadows.

"Only the dead can speak the true words of life."

THE PRIMORDIAL GUARDIANS

Before Hjardabristallum gave life to a larger population of dwarfs, he was aided by their kin long before a single word was spoken about Drytgastadl. In Loistefruden, the mythical land in the west was a home for many forgotten peoples and amongst them lived Hjardabristallum. By a great lake of Vosnja was Hjardabristallum's stone mansion, which had large halls, a beautiful harbour side and numerous smaller wooden cottages that delightfully filled the water front of the beach-side, north of the mansion.

In the stone mansion, which had the name Pälter, lived Hjardabristallum and a few clans of dwarfs, who traded and lived with the other peoples of the land. In one of the cottages near the mansion was born Tuldbydar, one of the greatest dwarfs ever to live. His reputation was crafted in the very early stages of his life, due to his charisma and sheer strength. When he came of adult age, Tuldbydar was assigned as the leader of the warriors, who protected the mansion and its dwarfs from beasts, bandits and other ancient troubles of Loistefruden. The name of Tuldbydar's spear struck fear into the hearts of his enemies, which included gaberleks and hurthallans, led by the dragon Hejesvim Gwlinvinvor.

Tuldbydar was also an adroit sculptor, who helped Hjardabristallum during the nights when he was planning the western sky and its pictures. Pälter's western hall had a library and a gallery of Hjardabristallum's creations, which sparked around short stone pillars, the glass ceiling and windows of the hall. In the room, the two crafted such magical things that not even the wildest dreams of mortals could achieve their magnificence. Only the statues of elder dwarfs witnessed the splendour of the nights, which gave birth to many stories. However, every now and then, some of the curious dwarfs looked secretly at the majestic night of creations through the large glass windows of the hall. Hjardabristallum was aware of the dwarfs, who woke up during the night in the village, which was on the southern side of Pälter, to behold his magic. He was not bothered at all, and sometimes deliberately made the whole hall shine with lights and echoing chants to entertain the curious audience.

When Tuldbydar was on the water front of Vosnja, he met Celn, lady of the lake and guardian of water. The two shared many stories and often the traders in the shores of the lake came to hear the tales. They were regarded as good days and Tuldbydar's life was full of excitement, which had been blessed with remarkable length. Celn loved the stories about Hjardabristallum's nightly makings, which fascinated the guardian of water so much that she stayed awake during the nights only to see a glimpse of its beauty.

Hjardabristallum drew so many illustrations in the western sky, that it could no longer bear their enormity. The creator had also caused a lot of attention and his magic was desired amongst his foes, who had been observing them far in the western forests and mountains. Celn wanted to help the creator of the western sky and spoke about a place, which the dwarfs had named Hulofrud, which lay in the lands of Drytgastadl. In the safe and secretive place of Hulofrud, one could build a new sky and hide the additional illustrations. Hjardabristallum liked the idea and ordered Tuldbydar to follow Celn to Hulofrud, where he would shape a new sky. The great honour made Tuldbydar cry a few drops of joy, as he hugged Hjardabristallum, who told him that also a gift would wait for him in there.

Tuldbydar, Celn and a group of dwarfs left for the east with their heads up high. The long journey ended in the northwest corner of the mountains of Folu, which hid a piece of land between the two lined mountains. Hjardabristallum had said that in there would wait the fallen pieces of his magic and from those he would have the power to build a sky. It was said that the powers would make the place remind of Loistefruden and the beauty of Pälter. Hjardabristallum told Tuldbydar that the last spell he should raise could be found inside a mansion that was called Dusp. When Tuldbydar opened the doors to the hall, a group of dwarfs approached him with a great delight, showing him a small bundle, which had a dwarven child. His name was Dörsmiten and he was Tuldbydar's son. Very far away, Hjardabristallum smiled that night behind his wide and long beard.

Tuldbydar spoke with the dwarf lady named Amna, who helped him to place the illustrations to the garden of Holdilalj. Amna's dedication was so immense, that her presence became one with the northern sky, which held many precious pieces of work of Hjardabristallum. Tuldbydar decided to keep the pictures under the vast canopies of the oak forest, which hid their magic from the outer world. A better age had begun for the dwarfs and they celebrated under the sun, moon and the stars, where Hjardabristallum looked over their pottering around.

Tuldbydar and Amna raised Dörsmiten in Hulofrud, where he learnt everything about Hjardabristallum and the enchanted skies. Celn kept going back and forth Loistefruden and Hulofrud, and told news which Tuldbydar was always eager to hear. Usually the news was good, but one day, when Dörsmiten was a young adult, Celn said that hurthallans and gaberleks had united against Hjardabristallum. A war had begun and the remaining dwarfs in Loistefruden needed their help urgently. Tuldbydar, Amna and Dörsmiten did not hesitate to return to Loistefruden, but the distance was too great and it would have taken too long to return by foot.

Celn in all her powers asked the three to trust her, as she was about to perform a mystic rite, that could allow her to take the three dwarfs with her to Loistefruden in a few days. The dwarfs needed to walk to the lake and connect with the water, and then they were to drown whilst holding Celn, who took them through clandestine layers of water. After a short thought, the three accepted the offer and Celn carried the flaccid dwarfs under the dark water. Ultimately the risky journey was worth the toll and the three dwarfs arrived to Loistefruden, where they had not been for many years.

Hejesvim Gwlinvinvor, the dragon leader of hurthallans and gaberleks had been destroying the serenity of Loistefruden and many of its peoples had fled their homes, leaving only the fighters behind. Hejesvim destroyed Pälter and Hjardabristallum's domain was shattered. Hjardabristallum decided to command the dwarfs to flee and find a sanctuary in the east, where he would meet them later. In here, Hjardabristallum gave a special task to two dwarven smiths to find a way to Hulofrud, where they would forge the sword and shield of Dörsmiten. The smiths were named Polvf and Eltur, and they left with Tuldbydar, Dörsmiten, Amna and Celn, who had not had much time to help the fight.

With his remaining energies, Hjardabristallum sent the four travellers back to Hulofrud and shone the silvery light of the western sky on his foes, who could not bear its pillars of brightness. Hurthallans and gaberleks, with their dragon leader, fled underground where the light did not burn them. Hjardabristallum was left frail from the deed, but it had saved time for the dwarfs, who were reorganising their ranks. Their enemies were doing the same in the depths, where the furious Hejesvim summoned his other servant, Morvgraza, the lava serpent. Simultaneously, Hejesvim began to speak poisonous words to the other powers of the world about Hjardabristallum's western sky, which made them push some of the illustration out of its cosmic frames.

Whilst Hjardabristallum, with the remaining dwarfs, gathered their powers and started to reclaim the fallen illustration from the depths, Tuldbydar was implementing a plan in Hulofrud. The dwarven smiths Eltur and Polvf were building a forge, west from what was eventually going to be Podfrud. Here, Tuldbydar's task was to protect their work and answer to all threats that could endanger the future of the dwarfs. During the years, Tuldbydar, Dörsmiten and the two smiths experienced many adventures, which were required to ensure the concluding coming of the dwarfs.

Celn told Tuldbydar news from Loistefruden and how she had begun to see dreams of how the land was disappearing into oblivion. She believed that Loistesse's time was coming to an end and its people were either leaving or forgotten to the shadows of time. Regardless, Celn informed that Hjardabristallum had a difficult situation with the gaberleks in the depths and recapturing the sky pictures had been an ordeal. The army of the dwarfs were stuck in the deep layers of the world and Hjardabristallum had left Loistefruden to help his dwarfs. He had become one with the western sky and its star, whose light helped the dwarfs out of the long dark, to the lands of Podfrud. Tuldbydar rapidly understood the purpose of the forge and how the little stone door ultimately revealed the dwarfs.

After some years of gathering the majority of their folk, the realm of Podfrud was established and the dwarven population began to grow. Tuldbydar and his son prepared to defend their lands, since they knew that, most likely, hurthallans and gaberleks inhabited the dark caves of the world here as well. The plan was useful, since the gaberleks had moved to a land in the northwest corner of Podfrud's region. The War of Ancestor's North was the first time when Tuldbydar was fighting in Drytgastadl, but he was as confident as he had always been. The war, which lasted roughly one hundred years, was a series of smaller clashes and the exceptionally long-living commander saw many of his successful warriors die of old age.

Tuldbydar heard reports from scouts, that they had seen a distant glow in the west, which they presumed to be part of the western sky. The ancient warrior began to contemplate whether their creator was trying to tell his kin to travel to west. Tuldbydar and his guards agreed that the idea of a distant glow was a worthy quest. The dwarf commander and his warriors left the young domain and promised to come back as soon as the final pieces of the sky were found. Dörsmiten and the elder dwarfs were left to be the wardens of their homes. Unfortunately, during the journey, Tuldbydar and his warriors were ambushed by a mountain snake. The ancient fighter was killed by the beast and his soldiers had to retreat towards the west. The soldiers could not abandon the mission and despite the loss, continued their quest further west. The spear of Tuldbydar was lost as well, which set a great shame upon Tuldbydar's warriors.

Somehow the mythic spear found its way to Hillfort Lands, where it was owned by several people. Gabyr Lord Gullof found the weapon after a battle with a group of bandits. During the several years in Hillfort Lands, the spear was called the Great War Spear of the North. Gullof had seen visions where the spear broke the curse, which made gabyrs fear the mountains of Folu. It was time for retaliation and Gullof with his hordes attacked Hulofrud and its garden of Holdilalj. The gabyr warlord struck the northern sky and lifted the curse, which allowed the gabyrs to enter the lands faster than before. Dörsmiten defended the land and the spear, which was in the hands of the gabyrs, was reluctant to serve them. Instead, the spear did everything to make their army weak, which gave the dwarfs the opportunity to obliterate the gabyr warband.

Dörsmiten and Gullof had a long and personal battle, which lasted for many days and nights. The dwarf warrior was better and he slew the tall and strong gabyr lord in the forests of Hulofrud. After the victory, Dörsmiten found the spear that had been tainted by the unworthy owners after his father's death. The blade of the spear had a hurthallan carving, which claimed that all possessions of the dwarfs belonged now to Hejesvim. This made Dörsmiten exceptionally angry and he decided to crush the arrogant hurthallans and their leader.

Dörsmiten called his warriors together and left to the northeast, where the hurthallans resided. The dwarf soldiers infiltrated deep into the hurthallan domain and found the cave where Hejesvim Gwlinvinvor lived during summers. In the cave, Dörsmiten charged at Hejesvim, who was surprised by the subtlety of the usually noisy and drunk dwarfs. The dwarf legend fought his foe and threw the spear at the dragon, which made it fall into darkness. Dörsmiten was badly wounded in the process and could not deny that his final moments were at hand.

Miraculously, the dwarf held on to his life till the band arrived to Hulofrud, which he considered a sacred place for his kin. In the northern hall of Dusp, which had tall and wide windows, Dörsmiten died and was buried. In his honour, Hulofrud mourned and celebrated the mythical dwarf, who had brought goodness to the peoples of the land. The light and green oak and birch forests whispered Dörsmiten's name, who had finally gone to the halls of his father.

OBSERVER OF THE THREAD THIN LIVES

Fydja was the only dwarf in the family of Porenhal, who had a profound connection with the past and Hjardabristallum. As a child, the dwarf lady stared at a large tapestry, which hung in the northern hall of Podtyr. No one could see its magic, but in her eyes it showed the same picture that could be seen in the western sky. The sky had faded and only a few dwarfs believed in its powers, which made Fydja sad when she tried to explain her visions to other dwarfs. The tapestry had matching illustrations and they were telling a story for the young lady, who was going to be the queen of Podtyr later in time.

In her early years, Fydja became friends with Douste Haskk, who was born into a family of warriors. His destiny was to become a grand commander in the army of Podfrud, which eventually entwined the two together. Douste could see the same magic of the tapestries as Fydja and the two spent many years discussing its stories and messages. When Fydja told her family that she could see Hjardabristallum writing and drawing in the empty the western sky, they laughed it off and told her not to believe too much in old legends.

"I saw ships, warriors and battles, which were close to a place named Pälter, and Hjardabristallum was there discussing matters with the long-gone soldiers of our kin. They all looked happy and confident, yet somewhat sorrowful and expectant. I had read tales of hurthallans and the gaberleks, who were no longer dwelling in our world. These servants of the dark were now threatening Hjardabristallum again, as it appeared that he lived in a place I could not recognise."

After Fydja was crowned, she continued her research on the tapestry, which had not caught anyone else's attention.

The queen saw a visualisation in the tapestry, as if Hjardabristallum was directly speaking to her. It explained how the only way to find him would be to find a way to the beacon of soil, which was also known as Kulus. In here, the brave dwarf warriors should fall and through their death, they would be taken to Loistefruden by Celn. The guardian of water had remained with Hjardabristallum and she had her ways to help the creator of the dwarfs. Hjardabristallum had the ability to predict certain parts of the future and he had seen the fall of the beacon of soil and Father Storm. It was a crucial opportunity for him to get his soldiers gathered, however, convincing them to die for the cause was a different matter. The majority of the dwarfs in the age considered Hjardabristallum to be a myth and his messages were ignored by most people, Queen Fydja Porenhal being an exception.

Fydja spoke with Douste Haskk and both dwarfs were willing to commit a great sacrifice to help their ancestral creator in the covert land known as Sondsirkkel. Commander Haskk, who was raised by the dwarf lady Amna in Hulofrud, had also an important part in the story, since his adoptive parent Amna had also raised Tiliasn Windesules. After his life, Tiliasn had been helping Hjardabristallum and Celn between Drytgastadl and Sondsirkkel.

Fydja asked Douste to dream of Tiliasn and tell him to open the original forge's stone door, which allowed their army to march in to unreachable places. Ultimately, when the dwarfs marched to the forge, Tiliasn opened the forge's little stone door and let the soldiers in. Fydja saw the army marching inside the forge, from the western fields of Tammarkaus and her wistful mind was contemplating whether the plan was the right choice. Many of the dwarf soldiers in the army had families and without them knowing, they were marching to a certain death.

Queen Fydja Porenhal kept following the tapestry and the western sky throughout the war, which made the illustration move frantically. Once again, the queen saw warriors, weapons and battles, clashing together like a wind against a wind, turning everything dark red. The images revealed that Tuldbydar and Dörsmiten were with Hjardabristallum and they led a regiment of soldiers. They were doing well against the hurthallans, whose warriors were at least two heads taller and had dishonourable manoeuvres in combat. Simultaneously, the queen saw how the fire serpent Morvgraza was slain and the army entered the Battle of Kulus.

The tragic end of the battle felt like an ice-cold blade through the heart. Fydja had lost a close friend, and many other dwarfs in the battle, and now she could only wish that her apparitions were true. Many details had changed in the tapestries and in the western sky, making her amber eyes look hollow. She could see deep forests, wooden cottages and cheerful dwarfs who were hugging and dancing. Amongst the dwarfs was Hjardabristallum, who saw Douste Haskk and expressed his gratitude towards him. Oddly, he also looked in the direction of Fydja's vision and smiled cunningly. She was not even there, but Hjardabristallum knew.

Ever since, Fydja kept observing the tales of the western sky and the tapestries, which were still hanging on the northwest wall of Podtyr's great hall. The stories spoke about battles against hurthallans and Hejesvim Gwlinvinvor, who challenged Hjardabristallum one last time. Fydja's family were known to have forged mighty weapons in their ancestral halls and every weapon had been drawn into their family book. Fydja had decided to use the book to help the warriors in their fight. The queen climbed on the top of the highest mountain of Folu and shouted to Eltur and Polvf to heat up the forge. Fydja threw the pages of the book into the air, which flew up towards the western sky where the two smiths were told to have dwelled inside a small cottage.

Certain tales told that the smiths crafted unearthly weapons for the dwarfs by using Porenhal's book, and sent them to warriors who could use their terrific powers to defeat the strong hurthallans. This changed the course of the battle, making Hejesvim Gwlinvinvor and its grim army retreat out of Sondsirkkel. Nevertheless, this was not enough for Tuldbydar and Dörsmiten, who had bottomless grudges towards the hurthallans and their dragon leader. Their weapons blazing, Fydja could see the whole tapestry setting on fire when the dwarf army began to pursue their foes. Suddenly, the whole western sky began to move from its frames and created a stream of star light towards the northwest.

Queen Porenhal knew that at the point where the light hit the land, the final battle between the dwarfs and Hejesvim would take place. Fydja assembled her armies and began to march towards the northwest, which was also known as the home of the gelders. Meanwhile, Hejesvim and its army rose from the depths and caused havoc in the land, acquiring the attention of the gelders. Hejesvim and its army was in bad shape and they needed reinforcements, which it tried to get from the gabyr warbands, that had been fighting the gelders in the land.

The war became a lot more complicated when the gabyrs of the north decided to join Hejesvim Gwlinvinvor and the hurthallan forces. However, they did not know that an army of dwarfs were marching towards them. Fydja heard from scouts and other sources of information that the gabyrs believed in a foretelling, which told of how a grand battle would be fought in the lands of the gelders. Ilgatn Hysc was the leader of the gabyrs of hanahathrul, who were also known as the servants of the forest and turning eye. They saw hurthallans as their ancestors, whose appearance in the world was a sign of the final battle.

When the dwarven army finally arrived in the lands of Pimenn, the situation was chaotic. Fydja, who travelled with the army, heard that the gabyrs had a magical piece of sky, which they called hurpathrul and it consisted of their black spells. For many years, hurpathrul had affected the northern sky, sending it dissonant messages, making its presence weaker. The gabyrs had even tried to reproduce similar forces from the sky, failing, and occasionally causing more harm to themselves than to their foes.

Fydja had a small piece of tapestry with her, where she followed the messages of Hjardabristallum, who wished that Fydja's army would crush Hejesvim and its servants in Drytgastadl. The final battle was at hand, which made Yrtar, the creator behind hurthallans, gaberleks and gabyrs appear in the battlefields. Yrtar's and Hejesvim's alliance was the worst event the northern part of Drytgastadl had seen for a long time, but it also united the dwarfs and gelders.

The final battle of Hejesvim Gwlinvinvor was fought in the winter and its wrath unmercifully whipped all belligerents. Hejesvim gave its heart to Yrtar, who passed it on to hurpathrul, as this was the only safe place to hold such a vulnerable part of the great dragon. Hejesvim knew that if it lost the battle, it could keep its heart safe up in the sky without losing its life. However, Hejesvim and Yrtar were not aware of Tiliasn Windesules, who was a close friend of Father Storm. The elf spirit saw the heart of Hejesvim in the hidden sky of hurpathrul and sent a message to Fydja, who could see a vision on her small piece of tapestry. The queen passed the message to Hjardabristallum, who revealed hurpathrul with his piercing light. Whilst the fight was going, Hejesvim became frightened and flew with its large wings towards the sky, to protect its frames and heart. All the way from the western sky, Hjardabristallum's manifestation threw a stellar spear, which on top rode dwarven heroes of the past, hitting hurpathrul directly. The war, which had lasted for two years, ended in that very moment, as Hejesvim fell from the sky and Yrtar disappeared after seeing his ally being defeated.

WRITTEN DEEP BY THE ANVIL

When Hjardabristallum sent his armies to the depths to collect the illustrations from the sky, the dwarven army became trapped in the deep layers of Drytvaarte. In the complicated chambers and corridors of the gaberlek realm, the dwarfs fought and lived for many weeks. Due to several reasons, a fair portion of the dwarfs became separated from the main fighting force, which kept moving towards the east. These dwarfs kept advancing north, as it seemed to be the only direction, which was not full of dangers. In the perilous depths, the separated dwarfs were led astray, as their names were called by numerous ethereal voices and chants.

The separated dwarfs kept travelling towards the sounds for many days and found a large underground gate, with decrepit walls that smoked quietly in the dark light of the tunnel. Dauan Elvarfastur, the leader of the separated dwarfs, knocked the gate and it opened, revealing another chamber behind it. In the large hall, which had several small spots of light hitting its stone floors, sat a group of heavily armed dwarfs. Dauan and his dwarfs were confused, but decided to approach the warriors.

In the chamber, Elvarfastur and rest of the dwarfs met Obaldak and Biidars, who were just like Hjardabristallum, an ancient force who protected the dwarfs. Biidars and Obaldak were not particularly close to Hjardabristallum, nor were they enemies, it just happened to be an intricate situation. Ultimately, Hjardabristallum was bitter about the separated dwarfs, who were saved by the two other dwarven protectors, as he felt the hammer of failure pounding his head.

Biidars and Obaldak could not care less about Hjardabristallum's opinions and welcomed the separated dwarfs to join them wholeheartedly. Dauan Elvarfastur had heard stories about the dwarven protectors when he was still living in Loistefruden, but had not met them personally. They did not like to live in Pälter and decided to move to Drytgastadl and build their home there. Some dwarfs had already joined them, which came as a surprise to Dauan and the rest of the new dwarfs. Nevertheless, unlike Hjardabristallum, the two protectors preferred to craft spells and hide them underground.

Their illustrations and pictures were in hidden places and chambers in the underground layers of Drytvaarte and this was also one of the factors which helped them to find the separated dwarfs. The home of the protectors and their dwarfs were in a place named Saundafruden and it was in the mid-north parts of Drytgastadl. The mountains of Myrfvaakel hid the home inside its thick stone walls, where the protectors and their dwarfs had lived for some time.

When Saundafruden was being built, many centuries before the separated dwarfs met the protectors, they were occasionally in contact with halmhendens, including their creator Stala. Obaldak and Biidars were very suspicious of Stala and his intentions, but did not consider him as a direct enemy. Old legends told that through many years of careful relationship, the protectors helped build many locations with Stala, including the beacons of day. When Hjardabristallum saw this, he was disappointed in Biidars and Obaldak, as he considered Stala a scheming snake, who ultimately wanted domination and destruction.

At some point, the beacon of soil appeared to the world, which was also known as Kulus. It was there to absorb all the excess spells in the world, so the balance of the magical breathing of the existence would flow steadily. Realising this, the two protectors had to hide their spells, thus creating many veiled places, that most likely were somewhere between the mortal layers of Drytvaarte. In places like these, the spells were safe, but also had the tendency to get the attention of other powers. Unsurprisingly, Stala had liked their ability to fold and hide spells into places in the world, which were unreachable by Kulus. Even Stala was inspired by these places and presumably used them for his own spells.

Ultimately, the separated dwarfs settled in Saundafruden, which quickly adopted the name of Saunfrud, as this is what it was called by the new dwarfs. There were also several other ancient spirits living in the lands and many of them were not too keen to see the new dwarfs arriving in their realm. They were worried that the dwarfs would eventually grow too ambitious in their stone halls and decided to take over specific locations in the world. For instance, the beacons of day had not been claimed by any realm so far, since they were well hidden in places unknown by the mortals. This all was changed when Kustnaw Korosk, an infamous gaberlek warlord emerged from the depths and claimed the western beacon of day as his domain.

The gaberlek warlord was one of the most ruthless and cruel beings in their ranks. His biggest desire was to get hold of all the beacons of day, which could presumably control the spheres of the world. The dwarfs of Saunfrud, who were connected to the creation story of the beacons, heard distant rumours of a great gaberlek army taking over the mountains of Hulumnoar. Due to this news, the dwarfs of Saunfrud established a council of the wise, which was also known as Foesth. Their purpose was to make decisions about the matters of the realm.

At the time, the most influential dwarf of Foesth was Avamagil Thoerd, whose word was highly regarded in the meetings of the council. She suggested that a dwarf army would be sent to the mountains of Hulumnoar to reclaim the beacon of day, which was taken over by their old enemy. The council agreed on the idea and sent an army of brave warriors towards the southwest. However, when the army arrived at the roots of Hulumnoar, the place had already witnessed a fierce battle. The commander of the army,

Dolvn Ufsat, travelled deeper into the mountain chambers and met elves that were burning the bodies of slain gaberleks.

Ufsat, a wise but short-tempered warrior, asked from the elf commander Virkelnas Araptru if they knew about the whereabouts of the beacon of day. The elven commander laughed and told that their army had come to conquer the mountains for this very purpose. The dwarf general's face turned red and he demanded that the elves leave the mountains, as the beacon of day was not the doing of elven craftsmanship, but a rightful dwarven claim. Virkelnas spat on Ufsat's face and told the dwarfs to leave before blood was shed. The dwarf general stood still and his eyes could have torn the world apart, if their veins had hands. Ufsat began to laugh frenziedly and struck his hammer across Virkelnas' jaw, breaking the elf's face apart. The dwarfs had come for a war, and a war they would get.

The Battle of Hulumnoar was one of the few conflicts the dwarfs and the elves had in the long history of the world. The nature of the battle was like a gale of steel, which was encouraged by both sides' will to prove their reputation as formidable and unyielding warriors. Virkelnas, who died of Ufsat's blow, was a tragic loss for the elven army, which organised effective counter attacks on the dwarfs. The bearded folk's casualties were tremendous, and the dwarf army had to pull out of the mountains, as they had not expected the elves to retaliate with such dedication. Ufsat barely got out of the halls before his army had to retreat towards the east. Ufsat understood that the army would need a lot more soldiers to defeat the elves, who had strong defences in the mountains. The army decided to head back home and prepare for another journey towards Hulumnoar. Meanwhile, certain dwarfs were assigned to stay behind and spy on the mountains.

A year after the clash, the dwarven scouts returned to Saunfrud and they had a mysterious guest with them. The scouts had met a dwarven protector, who came out of the mountain after the elven army had left it, failing to find the location of the beacon. The protector's name was Ikivästallum and he was Hjardabristallum's elusive brother. The ancient protector brought with him an anvil which had immense energy. With the presence of the anvil, Ikivästallum could hide the location of the beacon, making the elves very frustrated. After their leave, the protecting force revealed himself to the dwarven scouts, who nearly dropped their long beards out of surprise.

The protector walked in with the scouts, who were greeted by the council, but not by Biidars and Obaldak. The three seemed to have their disagreements and the mortal dwarfs watched the three arguing in the front hall of the city. However, Ikivästallum was there to make peace and hoped that he could take the anvil back to Loistefruden, after Biidars and Obaldak would write their messages on its cold steel. With their words, the anvil could protect all the dwarfs in the world and the anvil's eye would keep a watch over all the dwarven skies.

Obaldak and Biidars hesitantly agreed and touched the anvil, which caused a great light and the whole hall was filled with winds, which left the two protectors on the ground lifeless. Ikivästallum laughed maliciously and revealed his true self, who was not the dwarven protector, but a gaberlek sorcerer who had fooled all the dwarfs with his disguise. In the great shock, the soldiers attempted to attack the sorcerer, who blew another great wind on his attackers and began to run towards the northern balconies. From the great cliffs, the sorcerer jumped into the sea and disappeared, leaving Saunfrud in turmoil.

The horrific day left Biidars and Obaldak dead, which left many dwarfs with disheartening questions. Nevertheless, in the grimmest of days, the dwarfs gathered their strength and set their eyes on the northern sea, which was seen from the mountains of their realm. From the great balconies and platforms were seen several islands, where Ufsat believed that the sorcerer escaped with the anvil. The dwarfs came to believe that reclaiming the anvil back, the two protectors could be brought back to life.

This was the beginning of the great struggle which the dwarfs of Saunfrud had with gaberleks and gabyrs. The old enemies of the dwarfs had arrived on the islands, and their shores could be seen from Myrfvaakel's sides. For many centuries, the two sides fought on the islands and the controlled regions changed constantly, as both sides were unwilling to leave its damp and cold spruce forests. Eventually, the council of Foesth decided to build great towers on the mountain rooftops of Saunfrud's city. The idea was to use the towers to see even farther to the seas. It took almost a hundred years to complete the three towers and during that time a special magic was attached on their walls. Every dwarf who dwelled in the towers claimed that their eyesight was drastically improved and they could see details like a young hawk in its prime. Ilbjur Katl, who was one of the dwarfs living in these towers, saw a spark in the skies and a stream of light falling on one of the islands. At first, the dwarfs were not interested in the sight, but later they discovered that the gabyrs in the islands had suddenly become a lot wealthier.

The legend says that one of Hjardabristallum's illustrations fell and happened to hit one of the islands, which made its resources flourish. The dwarfs became alarmed, and interpretations began to circle about the sight. Ilbjur kept seeing one specific place in the island, which glowed when observed from the towers. According to Ilbjur, if the fallen illustration made the resources more visible, this could mean that the location of the lost anvil was also revealed, as it was presumably the most valuable and powerful object in the islands.

The council believed Ilbjur's story as it seemed to make sense and assembled an army of their finest naval soldiers, who were sent to the harbour of Jalkylm, a dwarven port and stronghold in the islands. This started another story in the history of Saunfrud, which ended up in the poetic book named Kylmwal. The book described stories about many fabled heroes and foes, who fought in the islands, seeking the distant glow. The anvil had become an obsession for the dwarfs and they were willing to bleed their ale-filled blood for its acquirement.

The conflicts kept developing throughout the years without a clear conclusion. While they were occurring, the dwarfs were enthusiastic fishers, just like in Podfrud. Saunfrud's dwarfs came up with their own speciality, salted fish in a barrel, and its reputation as a delicacy grew in the lands. It was delivered all the way to the south, to the town of Whalafryden, where the fish had become already so salty and fermented, that it put most of the dwarfs and other travellers off. Strangely, one of the visitors in Whalafryden, who had become a huge friend of the salted fish, had something to tell the dwarfs of Saunfrud.

The unnamed traveller claimed to have seen the powers of the anvil in the world. She believed that the lost anvil, which was still in the islands, had the ability to transform any metal into another metal. The protectors like Ikivästallum had used the anvil when he was creating his own hidden places in the world. The anvil could create impossible metal to impossible keys, which could only fit impossible locks, therefore making it a unique way to conceal one's property or spells. The dwarfs believed that if the gabyrs found the anvil, they could use its energy to also access some hidden parts of the world, with its metal-altering powers.

The times moved onwards and the eternal conflict did not seem to have an end. The dwarfs and the gabyrs had fought in the islands now for countless ages, which included several smaller and larger battles. Sometimes it took decades without anything happening and sometimes more happened in a year, than it had happened in the past hundred years. It was an exceptional story, that gave birth to many interesting dwarf clans in Saunfrud. For instance, the island dwarfs, who were descendants of the naval dwarfs, established a great clan named Tuonlturwe. These dwarfs were part of Saunfrud, but they preferred the island life and living on boats and ships. They were also very dedicated to building dimly lit rooms, where they could throw water on a stove and warm up from having the hot steam around them. These rooms were named turwenkeel and were believed to have a connection with the gelders, who were building similar cottages far in the east.

The most famous of all turwenkeel masters was Väinär Olsbalen and he was one with the secretive energies of the rooms. He also happened to be a captain of a fleet in the naval forces of Saunfrud and Tuonlturwe. He liked so much of turwenkeels that it became a standard to build these rooms into the ships, were the dwarfs could bathe in the hot steam rooms, after facing the icing tides of the seas. These rooms were considered sacred amongst Saunfrud's dwarfs and they could possess many unearthly features.

Some tales spoke of how the turwenkeels in the realm were magically connected to each other and from the dark corners of these rooms could one enter another, by just entering the dark under the wooden benches. This meant that sometimes the rivalling dwarfs appeared in their counterpart's room and began a fight, just because it was considered as quality banter. An even stranger occasion was when the dwarfs could move between the ships by entering the turwenkeel and appearing in another one, located on a neighbouring ship. However, one must remember that such tales were mostly told by very drunk dwarven naval soldiers, who tended to talk utter bollocks.

The anvil's reputation had spread far and wide and the dwarfs and gabyrs were no longer the only ones desiring its might. One day, a fleet of shore elves arrived on the same tides, which surrounded the islands. The elves were led by an elf captain called Surge. His presence attracted the attention of gelders, whose coastal towns he had been raiding in the past. Suddenly the dwarfs and gabyrs found themselves fighting two other sides, and they all had the desire to claim the anvil. Turwenkeel master Olsbalen was furious when he found out that Surge had found the anvil before the dwarfs even had a chance. The elf captain had taken the anvil and had begun to sail towards northwest.

A great pursuit began and Väinär Olsbalen's ship was just behind the gelder boat, which was reaching Surge's flagship. The dwarfs were falling behind, but Olsbalen and his crew refused to abandon the chase. Eventually, on that day happened something which truthfulness is open to a dispute. A story tells of how Olsbalen and his dwarfs got the idea to enter their ship's turwenkeel and enter the dark under the wooden benches, which were next to the great stove. Through the dark, the dwarfs appeared inside the gelder ship, which also had a similar room. If it had been any other ship, the odd plan would not have worked. The dwarf naval soldiers surprised the gelders inside their own ship and defeated them just when they reached Surge's flagship.

All the details of this part of the story were regarded as sailor's tales and in truth, it is most likely that the dwarfs managed to reach the other ships by using skilfully the tides and winds. The story about turwenkeels perhaps sounded better and more fitting for Väinär Olsbalen's mythic reputation. Nevertheless, what happened after the incident continued the nature and overemphasis of the incredible story. A large sea monster appeared from the depths of the sea and hit its gigantic caudal fin on Surge's boat, causing a major flood.

Surge's ship was plummeting rapidly and he attempted to jump to another ship in his fleet, with the anvil in his hands. The experienced captain jumped, but failed to reach the neighbouring ship, as the sea monster swayed the sinking ship. Surge fell to the sea, falling into the black abyss still holding on to the anvil. Surge could not let the magical item go from his grip and he began to drown. Whilst being unconscious, the anvil, which was taking

Surge even deeper, hit a golden chain that was weirdly floating and holding on to another character.

The anvil broke the golden chain and woke something, which began to take Surge and the anvil back to the surface. Simultaneously, Olsbalen was staring at the sea, where the golden glimmer of the anvil could be seen, returning towards the plane of water. Olsbalen's emotions were racing like wild horses and his heart was pounding like an axe being swung into a gabyr's head. A vast underwater blow shook the ships and two characters were seen soaring through the air, guided by the force of the flying anvil that was heading directly up to the skies. Until that moment, the crew of Olsbalen had never heard him cursing so loudly, as he was looking at the odd sight.

The anvil took Surge and the other character above the clouds, before the covert person opened his eyes and looked at the elf captain, who began to fall back to the sea. The character followed the falling anvil and the captain, which hit the deck of the gelder ship, where all sides had stopped fighting. First the anvil hit the deck, going through a layer of wood, followed by the captain who slammed directly onto the deck, causing a bloody mess. Lastly fell a bearded figure, whose head hit the mast, causing a sound of thunder. The gelders and dwarfs surrounded the fallen characters. Suddenly, the bearded man stood up and with staggering steps walked close to Surge's body and said that he was going to survive.

The battle ended in an odd way and Olsbalen demanded a name from the fallen bearded man. The man looked at Olsbalen and his eyes were shining with a familiar strength. The bearded stranger introduced himself as Ikivästallum, the crafter behind the anvil. Olsbalen and his dwarfs bowed in front of the dwarven protector, who said that he had been imprisoned in the abyss after the gaberlek sorcerer cursed him. The anvil was controlled by him, but so far it had been too far from his powers, meaning that Surge had performed a great favour by finding and stealing the anvil.

Since Surge died drowning, whilst holding the anvil in his hands, its powers could also bring back the dead captain. The fall, which would have finalised anyone's life, did not have such a substantial effect in this situation and when Ikivästallum touched the anvil and Surge's body, it made the captain breath again. Olsbalen wrote in his memoirs how the whole deck was quiet and the fighting sides had lowered their weapons in amazement. Ikivästallum told the gelders and elves to leave, as he could use the anvil's energy to sink their ships with a back-shivering tone in his voice.

Ikivästallum returned the anvil to Saunfrud's halls, where Biidars' and Obaldaks' tombs were. In the great hall, the ancient force touched the anvil and the resting places of the dwarven protectors, in hope of bringing the two back. However, too much time had passed since their lives were taken and the return of the two was too late. The dwarfs realised that perhaps the obsession with the anvil had made them unable to see the whole picture and passing of time. The world of the lost protectors was different and their return could be redundant. At least the anvil had returned to the hands of Ikivästallum and the protector settled on one of the islands, where he had a little wooden house and a forge.

Eventually, the gabyrs disappeared from the islands and many dwarf villages were built in them, sometimes bridges connecting their harbours. Saunfrud was flourishing with wealth and their old enemies were no longer present. One day, Ikivästallum left the realm as well, leaving the anvil inside his wooden cottage to be protected by the dwarfs. The anvil's powers had faded and it no longer looked like anything else than an ordinary piece of iron. The fire in the small forge had vanished and only Ikivästallum's personal belongings reminded the dwarfs of his deeds.

CRAFTERS OF THE WOODEN KNOWLEDGE

Väinär's family of Olsbalen was well known for their carpentry and house building. In the long past of the family, Karjaln Olsbalen journeyed to the east from Saunfrud and met many fascinating peoples there. In the land of Pimenn he was taught the powers of turwenkeel, before it was known by that name. The two spirits the dwarf met there were known as Tlaute and Pjyn and they befriended Karjaln. The dwarf wrote many stories and tales about the two spirits, who grew interested in the dwarfs and their world. Karjaln invited the two to Saunfrud, which was not easy since Pjyn and Tlaute needed a turwenkeel to survive, as they could not leave their original source of life. Karjaln decided to build a little cottage that was pulled by horses and it had a turwenkeel inside it.

During the journey to Saunfrud, Karjaln wrote a book of stories that consisted of Tlaute's and Pjyn's adventures. In due course, the book became an essential part of Saunfrud's folklore and was highly celebrated by many scholars. The dwarfs invited the two spirits to become part of their myths and legends, which coloured the rich past of their kin. Specific rites were set to respect turwenkeels, which were built in many houses in the realm.

The tradition continued in Väinär's family and was passed down to him, as he became a master turwenkeel builder. The dwarf spent many years learning the ways to build the rooms of steam and mystic. It was a very elaborate process, which required unnecessarily many rites to complete. Väinär also made friends with the two protectors of turwenkeel, who had followed the story of the dwarfs from the times immemorial. He had the craftsmanship and passion in his blood and the spirits favoured his presence.

Sometimes Tlaute and Pjyn invited the dwarf to join him in the turwenkeel and throw a lot of water on the stove, making the room hot and comforting from the troubles of the world.

The two turwenkeel protectors showed many places and stories to Väinär. The tale claimed that his understanding grew and the two spirits decided to reveal to him a secret skill, which included the darkest corner of a turwenkeel. Under the wooden benches of these rooms, one could access to other turwenkeels that were connected to the same world of Tlaute and Pjyn. It is unsure whether any of these stories were true and whether it could be done, but the dwarfs liked to write about it and explain the wildest stories after a good night of feasting and drinking.

Later in Väinär's life, the dwarf joined the navy of Saunfrud, which had been sailing the seas north from the realm's shores. Väinär, being a master of his craft, became a builder for the navy to build turwenkeels for the ships of the dwarfs. It was also exciting for Tlaute and Pjyn and their friends, who could finally sail the seas, whilst being inside their own sauna worlds. Pjyn and Tlaute also visited the sailing dwarfs in their turwenkeels and told them illusionary stories, capturing the dwarven imaginations. In the middle of the cold seas, these tales helped the dwarfs to comprehend in their hard lives.

Väinär spent many years with Tlaute and Pjyn, who taught him plenty of old magic singing and sauna rune reading. The dwarf used this knowledge to his advantage when he built turwenkeels inside the ships, as the dwarven sea soldiers liked their presence with a passion. Another tale adds that since Väinär was good friends with Pjyn and Tlaute, their ships were occasionally aided by Eldinvurtel, lady of the tides. Väinär's fleet was able to sail faster than many other collective of ships in the seas, and they rightfully received the name: Tater noses and fluttering beards.

Väinär, who did not have close relations with his family, joined the clan of Tuonlturwe, which regarded the tales of Kylmwal an important part of their ancestral lore. The elder of the clan wanted Väinär to lead the fleet, when Saunfrud sent their armies to reclaim the lost anvil. Väinär accepted the offer without hesitation, as the blessing of turwenkeel and the tides were on his side. Yet, the dwarfs were unsuccessful in acquiring the anvil and it was captured by the elves that had joined the battle alongside gabyrs and gelders. Väinär began to chase the elven ship, being just behind the gelder boats, which seemed to move faster than expected. The dwarf captain was disappointed and began to contemplate whether Eldinvurtel had abandoned their ships. Väinär did not know that the lady of the tides had left to fight a monster of the depths, which had been secretly summoned by the gelders.

The legend continued in the book of Kylmwal, explaining how Väinär saved the dwarfs from the predicament, by using his knowledge of turwenkeels. The captain claimed that he and his soldiers entered their turwenkeel in their ship and asked for guidance through the home of Pjyn and Tlaute. Apparently the two dwarven protectors rarely let any mortals enter their shadowy home of dim and steamy wooden rooms. The two protectors made an exception and let the dwarfs use a passage, which had not been witnessed by many mortal beings. Väinär and his warriors entered an interesting series of turwenkeels, where various people were steam bathing and telling stories.

When Väinär travelled through this unexplainable world, he saw many old forces and heroes enjoying the hot steam of the stoves. Some of the characters were gambling or drinking and some of them were engaged with more serious conversations. It felt like a place where the good and evil forces of the world had eternal armistice, a place of a break from the larger frame. Inside one of these rooms Väinär came across a man, who was enthusiastically betting with several other people in the shadowy and steamy wood chamber. There were only two bright lights coming from the right wall, which had two windows, revealing a bright summer day and a lake. The light revealed the man's face who invited Väinär to join the game. The captain knew that he had no time, but he loved a good bet, which this time was a mistake. The man laughed and collected his win.

"I do know that no one believes my story, I have accepted it already, but please do understand that our world has many secrets and only a few of us are lucky enough to witness their beauty. This room however had something different in it, there were people gambling and I joined for a fast round, which I lost as rapidly as I had started it. I promised to the man, that I would return and win my silver back from him. The man laughed and told me that his name was Abyss and he would be waiting for me."

One of the chapters in the book of Kylmwal explained that Väinär approached one of the rooms, which was guarded by gelder protectors. Nevertheless, these two guardians were known by Tlaute and Pjyn, who managed to overcome their powers. This gave an access to the gelder ship's room, which was their equivalent of a turwenkeel. From here, captain Väinär and his soldiers surprised the gelders, who were busy chasing the elven ship. The strange plan had worked and the dwarfs challenged the gelders in their own ship, causing absolute bedlam. The fight was ferocious and both sides lost many warriors, but its end was coming swiftly. The beast of the water had defeated the lady of tide and was approaching Surge's ship. With its large body it caused severe harm to the elven ship, which made its crew abandon it. Väinär, the rest of the dwarfs and the gelders saw the struggle and how Surge accidentally fell to the water, with the anvil in his hands. The whole battle ceased on the gelder ship's deck, as the whole purpose behind the battle was now deep underwater.

"I kept seeing a golden glow under the dark water, which hit something that looked like a chain. The golden shine expanded and moved like a whip in the water, leaving

sparks to the lonely depth. The anvil returned to the surface with two characters. From there its metallic glory continued its journey towards the sky, making the two other lads fly in its wake like birds in the sky. From there, they fell on the deck of the ship, causing wooden splinters to hit our bodies. One of these cheeky chaps got up and did something with the anvil, making the elven captain come back to life. It was impossible! I had personally seen the bloke's head open like a rotten tomato."

Väinär was the first dwarf Ikivästallum had seen for ages and his confused face gave a slight smile. The dwarfs felt his power and knew who they were standing in front of. This made all the warriors kneel in front of Hjardabristallum's brother. The battle had ended, as the gelders and elves knew that Ikivästallum could sink their ships with the flying anvil. Väinär, who had gone through unbelievable experience, commanded the dwarven fleet back to Saunfrud, where the anvil would find its original home.

After the anvil returned to Saunfrud, the situation in the islands began to alter as well. It took a long time for gabyrs to disappear, but the return of the ancient force had ignited the flame. Väinär kept studying the stories of Kylmwal and turwenkeel, where he kept meeting with Tlaute and Pjyn. Some dwarfs later told stories of how Väinär lost touch with Saunfrud and began to dwell more and more in turwenkeel, eventually being absent for long periods of time. The last time the dwarf was seen, he claimed that he had a bet with a man and it was time to go and claim his silver back.

GELDERS

Didly Didly Wazz

"It took me some years to realise that I am a son of the north. I yearn for the lakes and forests. I want to be buried in a place that cannot be found. I want to live forever in tales, but my resting place should not be found, as I am like the world of the old days. I want to disappear into the forests. I want to become the soil of this earth and rest in serenity, because I know that there will be people speaking my name. I have earned this - I have earned my place in the stories that live forever and they will talk about the son of the north under the wistful stars."

In Oblivion of Heroes, which was also known as Kajoste, lived Caolfveld, the shaper of thunder and ruler of tempests. His powers were enormous and his melodies reverberated in the firmaments over the land. Kajoste was full of different factions and old heroes, and many of the fighters were as old as the world. Caolfveld was a good friend of many powers, including the protectors of Husmyrsket, who later gelders and dwarfs met either in turwenkeels or torpas. The guardians of Husmyrsket had a furnace, where they had created the eternal flame of Palendeirn and its energy was bound to several objects. Vilhiildes, who were demonic beings, sent their forces to steal the flame, since they needed it to defeat Yrtar, the creator of hurthallans, gaberleks and gabyrs. Essentially, these were the elements of the great struggle of the gelders.

Caolfveld was caught in the middle of the adversaries between Yrtar and Atrurionas, the leader of vilhiildes. There was a foretelling of three strongholds, each requiring one element to destroy Yrtar, who tried to corrupt the vilhiildes and their leader. The time was running out for the vilhiildes and Atrurionas, who commanded his forces to attack the furnaces of eternal blaze. Caolfveld, who was friends with the protectors of the furnace, defended the forge, battling against vilhiildes and their commander Dusm. During the battle, the furnace broke and released its powers to the surroundings, enabling the vilhiildes to acquire two of its most crucial embers. Caolfveld managed to save one and bound it to his battle axe.

The war continued in Kajoste between vilhiildes and Caolfveld, who the creatures wanted to slay in order to receive the final ember from the silenced forge. Caolfveld took a fragment of the ember, which was in his axe, and threw it in the air. Whilst in the sky, Caolfveld summoned the greatest tempest Kajoste had ever seen and its lighting hit the heroes who resided there. Every hit of thunder bashed the old heroes into the soil, where they ultimately rose with refreshed minds and bodies. It was the day that gelders arrived in Kajoste and their relentless mind-set tore a great hole in the ranks of the vilhiildes. Never before had the vilhiildes feared anything with the same intensity.

After being defeated in Kajoste, Atrurionas and his forces left to Drytgastadl, where their third and final stronghold stood. The leader of the vilhiildes had heard that Yrtar was residing in the land as well, which made him forget about Kajoste and the gelders. Caolfveld was not accustomed to see such attitude from his enemy and decided to follow Atrurionas and prevent him reaching the mountain that was known as Odomnan. Caolfveld met the protectors of the furnace, who were called Leutel and Fjyn, siblings of Tlaute and Pjyn. The four protectors showed the mysteries of Husmyrsket, which could provide alternative routes to Drytgastadl's western parts.

Caolfveld took his gelders inside the cottages of Husmyrsket, which was considered an uncharted part of Kajoste. Caolfveld led his people to the dim and clandestine wooden chambers, where the old heroes were bathing in hot steam. The journey went well at first, but soon the gelders realised that they had been reconnoitred by hurthallans, who had also infiltrated the Husmyrsket. When Caolfveld and his gelders arrived to the greatest of all chambers in Husmyrsket, Yrtar suddenly appeared and tried to take Caolfveld's amber and axe. A fight commenced in the wooden hall, where light pillars pierced the hot steam. The old heroes who lived there became excited about the sudden fight and joined it without any particular reason.

The four protectors of Husmyrsket had made a rule that no battles should ever happen in their home. The ones who would fight, would fly out like birds beaten by a storm. When the first blood dropped on the floor, a great wind blew the gelders and the hurthallans outside the windows, which were far up in the western wall of the room. Caolfveld, Yrtar and their forces entered a world of dreamy waters, where they began to sink. Darkness and distant visions were finally broken by a great thunder of Caolfveld, who manifested himself into a storm that carried the gelders towards the bottom of the lake. However, no bottom was found and the gelders dropped out of the lake into air, as new land was seen beneath. With rain dropping from the lake that was now above in the skies, the gelders descended to the forests of Pimenn in Drytgastadl.

THE LIGHTNING BLOOD OF ASH AND FURY

Velankad, sister of Caolfveld, beheld as the thunder escorted the gelders to Pimenn's deep forests. Caolfveld recognised his sister, who had a baffled look on her face, next to a large lake, which had numerous islands. The two spoke to each other and Velankad saw Caolfveld's presence, as he had turned into thunder, a pure demonstration of nature's spear. Velankad and Caolfveld were not keen to see each other, as the two had their differences. According to Velankad, her brother had turned into a force filled with nothing but bloodlust. Their father Kalvkad had the same problem and he had disappeared inside the stone of Til earlier in time.

Velankad saw too many similarities between her father and brother. She told Caolfveld that he would not bring the bloodshed to Drytgastadl under any age. In return, her brother looked at her face and said that his people would do it for him, regardless of the outcome. Velankad saw the people who had come with the thunder and they had a name; gelder, meaning 'Lightning'. Velankad tried to ignore her brother and told him that he should join Kalvkad in Til, as it was the only suitable place for their nature. Caolfveld snorted and lashed the stone with his thunder, disappearing inside it. Velankad was now with the gelders and was aware that Til was the beacon of blood and it prevented vilhiildes accessing Drytgastadl. Til required blood to protect the land from vilhiildes and it left a controversial situation for Velankad. She was mindful that the creatures had come to Drytgastadl and the only way to remove them would be filling Til with blood.

Eventually, Velankad commenced the hunting tradition, when the gelders initiated the great hunt for hurthallans, gaberleks and later gabyrs, who lived east from their realm. It was an age of wonders and many tribes united against the gelders, who had sown the seed of war in their soil. However, there was only one who saw the opposite side of the situation and his name was Myrkutgar, the second mightiest force of hurthallans and gaberleks. The force of darkness knew that vilhiildes could destroy their kin in the long term and the only way to keep them out of Drytgastadl was to fill the stone of Til with his own unearthly blood. It left him no choice but to sacrifice himself and ride to battle to the stone of Til, where their army had a clash with Velankad and gelder warriors.

"I could not think of anything worse than living forever. Days would feel like nothing and years would pass by like days."

Myrkutgar hit the stone and it gained so much energy that the cycle of vilhiildes' end was initiated. The process took a long time, but it was final and irreversible. Yrtar could not understand the sacrifice of Myrkutgar and claimed that the hurthallans could have defeated the vilhiildes with their sheer numbers. In fact, Yrtar was so bitter about losing his closest captain, that he declared eternal war on Velankad and the gelders, who he thought lured Myrkutgar into the senseless deed. Yrtar's new aim was to capture the stone of Til and bring back all the fallen hurthallans and gaberleks. He was not alone and many shadowy forces of the lands joined him, creating sorcerous phenomena named hanahathrul.

Velankad heard about Yrtar's plans from gelder scouts, who had seen the new magic taking over the eastern parts of their land. Velankad asked help from the protectors of Husmyrsket: Leutel, Fjyn, Tlaute and Pjyn. They resided inside a world of their own and only way for them to travel the lands of Drytgastadl was to manifest into a steam or mist. The four protectors were allies of the gelders and wanted to remove the hanahathrul from their homeland, as it was affecting their ethereal presence as well. The gelders began to build torpas, mysterious wooden cottages which had stoves inside them. When the gelders needed the help of the four forces, water was poured on these stoves, creating steam that enabled their presence in Pimenn.

Velankad planned white and black torpas, which both had different purposes. The white ones helped the protectors move and hunt the hanahathrul in Pimenn and the black ones were dedicated for disparaging means. The gelders blessed their weapons in the steams of torpas, before they left for a hunt. For instance, arrows which were touched by the steam inside white torpas, could reveal the secret paths of hurthallans and their gaberlek sorcerers. The weapons blessed by the black torpas' steam could finish the task by slaying foes, which otherwise were impossible to see due the deceiving magic of hanahathrul.

Velankad was chosen to be the supreme leader of the gelders and she commenced great plans to build Jarndava, which was going to be built around the stone of Til. The island, where the realm saw its first days, was surrounded by a lake and several other smaller islands, which eventually all had white torpas, spying and protecting the dark magic of their enemies. It was an age when some of the gelders became very talented torpa masters and they could live inside the cottages, revealing the hidden areas of the hurthallans and gaberleks in the east.

Velankad, who was gifted with remarkably long life, saw her realm expanding as the centuries went by. The situation was a stalemate and both sides were too cautious to make daring moves. Nevertheless, it gave Velankad and her closest torpa masters time to search for the blind spots in the east, where the enemy practised their hanahathrul. Velankad was certain that the old foe would make a move soon and the gelders should prepare with all measures. The primary problem was that the blind spots of hanahathrul were constantly changing and the gaberleks and hurthallans were moving at the same pace, trying to stay hidden from torpa magic's eyes.

When Velankad was still residing with the gelders, she asked further help from the four protectors of Husmyrsket. Velankad ordered the gelders to pour so much water on the stoves, that the four forces could move inside the dense steam and travel towards the east. Meanwhile, the gelders built transportable torpas, which looked like small tents and regularly added more steam into their wandering presence. The plan worked and the steam began to patrol the lands of Pimenn, making the gaberleks and hurthallans afraid. At the time, it was the key force which kept them outside Jarndava and its outer villages.

Hurthallans and gaberleks never managed to get close to Jarndava, but the gabyrs of later eras had much grimmer schemes. This all happened by a pure accident, when the mist of the four was moving in the land and came near a lake, which hid a secret. Some of the gabyrs who had seen the mist coming attempted to hide. The only place they could hide was a bottom of a lake, which made them jump into the dark water. The four protectors glided above the lake and sensed the hiding gabyrs, who were running out of breath. Ultimately, they had to give in and the mist slew the majority of the gabyrs who emerged from the lake, gasping for air. However, one of the gabyrs was dragged under the lake, into a cave where aakas dwelled. The beings were also known as water witches and they were about to become a dangerous ally for the gabyrs.

The aakas hated Velankad's father, Kalvkad. The witches cursed Kalvkad and his family, as he had taken away their land when he arrived to Pimenn, several centuries earlier. The stone of Til was on their sacred site, which included many of their under-the-lake homes. Kalvkad had witnessed that the aakas could not bleed blood, just like the vilhiildes, and thought mistakenly that they were of the same origin, pushing them away from his new home. Later in time, Velankad began to receive concerning news from the east, where the gabyrs and the aakas were planning a great war by using hanahathrul.

Velankad eventually died of her age, leaving the realm mourning and somewhat lost. When gabyrs and their allies heard about the news, a vast war plan was put forward. The four protectors could no longer keep up with the sorcery and tricks of hanahathrul, which allowed some of the aakas to move underneath the lands and lakes near Jarndava. They had finally set a blind spot for the torpas and the gelders were in trouble, as they had to face an army that was ten times larger. The gabyrs were emerging from everywhere, even from the lakes, which until that day had been under the protective eye of torpas and the four forces. The Battle for Jarndava ended in a horrendous defeat and the gelders had to flee their dear home. It was an infuriating and humiliating defeat for the people, who could not feel fear. Yet, the gelders were not senseless and knew that there would be time to reclaim Jarndava in the future – it would just require careful planning and a yearning for revenge.

For several hundred years the gelders were itinerant clans, which travelled around the lands of Pimenn and Hillfort Lands, offering their skills and services for the local peoples. At the time, no permanent settlements were built and only a few wooden forts remained from this era, recapping the gelders of their years of homelessness. Some of the gelders grew impatient and wanted to recover the land of their ancestors. One of these gelders was Ulka Arkuus, who was a skilled hunter and well-known character amongst his folks. He had an enormous following and many gelder warriors swore on his name, as if he was one of their ancestral powers. Eventually, Ulka Arkuus decided to muster up a large band of warriors and conquer their home back.

The gelder army attacked Jarndava, which had become a decrepit place after almost three centuries. Ulka Arkuus and his cavalry charged over the bridges of olden Jarndava and caught the gabyrs off-guard. The courageous gelder warriors fought bravely, but the hanahathrul, which was residing in the old city, gave them significant hindrance by confusing their minds and visions. Ulka Arkuus was seeing his army battered down by endless hordes of gabyrs, who swarmed like rats, pulling his warriors off horses. The tale tells that Ulka Arkuus slew at least ninety gabyrs before he was mortally wounded and fell to the ground.

Gabyr commander Olkett laughed and decided to take Ulka by the stone of Til, where he pierced his chest with a large polearm. Olkett thought that it was the most humiliating way to leave the world, simultaneously avenging all the gaberleks and gabyrs, whose blood had been shed on it. When the blood of Ulka hit the stone of Til, his mind left his body and travelled to a distant place, where emerald-throated loons sang amidst the misty spruce forests. In here, Ulka met Kalvkad and Caolfveld, who were happy to see a familiar face. The two powers said that they had tried to return, but the curse of hanahathrul had kept them inside the stone. However, now everything had changed and blood of a gelder had touched their immemorial stone. The sky of Til commenced to glow and Kalvkad and Caolfveld took Ulka to the air, where they were taken by the light.

With a fiery storm, the two forces of the gelders appeared from the stone of Til and Caolfveld's axe began to cut the ranks of gabyrs like a scythe. Gabyrs panicked and the fire that touched the water created a familiar steam, inviting the four protectors back. With their aid, the air was filled with cyclones of thunder and a blaze that ravaged the aakas and gabyrs, making them retreat from Jarndava. To finalise the battle, Caolfveld threw his axe inside one of the windstorms, which struck pure death upon their foes.

Ultimately, the restoration of Jarndava began and the realm was back to its original glory by the end of the same century. Gelders learnt a lot from these hard centuries and their alliance with the protectors of Husmyrsket tightened. The guardians of torpa returned to the gelder realm and many sorcerers conjured their original energies. To avoid the protectors vanishing from the world, the gelders began to bottle the steam and mist, which they could carry on their journeys. The white and black steam was inside all-sized vials, which the gelder mages and warriors carried and used against all sorts of threats. For example, the people realised that by combining the two different colours of steam, strong whirlwinds could be summoned out of the bottles.

Gabyrs and their hanahathrul were no longer a great threat for the gelders, but their might could rise again. For several years, Jarndava remained peaceful and many gelders travelled east to continue their tradition as hunters and mercenaries in the ranks of the folks of Hillfort Lands. Moreover, another conflict was brewing in the south, when the mighty halmhenden Lord Vhyolan Rauwos was planning his vengeance. Vhyolan had first asked aid from the storm elves of Ikirias, but soon turned on the side of gelders, as the elves were not interested joining the cause. Vhyolan arrived to Jarndava and spoke to the leader of the gelders, Immos Veekel. The halmhenden lord was aware of the troubles, which the gelders had with the gabyrs in the past and offered them the city of Worlgaltrin in return of their warriors. Vhyolan was willing to give another home for the gelders and spell-crafting beyond imagination. Immos Veekel met with his wisest ones and decided to accept the offer, since the gelders needed another city.

Worlgaltrin had also a special place in the minds of the gelders, as it was seen magical and untouchable by the gabyrs, who feared the halmhendens and their creations. The losses of the past would never happen again, if the gelders had two cities and its sorcery would guarantee stability. Immos Veekel assembled an army, which shone in their famous shining scale armours, named silver pine cones. Vhyolan and the gelder commanders came up with a specific plan to conquer first Honedimn and expand from there towards the southeast. The aim was to bring all manfolk and their allied realms on their knees. These realms had caused most destruction to halmhendens and Vhyolan was crying for revenge.

Vhyolan and Immos planned a careful campaign against the realms of Aetari, Dyveln and Ylvart. The gelder armies began to move and their first task was to take over the trading town of Honedimn, which was not a challenge for the warriors. Some of the town's people managed to escape and made their way southeast, where the trading town of Lhorem was located. The three realms became aware of the gelders and their belligerences, as they received stories from the escapees. Meanwhile, the town of Honedimn was obtained and reinforced, as it provided crucial shelter and food for the warriors.

Due to challenging weather conditions, the gelder army was delayed and could not start their march towards Lhorem, which was their next target. By the time the army reached Lhorem, the defences of the town were a lot harder than expected. The attacking warriors managed to breach inside the town and briefly it seemed that the battle was won. However, later the tide turned in the fight and the gelders were pushed out of the town, which was a mortifying defeat for the gelders. In the battle, one of the gelder commanders was captured and slain. Before his death, the commander explained about Vhyolan and how he would bring end for Aetari, Dyveln and Ylvart. His message was received with varied thoughts, as the defenders perceived halmhendens mostly as legends of the yore.

The defeat was a shock for Immos, who swiftly met with Vhyolan and created a new plan. It was obvious that their foes would assemble a counter-attack and most likely it would take place in Honedimn. Immos decided to move the majority of his forces out of the town, making it look deliberately weaker. The idea was to lure the three enemy armies inside Honedimn and drain them with strenuous strategies. When the fatigued enemy army would think of a victory, a larger gelder army would appear from the west and sweep over them with a force. For his fortune, the plan was effective and the three armies were viciously defeated in Honedimn, making the survivors abscond in absolute horror.

The summer of the war was better for Vhyolan and the gelders, who sent parts of their army towards the east. Vhyolan wanted to get hold of Hulofrud, a sacred place for the dwarfs of Podfrud. The scheme was to attack Podtyr and Podmyr, causing enough chaos to take the attention away from Hulofrud - Vhyolan's primary aim. Soon, the Battle of Podtyr and Podmyr raged wildly, whilst a greater force of gelders raided Hulofrud. The dwarven defenders fought desperately, but their efforts were not sufficient. When the gelders pushed the dwarfs to the mansion of Dusp, a surprising aid arrived for the dwarfs; a storm elf army, led by Tiliasn Windesules. The elves crushed the gelders with their strong cavalry and the warband had to retreat west.

It was yet another defeat for the gelders and they began to doubt the war and its worth. Later in the year, Aetari, Dyveln, Ylvart and Podfrud marched to Galtreken to fight against the last gelders, who were still willing to fight in the war. It did not take long until distressing news arrived from Jarndava, telling that gabyrs had sent massive armies to take over their realm and all warriors were needed in the north. Vhyolan became angry and accused the gelders of being cowards. All the plans were forgotten and the war had turned into a despairing fight for nothing. Parts of the last gelders fell in Worlgaltrin, still believing in victory and keeping Worlgaltrin as their new home. These thoughts were ruined by the enemy armies and the death of Vhyolan, who was killed in Hurlgaltrin.

Gelders suffered immensely in the war and were short of crafters, farmers and more than anything warriors. The struggle with the gabyrs had not ended and the gelders decided to isolate themselves from the rest of the world and its conflicts. It did not mean that the people did not keep offering their services for the folks of Hillfort Lands, but no longer would they send their armies to fight other people's wars. Only much later in time, the gelders got a spark of exploration and the town of Kamahva was built to the shores in the west. From here, the gelders wandered around the world and their reputation began to grow like a flower made of steel.

"Peace cannot last when one's sword is sharper than one's tongue."

ORDEALS OF VELANKAD
PLODDENHALN

During a cold and rainy night, Velankad was born in Kajoste to a world of forgotten heroes. The family of Ploddenhaln carried an enormous amount of their past in their blood and their name was written in every book around the land. According to many, Kajoste would have never been the same if the family had not been part of its story. Velankad had to bear the burden of the name since the day she was born and many battles were waiting for her blade. Caolfveld and Kalvkad, who were her relatives, introduced her to the influential characters of Kajoste, who only seemed to care about their personal glory and achievements. Velankad did not look up to these people and was usually seen training by herself, ignoring the self-important warriors.

Ploddenhalns were not the only famous family in Kajoste, which meant that they had several rivals. One of the families was Yelstele, whose warriors had occasionally been fighting the Ploddenhalns. The situation was complicated since many elves from Selkelgen had arrived to Kajoste as well as becoming swords for hire. The personal conflicts between the elves had followed to Kajoste and many families in the land got involved. Velankad warned the people of Kajoste about the elves, but their services as mercenaries seemed to appeal to a good range of lords and ladies of the land.

Velankad, being often alone, was approached by White Hat, who was the protector of the mountain elves. The force told Velankad that he wanted true peace in the land and was willing to give a token of reconciliation, which was a simple piece of stone. Velankad was frustrated about the conflicts and took the token, despite being suspicious of White Hat's sincerity. The woman placed the stone into the hall of her family, as a mark of growth and willingness to move away from the time of battles. Velankad assembled a meeting, which included peace talks between Ploddenhalns and Yelsteles. Nevertheless, the elven mercenaries of Selkelgen were also part of the summit and they happened to be old enemies. Velankad tried everything to prevent the elven hired swords entering the assembly, but the family of Yelstele demanded their attendance, as a gesture of fairness. In Velankad's mind, letting the mercenaries inside was not the right choice, but perhaps the only way to find a solution for the violence. However, everyone agreed that all weapons would be left out of the hall.

One of the elven mercenaries was Hulfus Tonren and he was known to be as cunning as a fox and as striking as a wasp. What Velankad did not know was that Hulfus was there to kill his old enemy, who sat on the other side of the table. His opponent was called Kasdavf Morr and the two had a long and bloody past in Selkelgen. Hulfus, who was one of the mountain elves, looked at the stone of peace which, in fact, was a disguised weapon left by White Hat. Velankad thought that the stone would calm the impetuous warriors in the room. When the meeting was about to end, Hulfus and his soldiers touched the stone, causing a burst of colourful sparks. Suddenly, Hulfus and his warriors had weapons in their hands and the crowd panicked. Kasdavf attempted to run from the hall, but was caught by Hulfus' spear, slaying him on the doorsteps.

Velankad kept staring at the chaos, which had erupted through the treacherous stone. On that day, Velankad decided to leave Kajoste, since her anger and frustration had grown unbearable. Velankad happened to be a skilful shoemaker and she finally crafted her most precious boots, which could help her escape Kajoste forever. The boots she created were the key to getting out of Kajoste's never ending forests and mountains. Velankad bid farewell to Caolfveld and Kalvkad, who tried to convince her to stay.

Instead, the woman travelled towards the west, where she arrived in the forest of Tuolenwalo. She met five characters, who travelled the land's rivers, lakes and seas in the west with a small ship. The five adventurers were named Faedreksunne, Viliaspa, Moljvis, Galev and Afengunne and they welcomed Velankad with open arms.

For years, Velankad sailed and travelled with the five others, who showed her many forgotten and veiled places in the world. One of them was Hauesk, which later in time was referred to as Cellar World. In Hauesk, the five adventurers had a workshop, where they built boats and ships of all sizes. For instance, many elves came there to buy ships and Father Storm was an eminent patron of their ship house. In here, Velankad learnt to build boats and the business flourished for many years. Velankad observed the relations of the characters in the world for several decades and it became clear that Father Storm and the five others shared a mutual past. When Velankad finally dared to ask, she found out that all her five friends were ancestral spirits of the elves and they had given life to Mother Sky and Father Storm in the primordial days.

Velankad discovered how the five spirits, Mother Sky, Father Storm, Caolfveld, Kalvkad and Stala had fought vilhiildes in Kajoste. They had created the stone of Til, which defended Kajoste from the black sorcery of their foes. Til was a complicated magical stone and it could take anyone inside its own existence, but in exchange, it would fight against the vilhiildes and their dark ways. Kalvkad took the stone to Drytgastadl, since he had a feeling that it would be attacked by vilhiildes as well.

Some years after Kalvkad's departure to Drytgastadl, Velankad followed him and found the stone of Til, where her father was bound. There were many years of silence, which were ultimately broken by the arrival of Caolfveld and gelders. Velankad heard that vilhiildes had attacked Kajoste and as per usual, Caolfveld had been in the middle of the battles. When the stone of Til was no longer in

Kajoste, the vilhiildes could access there and they had tried to acquire the flame of Palendeirn. A piece of this flame was attached to Caolfveld's axe before he began to follow the vilhiildes, who presumably attempted to sneak to Drytgastadl.

Velankad had to accept her fate as a warrior and decided to take up her sword and fight, as it seemed useless to escape the conflicts. This time she did not feel sad, since she was facing vilhiildes and later hurthallans, who in her eyes were manifestations of evil. Vilhiildes and hurthallans also fought each other, but it was certain that their battles would not leave gelders or Velankad out. During these years, Velankad began to dream of boots, which ran in the fields towards the east. Every dream showed a place that Velankad had not seen before, but had a mysterious and definitive meaning. When Velankad concentrated, she could remember that the shoes were not moving by themselves, but they had a user who had long blonde hair.

Dream after dream Velankad came to realise that the character was the keeper of Til, an ethereal huntress. Velankad finally met the keeper, who introduced herself as Lufiat and the life-force of Til. She told Velankad that she would need the blood of their foes to keep her awake from the Til's sleepy numbness. Only the blood of the malevolent would keep her awake, as they gave her nightmarish energy, which prevented her falling asleep. Velankad gathered the company of gelder hunters, who Lufiat guided around the lands and they began to raid hurthallans and their wooden forts. The hunting warriors acquired several vials of blood from the hurthallans and other malevolent wanderers, who managed to sneak into Drytgastadl.

Velankad began to pay more attention to the vilhiildes, who were gathering their strength to defeat Yrtar, the force behind hurthallans. She learnt that the vilhiildes no longer needed Caolfveld's axe and Palendeirn's fire to face Yrtar, which was good and bad news at the same time. Nevertheless, the situation turned surprisingly simple, when a powerful hurthallan named Myrkutgar attacked Jarndava and the stone of Til. The ancient hurthallan spirit's plan was to die in the battle and let his blood flow on the stone of Til, which reduced the powers of the vilhiildes remarkably. The gelders and Velankad did not know that the easy victory over the enemy was a well-planned plot to prevent even worse creatures taking over.

Yrtar was furious about the loss of his finest commander and mainly focused on fighting the vilhiildes, whose plans had failed due the ultimate sacrifice of Myrkutgar. Eventually the vilhiildes' energies faded and they disappeared from the lands to unnamed places, leaving an uncertain tranquillity over Pimenn. However, Yrtar was not finished with Velankad and the gelders, who blamed them of luring his best commander to his untimely undoing. Yrtar had learnt dark magic from the vilhiildes and decided to use its might against the gelders. Ultimately, hanahathrul came to be, which was an undefined phenomenon changing places in Pimenn and parts of Hillfort Lands.

Velankad spoke to Lufiat, who knew many other protectors who could help the fight against Yrtar and hanahathrul. Velankad, who had now become the leader of the gelders, was introduced to Leutel, Fjyn, Tlaute and Pjyn. The four were guardians of Husmyrsket and were as equally concerned about Yrtar's actions and hanahathrul. They had arrived to Drytgastadl inside a ship, which had a room and a stove, as it was the only way for them to move in the world. The captain of the ship was Faedreksunne, making some pieces come together.

To help the four spirits of Husmyrsket, Velankad ordered the gelders to build cottages, which were named torpa. Inside these dim rooms, gelders could warm up during cold days, by throwing water on a stove, which projected hot steam into the room. At the same time, the steam and mist enabled the four spirits to move in Pimenn. When there was enough of mist or steam, Leutel, Fjyn, Tlaute and Pjyn could move within its flowing cloud and explore the world. Soon the four began to locate the blind spots of the hanahathrul, which helped Velankad and gelders in their attempt to defeat the enemy.

The most notable friend which Velankad received from Husmyrsket was the mist horse named Askiljae. It appeared through the steam of Velankad's favourite torpa and offered its services to her. The horse's body was a manifestation of thick steam, which glimmered in cloudy red. Velankad believed that Askiljae was the beacon of blood and the other spirit in Til, that Lufiat had mentioned every now and then. Velankad rode the horse and it struck fear into hurthallans, who could not escape its silent hooves and huff. Askiljae floated upon the land and it felt no fatigue or emotions, it simply existed and experienced life, as if it was motionless desolation with no depth. Lufiat met Askiljae as well and was happy that the horse had returned after being missing for centuries. Lufiat explained to Velankad that particularly vilhiildes were afraid of the horse, since they did not carry any blood in their bodies. The red liquid of life was poison for vilhiildes, making the horse a galloping weapon against them.

CHANTER OF THE MIGHTY MISTS

Immos Veekel was an orphan, whose parents had been killed in the wars with gabyrs. The gelder was raised by an old man, who lived northwest from Jarndava, where the young gelder experienced his first years. The old man, Sointumo, built string instruments and his little cottage was full of them. Throughout his childhood, Immos listened to Sointumo's tales and singing, which spoke about Husmyrsket and its guardians veiled in steam. The young gelder learnt how to make the same instruments and how to chant accordingly to the stories. The string instrument was called Lendelloin and Immos learnt to speak with the protectors of Husmyrsket, alongside its delicate tunes.

Sointumo was glad, as he watched Immos growing up and learning skills, which no other gelder possessed. The young gelder was diving into the secrets of Husmyrsket and the steam and mist gathered around him like dwarfs around barrels of ale. His greatest marvel was Lendelloin, which had thin strings of mist and with its music he could cast and summon numinous powers. The strings flew in the air whilst the tunes were filling the space, delivering spells to the nature that surrounded him. When Sointumo died of age, the old man left a book of chants for Immos, who finally got to learn the rest of the secrets regarding Husmyrsket and the instruments. Immos became famous and many folks acknowledged his abilities, even halmhendens.

Tuolan Rauwos, a significant halmhenden, met Immos and asked for his help, since their travelling company needed someone who knew everything about the mysteries of mist and steam. Immos, being a young chap, had no problems joining the halmhendens, who took him along to many campaigns, which mostly consisted of enforcing halmhenden influence. After a year, the company received an urgent task, which made Immos' role more important than ever before. In the mountains of Myrfvaakel an odd fight happened amongst hurthallans, who had built enormous caverns there. The scouts claimed that the hurthallans tried to imitate the gelder torpas, which also made the halmhendens alarmed. Tuolan said that the domains of Husmyrsket could possibly be destroyed and bring back many of their old rivals, who the halmhendens disliked as well. The place had to be kept peaceful, as it was fragile like a dry leaf.

One of the captured hurthallans revealed that their warband had travelled inside the caverns in search of an access to Husmyrsket and to

Adventurers in Husmyrsket

hunt down a commander who had betrayed them long time ago. Tuolan, Immos and the rest of the halmhendens decided to act swiftly and made a journey to the mountains, where it took considerable time to find the caves. Upon the discovery, the company did not see any traces of the hurthallans, but the place felt oddly familiar to Immos. Suddenly, the caverns looked like Husmyrsket and its endless small low light rooms of stoves with wooden benches on various levels. A great fire struck the company and everything was ablaze, waking Immos and the rest of the travellers from an illusion.

During the encounter, Immos experienced an ethereal revelation, which taught him new elements of Husmyrsket. Immos concentrated in his thoughts and could see landscapes of fire and smoke. The young gelder was no longer limited to the secrecies of steam and mist, but the smoke and fire followed his will as well. Immos learnt that fire, as per usual, was the most feared of them all in Husmyrsket, as it could bring down the whole veiled domain. Some rumours even suggested that Husmyrsket's fire was originally from Caolfveld's axe, which was also known as the flame of Palendeirn. Immos began to think that Caolfveld, whose tale had reached mythological proportions, spread his powers to the roots of the world, perhaps hiding parts of the flame underground. Immos assumed from the story, which proposed that the stone of Til's sphere was under the soil.

Tuolan explained that Husmyrsket was established to surround Loft World, also known as Blesk. Its purpose was to serve as a place of armistice that prevented anyone entering Loft World with ill intentions. Halmhendens had made an agreement with the spirits of the world, who got to dwell peacefully in Blesk. The halmhenden also clarified how parts of Caolfveld's flame were stored underneath Drytgastadl's soil, where it burnt in deep trees. The trees ensured that the fire did not spread all around, for example to Loft World. Immos was surprised by the story and became particularly interested in the flame, as it could be used against gabyrs and their hanahathrul.

Immos returned to Jarndava for a few years, where he quickly gained a reputation as a wise and strong leader. Some of his supporters suggested that he would become the new grand leader of the gelders, but for many, he was too young. His relations with the halmhendens were considered important, but he needed to put himself against many experienced hunters. Immos did not give up and he decided to gather a band of young gelders and travel east, where he could prove himself to the folks of Jarndava. His plan was to find all the ancient stone statues, which once belonged to the gelders, and build massive wooden forts around them. In these locations he also believed that he would find the flame of Palendeirn.

Eventually, Immos commenced his grand journey, which aimed to find all the statues that were believed to be gelder ancestors. The statues were also referred to as the hunting stones and each region's animals and foes would respect their presence. Every stone needed different blood and Immos gained it from his prey, which included animals and gabyrs. For instance, during the midsummer festivities, the gelders danced around the statues, which were smeared with the red colour to glorify the successful hunt. Nevertheless, Immos also realised that their presence was not appreciated by the giants, who lived in the same lands around Pimenn and western parts of Hillfort Lands. The giant folk were enemies of hill snakes, which the gelder loved to hunt due to their challenging nature. This caused a conflict between the two rivals over hunting honour and Immos decided to start building forts around the statues. Large logging camps were established and wooden walls began to rise around them. At the same time, Immos ordered some of the gelders to dig underground and find the eternally burning trees of Palendeirn.

"I remember another dream which I saw during my time in one of these logging camps. I was surrounded by

*unbelievably tall walls of wood and a wizard appeared from
the underground foundations of the fort. The wizard
brought out a fire tree from underneath, which had been cut
down after a night of work. I followed the company and saw
how they laid the tree on a river, south from the fort, where
its flames disappeared. The wizard rode on the log, which
was flowing towards west, keeping a soothing sound.
Suddenly, the wizard jumped and made the log fly in the air,
making it land perfectly on the fort's unfinished wall."*

One could say that Immos became relatively insane with
his majestic plans, but at least it seemed to impress the
elders of Jarndava. Immos was summoned to the city and
was asked to lead the gelder people with his ambitious
plans. Immos accepted the offer and his elevation was also
noted by a halmhenden named Vhyolan, who had many
spies around the world. Vhyolan, who happened to be
Tuolan Rauwos' brother, met Immos in Jarndava after he
had failed to receive help from the storm elves of Ikirias.
The halmhenden told that Tuolan had been slain by the
people of Aetari, Ylvart and Dyveln when he visited their
realms, as he was demanding back halmhenden heirlooms.
The tragedy made Vhyolan decide to set his foot on a path
of revenge, regardless of consequences.

Immos trusted Vhyolan, as he used to be Tuolan's
friend. The news about his passing made Immos' heart feel
emptier and colder. His nerves and eyes turned black as
Vhyolan's story continued regarding the injustice the three
realms had demonstrated towards halmhendens. Vhyolan
promised that the gelders would get Worlgaltrin, if they
helped him to destroy the three realms. Immos knew
Worlgaltrin well, as it was mentioned in many ancient
writings of their people. It was a halmhenden city, which
had the power to control many underground flows of magic.
For example, it was closely related to the flame of
Palendeirn and if the gelders would rule Worlgaltrin, the
flame would never stop burning. The hunting stones and
their prevalent energies would be strengthened and it could

possibly erase gabyrs and their evils from the land for all time.

A year before the War of the Returning One began, Immos and Vhyolan made an elaborate plan to defeat the armies of the three realms. Immos suggested that the destructive powers of the burning trees would be used to flame the armies. The plan was to wait until their foes would march upon specific lands, which underneath ran the roots of the elder trees, and then Palendeirn's flame could be ignited. One of these roots happened to be underneath Honedimn, which was an active trading city. Vhyolan and Immos departed and the gelder leader travelled to the fort of Laugeuvel, which was believed to be on the top of the core root of the fire trees.

The gelder armies caused havoc in Honedimn and Lhorem, which provoked the three realms to counter-attack. Vhyolan and Immos were waiting for the day, when the three armies would march to Honedimn and the flames could lash them to ash. Immos was keen to spread the flame underneath Laugeuvel, which had long ladders reaching down to underground caves, filled with fire trees. However, a story tells that Immos met Caolfveld in these caverns, who demanded Immos not to use the trees and roots as weapons, as the flame could spread too fast, reaching places like Til. Immos agreed and realised the madness he was doing to his own people and the world. The gelder leader regretted the decision to join Vhyolan, who had relied on his plans to use the roots as weapons.

After the strategy failed and Vhyolan ordered the gelder warriors to attack Podfrud and Hulofrud, Immos decided to draw back some of his warriors from the meaningless war. Only sometime later, gabyrs began to threaten Jarndava and Immos had to call back all the remaining gelders, making Vhyolan feel completely betrayed. Luckily, the disastrous war did not follow to Jarndava after Vhyolan was slain and Immos had time to get his mind together. In the end, Immos stepped down as the leader of the people and spent his remaining life studying the hunting stones and fire roots, making his writings an essential part of gelder folklore.

LOCATIONS

DRYTVAARTE
The entire world.

TAIVAARTE
The entire sky – 'Firmament'.

DRYTGASTADL
A continent, where the majority of this book's events take place. Often Drytgastadl was referred as Drytvaarte – 'The current world'.

LOISTESSE
Older continent west from Drytgastadl, original home of many ancient powers.

KÖRPIHIMGAT
A village in the western parts of Loistesse. A home for many spirits and powers before they moved to Drytgastadl.

KAJOSTE
Oblivion of Heroes, a place where many primordial warriors ended after the age of Loistesse.

HUSMYRSKET
A secretive domain, connecting several places with wooden rooms and chambers with stoves.

VÄLKEHTGEN
Old name for the western parts of Drytgastadl.

SELKELGEN
The home of the elves, before they arrived in Drytgastadl.

HASGASTADL
Home of the halmhendens.

ALASGASTADL

Home of the halmhaers, also known as 'Glass Bottle World'.

THE REALM OF NIGHT

Many legends in Drytvaarte suggested that this was the place where night resided during daytimes.

GLAUESK

The great cosmic fabric between Hasgastadl and Drytvaarte.

BLESK

Loft World, a realm of infinite dimly lit wooden rooms and a dwelling for spirits of many kinds.

KULUS

A well somewhere deep in the soil of Drytgastadl, providing a gateway for olden spirits.

HAUESK

Cellar world, a place of infinite spruce forests and lakes. Hauesk was full of various spirits, most of them leaning towards evil.